EQUINOX SEASONS DUET BOOK TWO

THESE
Unhallowed
HALLS

RE JOHNSON

Book Cover by RE Johnson Books

First edition 2025

Paperback ISBN 979-8-9927680-9-1
Ebook ISBN 979-8-9927680-8-4

To my fellow witches and spirit sisters who know that you don't

take fucks from anyone.

Unless they're your smoking hot professor or a seven-foot elder

god.

Content Considerations

This is a monster horror romance with several triggering elements. Presented below is a list of potential triggering content. Take your mental health seriously. You come first. If something triggers you, unexpectedly, take a step back.

I'd also like to mention that this is a work of fiction. Don't try this shit in real life, okay? Great. While there is a depiction of kink in the book, it is not a manual. If you are interested, I highly recommend checking out www.kink101.com.

If you'd like to read the story with no spoilers and understand what this type of horror romance might entail, feel free to skip these. But I did warn you. Lastly, if you're all good with the following, then maybe you're just a tiny bit fucked up. But don't worry. So am I.

- Breeding kink
- Cult activities
- Fisting
- Gore
- Losing virginity
- Mental health struggles, including depression and PTSD
- Mild medical trauma
- Monstrous transformations with two souls in one body
- Multiple penetrations
- Murder and violence
- Neglectful parents

- Oral
- Parental death (on and off-page)
- Praise and degradation
- Queer sex, including sapphic and achillean
- Religious persecution
- Sex in werewolf-like shifted form
- Significant age gap between love interests
- Size difference
- Squirting
- Stepsibling relationship
- Student-Professor relationships
- Supernatural horror
- Supernaturally-induced heats
- Voluntary possession by an ancient being

Playlist

If you're interested in listening while you read this carnival horror, dark academia baby, I've created a vibe playlist on YouTube. It's great for getting your spook on, with spicy tracks included for those key moments, and I highly recommend checking it out.

Some of the sounds are really disturbing, so if that kind of thing isn't your jam, be sure to skip or just do your own thing.

You can find the playlist here: https://tinyurl.com/TUHplaylist.

Prologue

A Beginning Through An Ending

Wren

Hunters had always tried to invade our lands. The barrier had been weakening by the year, and no longer could we hide the worst of the evils that lingered in the dark, seeking to infect our world and then the next. An endless cycle of devouring that would take everything in its path lay ahead for us all, and even the Winter Realm—my home and safe haven through the horrors of my life—saw its land and people changed.

There was much battle that lay ahead, and a child would not fare well in the clutches of the deep malevolence that sought to corrupt the entirety of the Winter Realm. Even now, Fierion did battle against the growing dark, seeking to protect a mortal world that had never loved him. Or me, for that matter.

But it had to do better for our daughter.

Fate and the strings that wove through every world from this to the far reaches beyond, and even into the World of Below, tied numerous destinies together. Though I would not see her grow, my child possessed the power of an elemental witch and the Winter King himself. She would line the years of history with her greatness, and some distant day centuries from now, the world would be made all the better for the strength that she brought with her into the realm of fallible mortal men.

"Be safe here, daughter." I walked to the wooden door, aged and rough with the effects of weather and time. "Bethany will look after you. She will teach you, protect you, and send the love I have in my heart to you each day until my last."

A day I feared was coming all too soon, thanks to the would-be god that harassed the Winter Realm.

"You must hurry, my queen. The king will be waiting for your return to launch the attack."

Renmier stood at my back, Fierion lieutenant, and I nodded solemnly. There was little in this world that I dreaded more than walking away from my child. Still, the most terrifying thing would be to watch her harmed under the might of this incomprehensible foe. None of us knew where this "deity", as he called himself, had come from, but the pain and anguish that coated his blackened being seeped out into the world, turning those loyal to us all in a bid for him to gain more power through blood sacrifice.

Failing to restrain my tears, I wrapped my knuckles on the wooden door, awaiting Bethany's approach. It did not take long, and she opened up with a look of horror and understanding on her face. She'd foreseen then. One whom I'd trusted for so long, who understood the craft and the ways of the witch better than

12

most, she'd always possessed such keen insight.

"You must protect her. *Please*." My words were a beg. "She will carry on. It is set into the fabric of the universe, but she cannot stay with me if she is to do so."

"Wren," Bethany croaked, her voice thick with emotion, "I have not seen you in so long. And now this? I have felt it, Wren. I have felt that dreadful malignance infecting the edges of the world. It will be here, too. Not now, not for centuries, but it *will* come."

"I know." I had felt it in my bones that the Winter Realm's stand would not be the last. "She will pass on our blood, the blood of witches and fae, and our line with come to fight it one day."

Bethany nodded, a mirror of my grim countenance on her lovely face. We knew. We knew, and we understood.

"He calls, my queen. Fierion cannot hold it back for much longer."

I turned over my shoulder toward Renmier, nodding and pointing toward the tree line coated in a fresh layer of snow.

"Tell him I am on my way." Renmier nodded, but I stepped forward, reaching up to put my hand on his tall shoulder. "And then get to your human. Do not let Sigurd die to this. Neither of you can be lost."

Recoiling slightly, Renmier's brow furrowed deeply as he shook his head. "My queen, I cannot. The king—you—need me."

"I need you alive to aid Bethany in protecting our daughter. Fierion knows. He understands."

Silence fell around our small group, a clandestine meeting to uphold the threads of fate. We needed to move quickly, all of us. This would not be the end, not for the faux-god, nor my line.

For my daughter.

Bowing, Renmier concentrated, letting Fierion know I would be returning shortly, and then he met my eyes again, briefly, before he took off into the woods to find the hut he'd been sharing with his human. I turned back to Bethany, depositing my daughter gently into her arms.

"Tell her always that she was loved. That her parent loved her *fiercely*."

Bethany could only muster a single nod, a tear sliding down her cheek. "I will. But...what do I call her?"

My mind churned. I'd been pondering it for quite some time now, wanting to give her something to be proud of, to lean on when she felt alone.

"She must be strong, like steel forged into the sharpest blade. As the heat tempers the iron, so too will she be Temperance."

"Temperance," Bethany looked down at the baby, a soft smile on her face as I allowed my steps to fade me into the background, "a child of two worlds. I will not fail you, Wren. I swear it."

But by the time Bethany looked up, I was already dashing through the snow-covered trees back to my Fierion.

One last time.

One

CHAPTERS CLOSE AS SWIFTLY AS THE WIND

TEMPS

"Lizzie!" I threw down the sweater I was folding to put in my suitcase, frustration making my temples throb. "Did you take my necklace again?! I told you a million times that I hate it when—"

But right as I spun around to storm out of the room, I crashed right into her. Lizzie stood just in front of me, laughing as I corrected myself and holding up the necklace. It dangled from her fingers, and I immediately pulled back, trying to ignore the heat that flared through my cheeks.

Three years. Three damn years, and I still react like this around her.

Wearing that classic smirk of hers, the corner of her full, dusty pink lips lifting as if to mock me and my suffering, Lizzie tossed her long braid over her shoulder and sauntered over toward the mirror, taking my necklace with her.

"Why don't I just keep it right here?" She opened the clasp and put it on, letting the little blue gemstone land right at her cleavage, which she brushed the tips of her fingers over gently. "It'll be safe and cozy, and if you want it so badly..."

Turning around to face me, Lizzie locked her deep hazel stare on me, and I could feel my chest tightening, not allowing me to take in the oxygen I so desperately needed. My heart was way too loud in my ears, and that pulsing feeling in my core needed to back the hell off.

You're twenty-two, Temperance Montgomery. You are an adult. Shake it off.

But then Lizzie was crossing the room to stand in front of me, the light-colored floorboard creaking under her soft steps. She got right up in my business, hardly a centimeter separating us, and I could smell the musky perfume she always wore, moss and cypress, blood and warm fur, with a subtle tinge of gunsmoke and sweet resin.

Something I only knew because I'd gone to the website where she bought the stuff and looked it up.

"...it'll be right here waiting for you."

"I...I..." My tongue was clumsy and too thick. I couldn't move, forcing myself to keep my eyes off the blue gem and the soft home where it now resided.

"Yeah, Temps? You what?" Lizzie's teasing voice did too many things to me, and I shook my head, stepping backward—nearly tumbling over the bed—and turning around to face my almost completely packed suitcase and backpack.

"We need to get moving. If we miss registration today, it'll be a pain in the ass tomorrow."

Lizzie scoffed, a sound I knew too well, and I looked up at the mirror on my side of the room, the one that reflected hers, and watched her spin around, rolling her eyes as she went back to her own suitcase, which was nowhere near packed.

"It's not like Night Grove is going anywhere. We'll be fine. It's like a fifteen-minute drive." In the mirror, I watched as she haphazardly stuffed things into her suitcase. The majority of our belongings, the ones we'd actually need for classes and such, had already been brought over to the dorms because Mr. Chamberlain insisted on helping out. "And you know for a fact that I'm only doing this because of what it is. A school for wi—"

"Lizzie, don't." I cast a glance out toward the hallway. I didn't hear my mom or Mr. Chamberlain, but I knew they were just downstairs, ready to see us off, since Lizzie wouldn't let her father drive us.

"Ugh, they're not listening, Temps. Chill." In a flurry of fabric, Lizzie stuffed her things into the suitcase, not being careful in the slightest, and then faced me again. "But if it'll keep you from having an aneurysm, fine. A 'post-graduate' school like this? Yeah, sign me up."

"Thank you. I'll…" I looked at my suitcase—the black fabric worn and aged just like the deep purple bedspread it was resting on—and then looped the buckle through my new backpack, the first one I'd bought for myself since high school. "…get my stuff downstairs and then we can go. And I feel like I should mention that Night Grove recruited us. It's not like we applied to go, so—"

"Exactly. *They* want us. Two hot step-sissies who have a little of that old black magic in their blood. If only my mom were here."

I wanted to point out that she was being less than conscientious again, but Lizzie had mentioned her mother, something she didn't do often, and it felt like a dick move to yell at her when she was clearly using humor to play off the lingering grief. She'd lost her mother a lot longer ago than I'd lost my dad, but one thing we'd both been able to agree on was that the wrong parent died.

Which, ouch, horrible thing to think, yes, but not any less accurate.

I wasn't like Mr. Chamberlain was a bad person. Lizzie's dad, who was, yes, *technically* my stepfather, was nice enough, but he was distracted. He worked long hours at the hospital, and he'd never been especially touchy-feely, according to Lizzie. That made things a lot worse when her mother had died back when she was young. He was that kind of man who just didn't see things if they weren't directly essential to his daily life. Brilliant but clueless.

Which was the opposite of how things had been with my dad when he was still alive. Mom was better then. After his passing, we both sort of drifted, but Mom never got back on track. Hell, she fell into a deep hole of weird new religious stuff, and where she'd been rather laid back about all that when my dad was still alive—even going so far as to encourage him to reconnect with his native roots since he was adopted and didn't know much about them—now, she'd just...*changed*.

I didn't feel like I could talk to her about this witch business with the school or our own heritage, for that matter. Apparently, we came from a long line of witches and spellcasters, even some medicine women on my father's side, per the Night Grove Academy recruiter. I'd hated that the man had known more about my family than I did and dug right into research mode.

A skill I was well-known for.

Sure enough, way back in the first records I could find from Europe, there was a mention of a woman who'd fled persecution, landing in Rockford, Massachusetts, when it was first being settled. Funnily enough, her name had also been Temperance.

I felt connected to her even though that was ridiculous, but hell, she was my family. The recruiter for the school had said that the faculty had been keeping an eye on our line for a while now, expecting magic to show up. I'd been the first in generations, and when I'd noticed that I could work some easy spell found online, I'd thought I'd gone nuts.

Until, that was, Lizze confessed to being able to do the same.

And something totally different, too.

Since I was young, I'd had an affinity for plants. A green witch, apparently, and alchemy, and I were regular buddies. I was mixing concoctions for as long as I could remember in some shape or form, and I'd gotten pretty good at doing it sneakily just before Dad died in a car wreck.

Tea and a few mushrooms couldn't stop a drunk driver from careening across the median and killing him, though.

Lizzie, on the other hand, wasn't the green girl I was. Oh no,

Lizzie's specialty lay in reading people, and she meant that pretty damn literally. She could touch you and see all your vibes, your secrets, what lay ahead for you.

Reason one million and two that I tried so hard to keep my distance from her.

Number one, of course, was because if she did, if Lizzie got too close, I wasn't sure I'd be able to keep myself from enjoying that *way too* much.

Sure, she'd only been in my life for three years, and we were both adults now, but Lizzie was still, in fact, my stepsister. There were rules, and I wasn't the type of person to just start breaking them willy-nilly.

You break one, and you might as well break them all.

It occurred to me that I'd been staring down at my bag for far too long now, and I shook myself, zipping up my suitcase and getting it down on the floor as I slung my backpack over one shoulder. This room wasn't much, but it'd been mine my entire life. I'd only shared it with Lizzie during college breaks, and that wasn't very often, considering how regularly she went out to do "other shit."

Her words.

So, leaving the place now, for what felt like a much more permanent evacuation, felt...weird. There was no time to be overly sentimental, though, and we both still planned on visiting the house during breaks. I just wasn't totally sure when those would be. We were headed to an academy for practitioners, and everything had been pretty mysterious about what precisely that would entail.

Circling my bed, I pulled my suitcase along the short-fiber
rug at the foot of my bed and parked it so that I could close
my closet. My bookshelves were mostly empty now, the books
having been carted off to the dorm in that moving truck that
came by yesterday. I was glad that the academy had allowed us
to have things delivered early. Our dean, Professor Owens, had
been very understanding about us coming to the school with
no other magic folk in our lives, and somewhat late in the game,
considering Lizzie and I had already graduated from college.

With oh-so-useful degrees in English and Art.

My plan had been to teach. I had no idea what Lizzie planned
on doing with a BA in Art History, but knowing her, she hadn't
thought that far ahead either.

"Girls! You should get a move on!" My mother called up the
stairs, and I snapped back to the present, forcing myself out of
the worry over the future and regret over the past—a limbo I
frequented more often than I'd like.

"Well, you heard Barbs, Temps. Let's roll."

Rolling my eyes, I adjusted my backpack and grabbed my
suitcase again. Lizzie had a way with nicknames, and "Barbs"
was pretty accurate with how warm and cozy my mom could be.
Following her out, I ran my stare over Lizzie's outfit again, both
admiring the way her slim curves looked in the black leggings
and the strip of flesh visible where her white crop top and leather
jacket ended, and feeling sorry for myself because I just *wasn't*
like that.

We trekked down the hallway, the white trim and teal walls so
bright compared to the deep blue I'd painted my room when I
was finally allowed. My style was very nightsky meets too many

books, while my mother was much more the "Live, Laugh, Love Your Obsession With Bird Motifs."

It wasn't horrible. It could have been *a lot* worse, but there came a point where I was pretty sure it was illegal to own that many cheesy block quote decor items and pseudo-rustic bird cage thingies that were always paired with some generic watercolor print.

At the foot of the stairs, said bird lover—who'd never actually gone bird watching or owned one or even given them so much as a second thought—stood clutching her little crucifix that she'd taken to wearing after joining that support group for widows and widowers. She smiled up at us, and then Mr. Chamberlain came up behind her, resting his arm over her shoulders.

"We're so proud of you girls. Drive safe and let us know when you arrive, alright?"

"Yeah, yeah, Dad. I'll text. We're twenty-two. Cut the umbilical."

"Elizabeth!" Mom said, her expression morphing from one of embarrassing nostalgia to horror. "Don't speak to your father like that."

I bit my tongue as Lizzie rolled her eyes, going straight for the front door with her stuff and snagging her keys off the hook that hung on the wall, another whitewashed piece with a tiny bird-shaped hole drilled through the back.

"He's got to be used to it by now, Barbs." Casting a look at me over her shoulder, Lizzie gestured at the door with her head. "Come on, Temps! Train's a'leaving."

And that was it. That was the big goodbye. I hurried along after

Lizzie, knowing with certainty that she'd leave me hanging if I didn't, and the door shut behind me as I tried to catch up. Lizzie slid into the driver's seat of her BMW M3.

Having a well-off doctor for a father had its perks.

Putting my stuff in the trunk, I made sure it was shut and then got inside next to Lizzie. She fired up the car as we buckled up— it always shocked me that she actually wore the damn thing— and then she hard-reversed out of the driveway and sped off down the road out of town.

"Witch school here we come!" She rolled down the window, sticking her arm out, and cheered. "Get fucked, normies!"

I couldn't help but laugh, and then, of course, Lizzie was rolling down my window. I would only be twenty-two and a new student at Night Grove Academy once right? So what was the harm in living it up a little? This was going to be the best time of our lives, finally able to use our gifts and grow them. For the first time in a while, I finally felt like things were looking up for "Towny Temps and Her Terrible Back Luck."

Sticking my hand out the window, I mimicked the way Lizzie when up and down like riding a wave and smiled from ear to damn ear.

"Here we come, Liz." My voice was too quiet for her to hear over the roaring wind that launched our hair this way and that. "Here we come."

Two

Into The Night & Into The Grove

Temps

Looming on the edge of the water just outside of Rockport was an intimidating building up on a hill. Thick trees surrounded it on the three sides that didn't face the ocean, and it stretched up into the sky like something out of a horror movie. I could see Dracula himself walking out of those imposing double doors at the front, and the building didn't lack for Gothic architecture. Steeples aplenty topped each turret-like tower, and there was a large bridge that connected the grounds to the road we were on.

"Jesus, it's like going to fucking Hogwarts. Minus the transphobia, I hope." Lizzie pulled the car through the exterior gate that led into the school, and I had to agree with her.

The place was exactly what you'd imagine an academy for witches and magical practitioners to be like. However, it was more somber than I would have thought. The sky here looked like it was going to rain at any moment, the sun barely getting through the clouds, and the fall leaves were left to pile up along the sides of the slim road.

A heavy weight in the air settled over me, and as we pulled up to the parking area just before another gate, it was far from what you'd call modern. Still, that held a certain charm. Stepping onto school grounds felt like stepping back in time and across the ocean.

A veritable Victorian England theme park.

"Temps, if I have to walk on fucking cobblestones, you're buying me new shoes."

Laughing, I rolled my eyes, starting for the trunk of the car to get my stuff. "We've been to Salem a million times because we're so close, and you've never complained then."

Lizzie responded with something, but I was so distracted by the sights around me to hear more than the tone of her classic sarcasm. The school was gorgeous, and through the gate ahead, I could see a set of stairs that led up into a mist that appeared to be perpetually hugging the ground. It smelled like wet leaves and fresh earth, and if I peered through the parking lot toward the back of the academy, I could make out an ancient graveyard.

This was exactly the kind of vibe I was looking for. I was ecstatic, picturing all the long dark hallways and enormous libraries filled with more books than I could conceivably read in a single lifetime. Though I'd try.

"Are you even listening to me?"

Lizzie was up in my face then, and I yanked myself back, my butt hitting the trunk of the car. "Sorry. I was thinking about what's inside. I'm just—"

"Let me guess. You're thrilled because this is something out of a dark academia wet dream? Yeah, I figured." Lizzie turned over her shoulder, glancing up at the massive structure where we were headed. "I'll hand it to you. A witch school right outside of Salem that's *this* in love with Gothic architecture is pretty damn cool. I just hope they don't have some dumb no-alcohol policy."

"We do not, in fact, Ms. Chamberlain. Though that applies to functions outside of class, not during."

Both of us jumped slightly at the sound of a new voice. When I peeked around Lizzie, an older woman, probably in her forties, stood with her back to the gate just a few steps from us. I definitely didn't hear her approach, and I had a feeling she hadn't *walked* up to us.

"And you are?"

Ugh, leave it to Liz to be less than subtle.

Chuckling, the woman stepped forward, extending her hand. She was poised, effortlessly graceful, and I was captivated by her yellow eyes, which bore a striking resemblance to those of a hawk. Her salt-and-pepper hair was pulled up into a severe bun, and she wore a tweed suit in dark charcoal with a purple silk button-down beneath her slimming jacket—peak English professor vibes.

"I'm Professor Owens, dean of Night Grove Academy. I'm here to escort you both to your room."

Did she say room? As in one? A singular room. That I have to share with Lizzie. Lizzie.

"Umm, I'm sorry, did I hear you correctly? Are we rooming together?" My heart beat furiously against my ribs, ready to break the damn bones so that it could get the hell out of here, and I was nearly about to help the thing out. Being dead seemed less problematic than rooming with my too-stunning stepsister.

Looking over at Lizzie, she just smiled, and it was way too knowing for my liking. Which, of course, could mean only one thing. She'd done this. *Goddamn it.*

"Yes, of course. Your request to room together was honored immediately. I assumed that Ms. Chamberlain had told you."

I rolled my lips between my teeth, trying to steady my breathing as I considered the fact that I was going to be spending a lot more time with my stepsister, and this time, I didn't have the constant vigilance of my mother to rely on when it came to Lizzie's behaving. Any time we were alone, she teased me, pushed buttons that she really shouldn't have, and that was *with* the potential to get caught. Without it, I didn't know what she would do.

Or if I'd be able to keep myself from following suit.

"Eh, must've slipped my mind." Lizzie looped her arm through mine, pulling me forward. "But this'll be great. I could never have my sweet Temps too far away. I'd miss her way too much."

On the surface, that sounded sweet as pie, but I could hear sin snaking around in the background.

"Oh, I can see how close you two are. That's delightful. Oh,"

RE Johnson

Dean Owens crossed the uneven drive into the school with ease despite her four-inch stilettos, waving a hand at our suitcases, "don't worry over those."

The bag disappeared in a whoosh, and even though I knew that kind of thing was going to be happening on the regular here, I was still taken aback. Magic wasn't used in the world at large. They still didn't know it was a thing at all, aside from the handful of witches and creatures that hid in the shadows. Lizzie beamed, chuckling under her breath and pulling me closer.

"Amazing. You *so* have to teach me that."

Dean Owens smiled back, gesturing toward the gate. Now, we had only our backpacks, and as we stepped up to the intricately detailed wrought iron, with motifs of leaves and bats depicted in the metal, it swung open for us.

"Well, that will be on your spellcasting professor, and we actually have a brand new professor this year. Or I suppose I should say a returning professor. Professor Harkert taught at Night Grove previously, focusing on alchemy." My ears perked up, hearing the word that could set me into a delighted ramble if allowed. "But he has joined us to fill the absent spellcasting position at the last minute."

"Why'd he need to step in so last-minute?" Lizzie walked a bit ahead of me now as I trailed back near the dean. "The previous one die?"

Stiffening, Dean Owens cleared her throat. "As a matter of fact...But let's not dwell on such sadness. Professor Harkert is renowned for his abilities, and I'm certain he will do an incredible job. He'll be sure to cover the basics of presidigitation and telekinesis as well."

"Sounds good to me." Lizzie turned over her shoulder with a flashing grin. "Where we headed, teach?"

Christ. Can she not be chill for even thirty seconds?

"It's Professor, and we are proceeding to the left up the stairs. You'll be boarding in the south wing of Foxglove Hall."

Conversation died as the three of us walked up the steps I'd noticed. Inside the gate, it was like walking into a new town. Everything was exactly how it would be if we were back in the early days of America, complete with the cobblestones Lizzie had been worried about. I wasn't going to hear the end of that one.

The various wings and buildings of the Night Grove campus stretched up and around us, the stone pathways connecting the sections like a spider's web. I could see stained glass in nearly every window that faced us, and the bricks used to assemble these formidable, foreboding structures were dark, with vibrant green ivy crawling over them. Pumpkins and autumn decorations already poked out from doorways and windows, too. Mabon celebration was clearly in full swing.

Tonight was the fall equinox, after all. If the campus were anything like Rockford or Salem, Halloween would be celebrated immediately after and all the way through until the end of November break.

Witches do love us some spook season, after all.

"We'd love to see you both down at the Midnight Mabon bonfire once you're both settled. It's customary to begin the semester on the eve of the fall equinox to harness all the magic it possesses, and as you've likely noticed, Samhain is a fairly big deal around here."

Lizzie and I both chuckled at that one, and I nodded up at the dean, who stood so much taller than I did in those heels, though I had a feeling she'd still tower over me even out of them. Lizzie was at least around my height, just an inch or so taller. However, that did put her lips level with mine when we stood too close.

Stop. You can't think like that, Temps.

"Count us in," Lizzie replied, happily skipping up the stairs.

A dark midnight bonfire with my stepsister. Sure, what could go wrong? Ugh.

We'd barely gotten settled in the dorm room, which was just as stately and filled with dark wood trim as the rest of the academy's interior, when Lizzie dragged me out of the room to "explore." As much as I wanted to stay back in the dorm—and maybe pretend to be asleep when Lizzie went to the bonfire—I had to admit that I was interested in seeing the rest of the campus. There were so many buildings and dorms, but the sun had set fast after we'd arrived. Or at least it had felt like it, considering it was the night before the equinox and all. And that had meant that I wasn't able to get a good look at the structures in the light. Even still, the place was lit up by glowing street lamps that flickered beautifully, and I'd swooned over them plenty.

"And look at that, it's about midnight. I managed to keep you walking around this place for a full three hours." Lizzie smirked over her shoulder at me, still wearing the same black, low-cut shirt that sat off the shoulder, even though the temperature had dropped considerably since the sun went down. "You have no choice but to go to the bonfire with me. No pretending to be asleep."

I gaped at her and then stomped my foot down, crossing my arms over my chest, which was thankfully covered in a thick black sweater because I *wasn't* getting cold. I *hated* to be cold.

"Don't read my mind, Elizabeth." She narrowed her eyes at me, dropping her head over her shoulder as she mirrored my arm cross. "We talked about this."

"I'm aware we talked about it, *Temperance*. And it doesn't take a mind reader to know that was your plan. I've lived with you for three years, dude. I know how you get out of things."

We were at a standoff now because I didn't think she was lying to me, but she'd still manipulated me into staying out when she *knew* I wanted to go back to the dorm and avoid the raucous socialization.

"Come on, Temps. I want to meet people and see what the community is like. This is as new for me as it is for you, and believe it or not, I want to make some friends." I eyed her. "Okay, at least some acquaintances. *Plus*, I want to do this with *you*. We did it. We made it to the academy without our parents freaking out and shit. Let's celebrate."

Dammit. She had me there. I couldn't deny her when she was actually being genuine with me. It would forever be my weakness. Lizzie said so much as one sweet thing that she actually meant to me, and I was a goner.

"Fine, but you owe me."

Walking over to her, I looped my arm through hers, a dumb move but one I was doing anyway because I was nervous as hell to make an ass out of myself at what could like be a Mabon bacchanal.

"I will let you have all the time with the dusty, old books tomorrow. Promise." She practically crooned the words, leading me to the center of campus where we could see the glow of a fire even from here.

It had to be huge, and I was glad I'd chosen to wear my thicker leggings and boots so that walking across the cobblestones didn't hurt my feet so much. Lizzie was at the very least covered there because she never went anywhere without wearing her trusty Docs. She could use that leather jacket she liked so much with the chill in the air. However, I supposed that the fire would be able to keep us warm enough.

We arrived at the bonfire a few minutes later, our walk filled with casual conversation about what our classes would be like. Obviously, I was most looking forward to Alchemy 101, and Lizzie was excited for the telepathy course she'd signed up for. By the time we reached the massive inferno that towered into the sky, I was ready to stand by the flames and warm up.

"I still can't believe you're not cold."

Lizzie smiled, unhooking her arm from mine and doing a little spin as she closed in on the fire. "Who could be cold around you?"

My cheeks heated, and I swallowed hard. I wasn't about to respond to that one, and unfortunately, Lizzie was already weaving her way through the massive crowd toward the front so that she could have ring-side seats to the fire's flickering yellows and oranges. At least it would be warm if also densely packed with bodies.

"Wait up!"

Hurrying up to her, I made sure I didn't lose Lizzie in the crowd, grabbing her hand again so that we didn't get separated. All she did was laugh and smile at me, and damn her for being so damn gorgeous in the light of the fire.

For too long, I was silent, just staring at her while Lizzie danced without letting go of my hand, her movements matching the beat of a drum circle I couldn't see. Her full lips were split into a wide grin, her loose braid bouncing this way and that as she forced me to dance with her. I shook my head, smiling even as I cursed my lack of rhythm and frail body.

Years of being a "hospital baby" had taken their toll, and even just remembering it made the scar on my chest burn. It was this dumb psychological reaction, my useless embarrassment over the fact that I'd had heart troubles as a kid and needed surgery. Three, in fact. But once I'd grown into an adult, all that was required was the annual check-up to ensure the old ticker was still working correctly.

I was all good now, really, even if the genetic abnormality had made me the "runt of the litter," so to speak. I was short, thin, and just a bit too delicate-looking. Not that I was. I could run and do sport, not that I was interested in that, but all in all, I was normal.

You know, except for being a witch…and attracted to my stepsister.

Don't go there, Temps. Your mother would have a coronary.

And even when I was objective, I wasn't sure that her reaction wouldn't provoke a literal heart attack. My mom's weird obsession with religion since Dad's death had gotten less than queer-friendly. She'd never said anything about it before, but now, it was all "it says in the book" this and "it's just not natural" that.

Stupid.

"Ooh! There's Mabon cider!" Lizzie's voice threw me out of my thoughts, and I looked up to see her pointing at a quaint little stand off to the side. "Want some?"

"Sure." I nodded, forcing a smile. "Grab us both one. I'll wait here and hold our spot."

"Cool, cool."

Lizzie ran off, and I waited by the fire, going utterly still and silent. I had to pry my eyes away from watching her leave, her skirt swishing just below the curves of her ass as she did. I hated how I couldn't stop myself from fawning over her as much as I did. I felt weak for not being able to keep myself in check, but at least I had the company of the fire to keep me distracted for a bit.

I let my mind go empty as I stared into the flames, eventually holding out my hand and twirling my fingers to make the ones closest to me dance how I wanted them to. People nearby, witches who played tricks on each other or held polite conversation like the adults they were, created a din of constant sound all around me. But as soon as I'd gotten comfortable in the moment, the group closest to me left, leaving a hole in the gathered crowd.

Unable to keep myself from glancing that way, I stared across the courtyard toward the next person to take up space on this side of the fire.

Oh.

The man standing there was staring right back at me, our eyes meeting and holding like I was under some kind of spell, which wasn't totally out of the question considering where I was. I needed to look away. It was bordering on rude now, but I just *couldn't*.

He was older than me for sure, but the man was undeniably attractive, his dark hair curled and falling over his forehead in little curly-Qs that I wanted to run my fingers through. He had a thick beard as well, manicured and trimmed, but dark and framing his full lips. I couldn't tell what color his eyes were in this lighting, but they peered into me regardless, the light catching on streaks of white that cut through his bangs.

I had to assume he was a professor here, wearing the apparently standard tweed jacket over his shirt. It was a brown color, muddled in the glow of the fire, and a soft-looking scarf wrapped around his neck.

He even has a vest on. Fuck, Temperance, no. Stop staring. You're being a weirdo.

But as I stood there, finally able to pull my eyes away for just a moment before I was looking back up again, the professor was crossing the distance, headed right toward me.

"Oh no." I fumbled in place, looking this way and that for some escape route I could take back to the dorms, but every other inch of this place was crawling with students and faculty. "Shit. Shit, shit, shit."

This was bad. Had I broken some unspoken rule? Was I not supposed to stare at handsome professors for another reason besides the fact that it was sort of rude? *Oh, my gods. I'm going to get kicked out of school on the first night?! Do something, Temps!*

He was closing in on me, and all I could do was start practicing what to say to him in my head, ways to plead for him not to throw me out on my ass. Why did my damn hormones have to be such assholes? I was just beginning a new chapter of my life, and already I was plagued with this nonsense that was now stretching beyond Lizzie and to *another* forbidden person—a professor.

"Hey," Lizzie was suddenly in front of me, and I'd never been so glad to see her in my entire life, "you want to head back? I did drag you out, and I *suppose* I can be nice."

I shot a glance past her shoulder, watching the professor stop short and then dart his eyes away, turning around and getting the hell away from the fire about as quickly as I wanted to.

Keeping my voice as level as I could, I plastered on a grin and took the cider she offered me. "Yes. Yes, I do. Thanks, Lizzie."

"Of course, Temps. What are sisters for?"

Three

DARK DREAMS PORTEND VIBRANT VISITORS

LIZZIE

I could still smell the bonfire clinging to my skin even as we walked back inside the dorm room and shut the door. Turning the lock over, I watched Temps finish off the dregs of her apple cider, spiced with cinnamon, cloves, and a healthy pinch of damiana. She wobbled slightly as she leaned against her bed, a long twin that sat on the wall across from mine, and pulled off her boots, letting them drop at the foot of the bed.

I wasn't cold, my skin still humming from the feeling of being so close to so many people intimately involved with magic. I could sense it dripping from them like a pungent perfume, thick scents of witch and wielder mixing with the incredible smell of an enormous campfire.

Walking over to the window that sat between our two beds, I pushed the pane open a crack on my side, letting in the fragrance of the fall night air.

"Lizzie, I'm going to get cold." Turning, I raised my brows at Temps, smirking just a hair. "Do we have to have it open?"

"Pull on an extra blanket." I needed out of my own shoes and clothes, so I hit up the closet to change, not bothering to hide shit because I *wanted* Temps to look. "Or climb into bed with me."

It was quiet as I kicked off my Docs and then pulled my shirt over my head, tossing the black fabric of the lacy tank on the floor of the closet. I wasn't wearing a bra, never really needed one, so it was the skirt next, which wound up in the same pile as everything else. Reaching into the small dresser that sat inside the closet, I pulled out a white tank top for sleeping and considered whether I wanted to wear my socks.

I decided to go without and pulled them off, chucking them into the closet behind me as I turned and sauntered back to the bed. Without looking up, I could feel Temps' eyes on me, the way my skin felt warm and humming with electricity whenever she did, particularly when we were in one of the "changing room" moments. A breeze wafted in from outside, coasting over my skin and making my nipples harden.

Gods, I hope she's looking. Eat me up with those pretty brown eyes, Temps. Better yet, come over here and—

"Your first class is at nine, right?"

I looked up to watch Temps hurry over to her separate closet and stand just inside it with the door angled over to hide her from view. Sighing to myself, I gave up fiddling with my tank and pulled it on over my head, mentally cursing the damned

42

propriety that kept her from being mine.

Because she was. Temps was all fucking mine, and one day soon she was going to realize that.

There wasn't a chance in hell I was letting anyone else get their hands on her. Not that Temps was big into dating or anything like that, but if some "Chad" thought he was going to try something with the hot new girl, he'd have another thing coming.

"Yeah. You?" I asked, stretching out on my bed with my hands behind my head.

"I have one before that at eight." The closet door still hid Temps, and I stared at it, trying to work those telekinetic muscles and make it swing open just a hair further. "Do you need me to wake you up before I leave?"

The dark wood panel, so similar to the elaborate trim of the entire college, moved silently just enough for me to get a glimpse of Temps' back. My being *ached* to touch her skin, so soft and delicate, these graceful lines and curves that made up her form, and went straight to the core of who I was. From the first moment I'd seen her three years ago, I knew one thing.

Temperance Anne Montgomery was meant to be mine.

Everything about her was crafted in perfection, sent down from the angels above, or maybe delivered by demons to tempt even the heartiest of souls. I wasn't hearty. I went after what I wanted. I delved deep into the worlds of sex and kink, had as soon as I learned about it. Sure, I hadn't gone as far as actually fucking someone yet, just platonic sessions at a kink club in Salem, but that had everything to do with the sweet piece of ass I was staring at right now.

If it wasn't going to be Temps, I had a damn strong feeling that it wasn't going to be anyone.

Her deep, brown-black hair slipped over her shoulder as she stooped to pull out a pair of sleep shorts from the bottom drawer of her dresser, making that plump little ass of hers stretch the fabric of her boyshort panties—mint green with little white polka dots.

"I'm sure I'll be up."

My eyes were pinned to Temps. If I were a dude, I'd be rocking a massive boner. As it was, I was wet as hell, and I had to adjust in the bed, rubbing my thighs together to ease some of the near-constant strain I dealt with on the regular thanks to my stepsister.

Standing again, Temps finished pulling on her sleep shorts and then grabbed a similar tank as mine from her drawer, getting it over her head and pulling free the long layers of her wavy hair. I wanted to run my fingers through it, grip those strands as she tasted me. Another hard cut of arousal washed over me, and shit, I didn't know if it was the equinox or what, but I was dying over here.

"Okay." Temps turned, stepping past the door of the closet and closing it before climbing into her bed and throwing the covers over herself. "I'll see you at spellcasting after, yeah?"

"Yup."

"Well...night, Lizzie."

Glancing over at her, Temps offered her classic too-cute smile,

and I couldn't l

"Night, Temps.

Crreeeaaakkk.

I bolted upright in the bed, my heart pounding a million miles a minute as I glanced around for the source of that noise. This was a new place, and yeah, I wasn't used to any of the sounds that filled the hallway just beyond our room, but something felt off. It was nearly pitch black. The light of the moon cutting in through the curtains just above my head was the only source of light.

This academy was gorgeous, but it was also kind of spooky. Our room was wood floors and squeaky closet doors that you had to push on a little to get latched, the Montgomery-Chamberlain household not so much.

But there was no sign of that noise or what made it.

I waited in the dark, leaning up on my elbows in bed and peering into the black of corners. I didn't know what it was, but my instincts were telling me something was up. Psychic bullshit wasn't one-hundred percent, though. I couldn't rely on my visions and feelings like a crystal clear map. They were more like suggestions, accurate but vague.

Unease. Just this sense of dread that wouldn't let go.

Still, I couldn't get even a generic reading. It was just this "vibe," and while I did run on those, they weren't exactly useful right now. There was no use forcing it either. That's not how my visions worked or my intuition. I needed to let things percolate sometimes.

A total pain in the ass.

Rolling onto my side, I flopped back down onto my pillow, not exactly content to just wait things out but not given much of a choice either. What was I supposed to do with "the air feels weird, too tight" anyway?

Nothing, that's what.

I closed my eyes, sucking in a deep breath through my nose to try and recenter myself. As much as Temps and everyone else, for that matter, though my insomnia was because of my high energy, it was actually the result of being too keyed into people's minds and emotions most of the time. It was hard to get your shut eye when a couple few doors down was fighting and spewing their hatred into the air like a cloud of noxious fumes.

"Mmm..."

An eyelid popped open, and I looked across the room at Temps, who was thoroughly asleep. She was dreaming, going by the vibes she was giving off, and I could just start to pick up on the invisible heat in her aura as she lay on her back in the bed.

The weird vibes weren't coming from her, which was good. And that should have been enough of a relief to let be go back to sleep. But my pretty little Tempy was breathing a bit hard, and the more I focused on her, the more I could sense the distinct nature of her current REM cycle.

"Oh, hell, yes. That's a sex dream."

I kept my voice quiet, not wanting to wake her up, and then extended my awareness to Temps' mind. It wasn't exactly invading her thoughts like she'd yelled about before. It was just a small vibe check, just a tiny, baby little peek at what kinds of thoughts might be rumbling through her head during this particular type of dream.

What's in that head of yours, cutie?

Pleasure, arousal, and enough pent-up desire to not have me flat on my ass. And that was just a cursory, surface glance. Damn, my step-sis was in desperate need, it seemed, and there was no way in hell I was going to let some piece of shit take something that precious.

Oh, no, no. That belongs to me.

It wasn't until I was leaning over Temp that I realized I'd gotten out of my bed and gone over to her. I was in way too deep to her aura now, damn near being animated by her dream's vibrations. Sure, there was my own desire for her, the cloying ache inside me that demanded I taste and touch and fuck every goddamn part of her, but it was the combination that was proving especially potent right now. Standing there, I hovered my lips over hers, breathing her in without touching her. My fingers moved without prompting, gliding over her sleeping form just above her skin.

Her energy hummed against my flesh, the lust pooling right at her sacral core. I could taste her desire on my tongue, working the heated waves of her essence right over her pussy, mournfully hidden from me by a blanket and a set of shorts.

Gods, to fucking touch her for real...

I clamped down around nothing, imagining her fingers inside me, and with whatever power was magnifying her dream, it was enough to have us both groaning low as the distant sensation of release washed over us.

"Fuck, that was—"

Temps shifted in the bed, and I practically leaped from right there all the way across the room to my own. Something had just happened there, something to do with the surge in energy I'd felt, and for as off as that had been, I was ready to do whatever had just happened with Temps all over again.

Soon. Soon she's  *the bullshit*
that's been keepi

The energy of the equinox was pumping even higher as I slid into a seat next to Temps in Spellcasting. As far as classrooms went, this one was an academic's vision of heaven, and I could feel my stepsister buzzing with excitement as she settled into her seat. We were in a large, auditorium-like room with rows of seats that resembled a stadium. The floor and desks built into the structure were a deep, chocolatey brown, and a massive blackboard—chalk and all—stretched across the wall behind the professor's desk.

He hadn't arrived yet, this Professor Harkert, and as far as I was concerned, we were annoyingly early. Class was set to begin in like five whole minutes. I could've snagged a coffee on the way here. Shucking off my leather jacket, I admired the modifications I'd made to the school uniform—we were adults for fuck sake and didn't need a dress code—and leaned back in my seat so I could kick my Docs up on the ledge in front of us.

"Can you believe this is real?" Temps' voice carried that lilting tone of wonder, and as much as I wanted to tease her about being such a nerd, it seemed mean to burst her bubble. "This place is gorgeous. Did you see the walkways?! Stone arches and floors. Gargoyles!"

Shaking my head, I knocked her with my elbow, thinking she still looked damn good in a knee-length plaid skirt and blazer.

"Think any will come alive and turn out to be hella cute?"

"That is exceedingly unlikely."

A voice richer and deeper than the chocolate wood around me cut through the room, and everyone went silent, even me. When I looked down to the front, following Temps' gaze, I was hit square in the face with one of the most beautiful sights I'd ever had the pleasure of witnessing—and with Temps right next to me, that was saying something.

Our professor was *hot*.

His voice held the hint of a New England accent, and for the first time in a long while, I watched utterly speechless as he set down his large satchel and pulled out the chair from beneath the long mahogany desk. My first thought was, of course, how fucking good it would be to be thrown across that desk by said hunky professor, shortly followed by getting Temps to join.

"Oh no."

My girl's whisper had me shaking out of my head, turning toward her, my brows knitting together when I saw the look of abject dread on her face.

"What's up with you?"

Temps looked over, her cheeks stained pink beneath the warm tan of her skin. "Forget about it. Don't, umm, just forget I said anything."

Flustered, nervous, mortified, my step-sis was balls deep in all of it, and I didn't know why. "Oh, ho, ho. What's this all about?"

"Lizzie," Temps looked away, facing the professor again as the sound of chalk scratching across the board filled the room, "just stop. We need to be quiet."

I opened my mouth to rebut, but anything I was about to say died when Professor Harkert broke the quiet again.

"That you do. So why don't you both try it out, so we can begin class?"

If Temps could turn an even brighter shade of red, she did. Unable to push for more details right now, I narrowed my stare and turned back toward Mr. Stuffy.

Hot but stuffy.

Still, as soon as our eyes met again, the challenge burning deep in my chest in a constant, silent demand that I give him something to think about, the tension radiating through my shoulders relaxed a bit. The deep navy of his eyes, framed by smart eyeglasses with thin wire rims, was nearly impossible to look away from, and I swallowed hard as he drilled that gaze into me and came around to lean on his desk, his expression stoic yet smug.

He was wearing a tweed blazer, complete with elbow patches, and a vest beneath it over a white button-down shirt. His pants were dark brown, and I just knew he was the type of guy to call them slacks. Just then, his eyes flicked to Temps with the same intensity, and the entire classroom felt like it dropped away into nothing, becoming just the three of us.

"Good morning. I'm Professor Harkert. I will be taking over this semester as your new instructor for basic spellcasting. It's nice to see so many new faces joining Night Grove." Harkert's attention swiveled back and forth between Temps and me, and I almost vocally mused about how the rest of the class was going to feel left out. "My specialty lies in alchemy, but I have accepted this position to—"

"If your specialty is in alchemy, why aren't you teaching that?" A voice sounded from the right side of the room, and all attention focused there on a student with straw-blonde hair in the customary uniform, pressed with so much starch that I was surprised it didn't crack.

"I suppose it's better to just get this over with." Harkert looked down with a sigh, pushing off the desk and returning to his seat. "I have just recently returned to Rockport after doing extensive traveling, where I lectured on modern alchemy practices. Since my return was rather abrupt, I was not able to get into the alchemy teaching post until next semester, and this class required a professor."

"Because the other one died, right?"

Blondie beat me to the question, and I shot her a look even though she wasn't paying attention to anything but Harkert. I hated her immediately, every vibe detector in my brain going off with warning bells that she was a bitch in sheep's clothing.

"If you must know, Ms..." Harkert looked down at a pad of paper he had open on his desk. "...Mitchell, Mr. Morrison was actually found dead in what is presumed to be a grisly murder. That the answer you're looking for?"

Oh, I like *him*.

"Apologies, Professor." Blondie clammed up, and after that, class progressed like a ride on the bullet train. Before I knew it, Harkert was wrapping up what to expect in his class this semester, and there hadn't been a single moment that he hadn't entranced both Temps and me. It was nice to know she had good taste when it came to guys, too.

"I'll see you all tomorrow. Make sure that you have your books for..."

Harkert's words died off, and the entire room turned toward the window to the left as jaunty music played loud enough for us to hear all the way in here. My nerves tensed at the sound, but several of my fellow students ran over to the glass, peering out into the misty, gray morning.

We were on the side of campus by the entry gate and parking lot, and just down the long driveway was a little truck bouncing along the road. I'd have taken it for a fucking ice cream truck if it wasn't for the very obvious circus and carnival aesthetic going on. Wind howled outside the room, and in a whoosh of faded yellows and red, several sheets of paper plastered themselves across the glass, as if the truck had let them go in the breeze, hoping they'd land somewhere people would see them.

"Oh hell yes, let's go check it out!" a taller male student cried out, and the class emptied in a hurry aside from me, Temps, and our professor. I stood up, gesturing at the window with my head as I slung my bag over my shoulder. Temps rolled her eyes but followed me down, and we walked up to the window to read the flyers that were still stuck to the panes.

Come one, come all to the Illusion de Lumière Carnival! Death-defying stunts, fire-breathing, soaring through the sky on the flying trapeze, and more! Don't miss out on this once-in-a-lifetime experience. Spooks and sweets for all! Corn maze! Fun house! Games! Every night from now until November 1st.

"A carnival? Already? It's still September." Temps turned away from the window, shaking her head as we crossed the room toward the exit.

"It's Rockport by way of Salem, dude. Spooky Season begins when the first leaf turns orange."

She laughed, but I definitely didn't miss the way her eyes tracked over to Harkert as she passed, or the way his own followed her right back. The energy wafting around was something else, making me feel like I'd smoked too many clove and wormwood cigarettes. I hurried along after her, though, ready to snatch up one of those flyers the moment we got outside.

As I passed Harkert, I flashed him a grin, certainly laying it on a little thick. "See ya, teach."

He leveled me with a stare, the muscles of his jaw working as he clenched it. "Ms. Chamberlain."

"Oh, come on. Lighten up." I reached the door, pausing to grip the jam and turn up the heat on my stare, ever so grateful that I'd cut this skirt to hit me at the mid-thigh. "It's Lizzie."

He didn't say anything, and Temps called for me down the hallway. Still, as I took off after her, I could feel the burn of Harkert's eyes on my skin.

This is going to be fun.

Four

TEMPERING TEMPTATION OFTEN REQUIRES TURMOIL

CALEB

That class was...not normal. When I'd come back here, agreeing to fill Mr. Morrison's class because of his extremely untimely demise, I'd done so on the condition that I be allowed to simply exist and teach. I wasn't looking to perform "tricks" for our students, nor was I interested in putting on a show, leading study groups, or serving as a faculty advisor to anyone. I had traveled to get away from Rockport, and coming back was no small feat.

Dean Owens had assured me that it would be "an effortless transition." About that.

"Ugh," I pinched the bridge of my nose under my glasses, pushing them up and then just taking them off altogether, "I do not have time for...*interesting* students."

Still, even in the empty classroom, I could feel both their presence, lingering in the space around me like ghosts bent on disrupting

my day. One semester, that was all I was meant to teach in this class, and already there was a complication that should *not* have been happening.

Ms. Montgomery had caught my eye at the bonfire, and I'd only prevented myself from going over to speak with her because the other one appeared. Now I'd learned that Ms. Chamberlain was also attending my class, and I was just as "affected" by her. Worse slightly because, unlike her friend, "Lizzie" was decidedly more aggressive about her interactions.

A trait that brought out the dominant side of me that wished to provide punishment for such a smart mouth.

No. You will not even entertain the flimsiest notion of this. You are their professor. Book closed.

Unfortunately, my mind was not entirely my own this morning. I'd been so distracted by the relocation, moving into my new flat, unpacking here at the school in the office I'd be using, and trying to avoid having a massive breakdown from simply returning here, that I'd neglected the more animal part of myself.

I hadn't been to a club or reached out to any submissives in the usual chat to aid in relieving some built-up tension.

My thoughts swirled back to the women in my class, the ones who were nearly twenty years younger than me.

Ms. Montgomery had warm, tan skin, a smattering of freckles across her nose and cheeks. Her long, almost black hair dripped down her back in tumbling waves, and she gave off such an air of innocence and inexperience that I could hardly stand it. Everything about her had portrayed this image of delicate fragility, one that I couldn't keep myself from zeroing in on with the intent to break it.

Her friend, on the other hand, had been the total opposite—a woman of fierce attitude and obviously sexuality. Similar yet different, her deep-colored skin was complemented by a long braid that effortlessly flopped over her shoulder, with wisps of hair framing her face, a style that remained perpetually messy. Her eyes had been hazel, where Ms. Montgomery's had been a deep brown.

And both of them had possessed pouty, full lips that would look so very pretty wrapped around my—

"Stop, Caleb."

The echo of my hand slamming down on the small classroom desk slowly faded in the silent room. I clenched my fists, forcing myself to breathe evenly as I got up and erased the board behind me. Wind continued to howl outside, and then rain pelted the window as thunder cracked outside. Rain was so common on Night Grove campus that I almost didn't notice it, but the flapping of paper against glass got my attention.

A carnival.

I stared at the flyers that quickly soaked up the water cascading down from the deep gray sky. The fact that a traveling circus of sorts had come to town was rather surprising. The fact that they were flinging their posters at a magical academy was nearly impossible to imagine. There was no way the performers could know what we were. The dean and school board had done everything in their power to keep the truth of this place a secret since its creation centuries ago.

And yet, students would undoubtedly flock to it—any excuse to indulge themselves.

It made me nervous. Interacting with humans too much could be a recipe for disaster. Immediately, *reflexively*, I flinched, unable to stop myself. My pulse began to tick upward, and I reached up, desperately loosening my tie. This was precisely why I didn't want to come back here. Things were different abroad. The states were—

Crack!

I jumped, unable to stop myself. The thunder continued to rumble, low and loud, rocking the room, and I couldn't escape it. Too fast, I was breathing too fast, and my heart was beating too quickly. Black pushed in on the edges of my vision, and vertigo made the room tilt on its axis.

"No, no, no. Breathe, dammit. Breathe, Caleb."

But I was seeing it all again. It was too late.

My parents stood before me in a hallway—our old home. We were just talking, a stupid conversation about dinner or what to do that night. I couldn't remember now. But I could remember what came next. I would *always* remember what came next.

Twenty years, and the wounds were as fresh as they ever were.

I saw the door launched inward, kicked in by the man now standing on the other side of the threshold. Curses and threats shouted through the air were the appetizer to the main course of breaking and entering. An entire crew of them—humans...

hunters—shoved into the house, flinging me to the side as I rushed to help my parents, to keep them out of harm's way.

It had been of no use. I was still only a young man, no older than my students now. Twenty-two and I watched the life I loved, the parents who'd raised me, protected me, and loved me fiercely, as it was torn from me, casting me into shadow and pain.

I couldn't breathe, observing from too close a distance as it unfolded in front of me all over again. The doors were slamming around me, and my parents were screaming. I could feel the iron grip of the oldest man there as he commanded his followers— just men who'd fallen into the leader's web of malice—to kill my parents, to leave me alive so that I could carry this warning to "all you fucking heathens."

The men slit their throats, one after the other, blood pouring from the wounds and soaking into the carpet at their feet.

I had screamed then, until I couldn't, until the authorities poured into my home, dragging my frozen, shell-shocked self out of the house and into the back of a vehicle. They were gone, just like that; my parents had been eliminated from this reality, and all because they were different.

Because we were all different from *them*.

"Professor Harkert," I looked up to see a member of the faculty with her bag standing at the door, "I'm supposed to teach in here next period. Did you—"

"Apologies." I stood up, gathering my things quickly and hurrying toward the door. "I got distracted. Have a good class."

"No worries at all." The woman, Professor Kirby, if I

remembered correctly, smiled, her easy-going expression so calm in the face of the turbulence that still racked my mind. "You too. Have a good class, I mean."

She didn't need to know that I didn't have any other classes today, so I just smiled and nodded back, getting out of there as quickly as I could without being rude. I headed to the faculty building just a few minutes away from where I'd taught spellcasting and proceeded directly to my office. Boxes were still stacked in the corners, the bookshelves bare as I hadn't had a moment to fully unpack everything yet.

Slumping down in the seat behind the large oak desk that sat at the back of the room, I sighed, dropping my head into my hands. This was not how I wanted to start the school year. I couldn't even make it a single day before my PTSD symptoms reared their ugly head. And yes, I'd been struggling for some time, but being back here, where everything happened, it just made it so much worse.

I went into my bag, pulling out the small set of keys I always had with me, and used the smallest one to unlock the top drawer in the desk. Inside was my stash of necessary items, and I took out the bottle of Prozac and whiskey, using one to take the other. I'd forgotten to take the medication this morning, maybe that was why everything felt so much harder today.

It could also be that I hadn't been in Rockport for about two decades and had been met with a problematic student encounter not five minutes out of the gate.

Images of the women in my class resurfaced, and I groaned, thoroughly annoyed with myself. Where the human society at large was rather prudish and full of assholes that would kill you as soon as look at you, witches and other creatures tended to be a bit more on the "eh, fuck it" wavelength.

Though they're both rather abysmal when it comes to the treatment of mental health.

Enjoying the burn of the alcohol down my throat, I put things away as I considered what the hell I wanted to do this evening. This would likely be one of the last times I didn't have papers and assignments to grade, and stressed was a mild way of putting how I felt.

I was also still pretty damn wound-up from seeing Ms. Chamberlain and Montgomery.

Pulling up the school email I had for announcements, I noticed the distinct lack of any news and signed out as quickly as I'd logged in. I couldn't just go back to my apartment and sit there. Last night had taken everything in me not to devolve into a mess about seeing...*Temperance* at the bonfire. I'd wanted to do things to the image of seeing her there, bathed in the glorious orange glow of the fire, that were beyond inappropriate.

And after class today, it was that much worse. "You are such a piece of shit."

But unfortunately, I was a piece of shit who also needed to get this out. I couldn't let myself bottle it all up as much as I wanted to. I'd combust and take too many people along with me, something I remembered from the years immediately following my parents' deaths.

My phone buzzed, and I picked up to see a message from one of the few "social" contacts I had.

Elaina: *Hey, you swinging by the club now that you're in town?*

We'd love to see you. ;)

As far as timing went, Elaina was right on point. Going to The Knotted Broomstick to relieve a bit of tension sounded as good a plan as any. And gods knew that I hadn't been tending to my kink needs very much over the past few months.

Looking down at my screen with the faintest hint of a smile, I shot back a text, feeling a bit more hopeful now—even if I knew without a doubt that a certain couple was going to be in my thoughts while I found someone to play with.

Better that, though, than actually *acting* on it.

Me: *Yeah, I'll swing by this evening. It's been a while, and I have some stress to burn off.*

Elaina: Perfect. I'll be looking forward to it. See ya then!

I didn't bother to send another text back. Elaina and I weren't like that. We may have fucked a handful of times, but it was all just for the scenes. No strings, no messy feelings, and both of us liked keeping it that way.

So it was settled. I'd get what I needed off my chest, allow myself to let go for even just an hour or two, and I'd be back to myself in no time.

As long as I could keep my distance from those *witches* in my class.

Five

WHEN TWO PATHS MEET, FOLLOW WHERE THE WIND TAKES YOUR FEET

TEMPS

"Come on! It'll be fun. Don't you want to have some fun for once?" Lizzie stood in front of me as I sat on my bed, glaring at her as she held her hands up to her chest, begging me to go to that stupid carnival. "We'll go together and get popcorn and shit. *Please.* The parental units are nowhere in sight, thank gods, and I need to have some fun. We cut the bonfire short last night, too. So, you know, you owe me."

"Uh!" I gaped at Lizzie, my mouth wide open, before I snapped it shut and leveled her with another glare. "You were the one who said we could leave!"

"I was being nice, and you know it."

With a sigh, Lizzie pushed up from the floor, where she'd actually been kneeling to really drive the point home, and stomped over to her bed. As she crossed one leg under her, she folded her arms, managing to lift the subtle curves of her breasts, which were already way too visible in the tank top she'd decided to change into.

"Temps, we need to go have some fun. Studying isn't the only reason we're here. We've *never* been able to interact with other witches. You know some will be there. The flyers were all over the school. This is the perfect opportunity to actually forge some connections with our classmates."

I narrowed my eyes at her, mirroring her arm cross as I huddled down into the thick, black sweater I'd put on. It was knitted with massive, chunky yarn, and I loved it. It was also exactly what I wore for *nights in*, ones when I knew I wouldn't be dealing with people for the rest of the day.

"Don't you squint at me. Yes, I know I hardly care about being buddy-buddy with anyone, but these are witches. The odds they're cooler than the dumbass townies we usually meet are astounding. And besides," she eyed me all the harder, leaning in to make her point, "it's just a carnival, Temps. It's not like I'm taking you to a rave."

"You're not trying to take me to a rave because you have before, and it failed miserably."

Throwing myself back on the bed, I stared up at the ceiling, kicking off the slippers I'd thrown on and hoping that Lizzie would just drop it. But a moment later, the bed was dipping as she hopped in, towering over me on all fours.

Shit.

RE Johnson

Having Lizzie on top of me like this made every nerve in my body hum with white-hot energy. I could feel the blush starting in my cheeks, the smell of her dark, spicy perfume hitting me as her braid swung down over her shoulder. Lizzie's hazel eyes were a masterpiece this close up, all flecks of greens and blues and browns, and my breath caught in my chest.

"If you don't come with me, I'm going to drag you to the witchy sex club I want to try out instead."

My eyes flared wide as the shock of her words hit me hard. I was speechless for a moment, my mouth hanging open again, and I could hear my pulse in my ears, clear as day.

"You wouldn't," I managed to eke out.

"I would, Temps. In a damn heartbeat."

It was a standoff for several beats, the two of us staring at each other and waiting for the other to blink. A tiny voice in my head—one I always tried to ignore and push to the furthest reaches of my mind—piped up with the comment that going to a sex club with Lizzie would be a dream come true. But I shut that down quickly.

What would you even do there? You have no idea what sex or kink are supposed to be like. You're the most vanilla, untouched bookworm on the earth.

Lizzie cocked a brow, seeming to read my indecision and annoyingly impossible to deny curiosity. I chewed on my lip, my stare breaking from hers as I sighed.

"Fine."

"Yay!" She bounced me on the bed as she celebrated, a massive grin on her face, and then, before I could stop her, Lizzie was leaning down, planting a featherlight and hummingbird-quick peck on my cheek. "Get changed. There's no way you're going to a carnival in your homebody clothes."

She was scampering across the room in a flash, getting herself ready with the last few touches since she'd already changed into a black, leather miniskirt and a mesh tank top with a black bra beneath it. She looked like something right out of a Killstar ad— hot, goth, and signalling questionable morals.

It took me way too long to get moving, frozen in the bed and still speechless because Lizzie had deigned to kiss me, even if it was just on the cheek. Still, I'd agreed to this, so I needed to get ready, regardless of being trapped in the definition of bi panic—a likely truth about myself that I refused to acknowledge. Not with my mother and years of homophobic classmates haunting me.

I sighed again, pushing myself up off the mattress. I still hadn't started getting ready, and Lizzie was already onto the black lipstick and fretting over which earrings she wanted to wear. The sweater I wore certainly wasn't cutting it if I was going to be going to a carnival with my undeniably attractive stepsister, so I wandered over to my closet at last to find something to wear in my collection of modest, no-frills attire.

Again—and unsurprisingly—I stood there, not moving or making a decision as I looked over my clothes. I hated all of them. I always had, but they were cheap, covered me up, and a majority had been given to me by my mother. Aside from that comfort sweater, I didn't pick any of these out really.

I didn't know how, which sounded pathetic. But I wasn't sure what I liked.

"Are you going to stare at your clothes until they magically pop off the hangers and dress you all by themselves?"

Dropping my head, I grumbled only loud enough for Lizzie to just make out. "I don't know what to wear. I...I don't have stuff like you."

There was a beat, just one, and then Lizzie was at my side, draping her arm over my shoulder. "Oh, hun. I can help, and we're basically the same size. You could wear something of mine?"

I whipped my face to her, gaping at Lizzie as she smirked at me. "You want me to wear something of *yours*? Are you nuts? I don't have the...*assets* to pull that off."

"Oh, sweet, sweet stepsister of mine," Lizzie pulled me along after her toward her closet, "I beg to differ."

***

"Lizzie, are you sure about this? I feel—"

She yanked away my hand as I pulled down at the black miniskirt she'd put me in. It was the twelfth time at least that I'd been caught doing it.

"You look fabulous. Stop fidgeting."

Her classic smile hit me, and my cheeks warmed despite the crisp autumn air. We'd determined that the carnival wasn't *too* far of a walk, at least by college student standards, so we were crossing through the dimly lit streets of the Old Downtown portion of Rockport. I was exceedingly grateful that I persuaded Lizzie to let me wear a flannel over the black tank top she'd grabbed for me, especially considering it was tight as hell and showed the barest sliver of my midriff. I'd also been *graciously* allowed tights beneath the skirt, which I was happy about, even if they did have a few strategic holes in them.

"How much further? I'm freezing."

I glanced around us, eyeing the dark streets and alleyways for any sign of danger. It was just my luck that some psycho would come popping out of the shadows to mug us or worse.

"A few more minutes, freeze baby."

We walked in companionable silence for a few more moments, and I did my best to resist the urge to pull down the skirt with each step. At least I had my comfort boots to make me feel a bit better. Lizzie had said they actually went perfect with the outfit.

"I think it's going to rain. We should hurry up. I won't see those curls sacrificed to the water gods."

Lizzie had taken the time to actually curl my hair a bit, which was damn hard considering the stuff had a mind of its own. Wavy it could be, but not in any sort of smooth, uniform style.

Pulling me along after her, we rushed down the streets toward the glowing lights that we could start to see poking out through the gaps between buildings. We zigged and zagged through the alleys to get there as quickly as we could, and then Lizzie pulled up short as we passed by a building that was stuck in the back of the street, seemingly purposefully out of sight. There was a single, glowing neon sign over the door that read, "The Knotted Broomstick."

"What? Why are you stopping?"

Snorting to herself, Lizzie shook her head as she chuckled. "Well, would you look at that. It's the sex club I was threatening you with."

My stomach sank, and I stepped backward instinctively, my eyes as wide as saucers, no doubt. "Lizzie, did you—did you do this on purpose?!"

I was still shaking my head as I backed up, eyeing Lizzie with horror. She turned around, though, also shaking her head.

"No! It's just a funny coincidence. You need to—Temps!"

Flinging out her hand, Lizzie's eyes went wide, and I was a few seconds too late in realizing that she was telling me to stop walking. Instead, I plowed right into someone behind me, making us both grunt as I stumbled and began to pitch toward the ground, face-first.

"Shit!"

All I could see was the asphalt coming up to greet me when a hand wrapped around my bicep and pulled me back onto my feet, saving me from making a total ass out of myself.

"Professor?"

My pulse was still racing when I heard Lizzie, and it just got worse as I swallowed hard and began to turn around, seeing the impressive blue eyes of Professor Harkert locked onto me. He let go of my arm since I was capable of standing on my own at this point and stared between me and Lizzie, his brows down in a deep furrow.

Oh fuck.

"Ms. Montgomery, Ms. Chamberlain, what are you doing

outside *this* particular building?"

Wait, did that mean he knew about this place? Lizzie's sex club? Okay, that wasn't totally impossible. It was more than likely that word about a place like this got around town. Hell, he might have even needed to keep students away in the past.

"What are *you* doing by it, teach?"

I turned over my shoulder to glare at Lizzie. I could kill her right now, and all she did was just smirk at me before focusing on our professor again.

Harkert cleared his throat, and when I looked back at him, he shook his head, his jaw tight. "I assure you both that I am not entering. I am on my way to the carnival. And you?"

"I couldn't convince Temps to go, so yeah, we're headed to the carnival, too."

"Lizzie!" Rushing up to her, I glared, wishing that for once my stepsister would actually listen to my chastising, but that was as likely as it raining gold.

"I see."

I couldn't keep myself from turning toward Harkert again, shaking my head as I raised a hand, feeling like I needed to defend myself. But as I fumbled all over myself, I noticed our professor look over my outfit, and it wasn't utter disapproval that lingered in his eyes. *Was that—Nope, absolutely not. Don't even kid yourself, Temps.*

I also noticed that he wasn't wearing his glasses at the moment, his body covered by a black suit jacket and matching pants. A deep maroon shirt poked out from underneath, the top buttons undone. He was gorgeous anyway, that had been the entire problem, but like this, with this air of confidence and ease about him, my core was practically weeping for him.

Kill me. Just end it now. I can't take this.

"Well, if you're going to the carnival, why don't we all go in together. We can sit as a group and chat before things get started?"

Was Lizzie's plan to mortify me into an early grave? Because she was doing an excellent job.

"You don't have to say yes," I blurted out. "Lizzie has a habit of making herself right at home with anyone. You know, inviting herself into *everything*."

The last few words were spoken through gritted teeth, and Lizzie shot me a withering look. I nearly buckled under the weight of it, but she wiped it off quickly, flicking her attention to Harkert as she reached for my hand and squeezed tightly.

"I know how to make *any* gathering more fun is all. So how 'bout it?"

Harkert stared at us, his eyes only briefly flicking toward the sign over our heads, like he didn't believe for a moment that we had been planning to go to the carnival. His narrowed eyes were accompanied by rolling his lips into a stern line, and I felt so stupid for eyeballing his mouth way more than I should have.

Sucking in a deep breath through his nose, Professor Harkert turned sideways and gestured down the street toward the sounds of music and bright lights filling up the otherwise quiet part of Rockport.

"After you."

Six

Secrets Are Shrouded In A Bit Of Smoke & Mirrors

CALEB

What were the fucking odds? Had someone cursed me? Hexed me for the evening? Was this some godsdamn prank Elaina was pulling? Because what in the ever-loving hell could explain how I'd run into the only two people in town I was desperately trying to avoid on my way to a fucking sex club?

I fought back the urge to groan as I followed behind the two of them—Temps and Lizzie—as we made our way the few more blocks to the carnival. I hadn't wanted to go to the stupid thing from the moment it was announced, and now I *really* didn't want to go. Being shut in the dark with those girls was going to kill me.

Plus, explosions and I had a bad relationship, and gods knew the place was sure to have fireworks or some shit.

"Oooh! Look how fun!" Lizzie shouted ahead of me, yanking on Temps' arm as she pointed off to the side. "There's a house of horrors! Let's go in after the show!"

"Lizzie, you know I hate that kind of thing. I don't like being jump-scared."

I hated to admit it, in fact, I wasn't going to at all, but I knew somewhere in the back of my head I'd imagined being the scare actor chasing them both down through the haunted house. And that was way too appealing for my liking. Just picturing Temps screaming as she ran away, and I was ready to—

"Oh, come on. It was hilarious to watch you punch that one guy right in the face." Lizzie snorted, laughing as she pulled Temps along as we closed in on the front entrance of the carnival's circus tent, faded red and white stripes illuminated by glowing string lights.

Oh, well, that was not what I was expecting. "You punched someone?"

Temps turned over her shoulder toward me, and I quickened my steps, pulling up alongside her. The flush under her cheeks deepened as she looked sheepishly between Lizzie and me. That look of embarrassment had my cock kicking against my zipper.

"It was an accident! He jumped out from a corner, and my first instinct was to swing!"

I couldn't help but laugh, smiling as we walked up to the ticket booth. "That's not a terrible instinct. It might come in handy someday."

"Huh," Lizzie turned down the corners of her mouth, "that's

what I said."

I nodded back at Lizzie, joined with her in a private understanding of each other, and I was smirking at her before I could think better of it.

Warning, Professor Harkert. These are your students. Pull up. Don't get sucked in.

"Welcome, folks! Get ready for the show of a lifetime! Get your tickets here, and be entered into an exclusive giveaway for a behind-the-scenes look with Ring Master himself!"

Temps was already at the counter as Lizzie and I walked up behind her. Lizzie squeezed in next to her stepsister, clearly not giving a single fuck about anyone who was standing in the other line. I rolled my eyes, stepping to that other side and waiting for the next cashier to open up so that I could buy my ticket. At least, this would actually be cheaper than going to the club, far less money spent on cover and drinks, even if The Knotted Broomstick did have a three-drink maximum.

We paid quickly enough, and then Lizzie was dragging Temps toward the popcorn vendor. I could tell that Ms. Chamberlain pulling Ms. Montgomery somewhere was par for the course. Still, there was something in the way Lizzie looked at Temps while they waited for their popcorn that struck me. It was ridiculous of me to assume, but there was something familiar in that expression, in the way Lizzie tracked Temps' movement, because I was guilty of it myself.

No. You're seeing things. Just make nice and get the hell out of here.

And then the two of them were running back toward me, and it was Temps this time who I caught lingering her stare on Lizzie.

Am I seeing things? Jesus, do I need to get laid that badly that I'm turning the two girls I need to stay away from into a porn stereotype?

"Let's go, teach." Lizzie looped her arm through mine, surprising me and knocking me off balance just slightly. I corrected easily enough, and she grinned up at me as she pulled both Temps and me along into the tent. "Show's getting started soon."

I didn't know what it was about her, but I found myself as helpless to resist the pull of this woman as she happily led me into the circus portion of the carnival, as her stepsister did. She was enigmatic that way, and I looked across her at Temps with a brow cocked.

"She's rather demanding, isn't she?"

Temps laughed, her stunning, sweet face lighting up. "Oh, you have no idea."

Lizzie rolled her eyes. "You both love it. So shush."

Oh, I like that. Note to self, make Temps smile more often, and make Lizzie act like a little brat, too.

The thought was so unbelievably wrong, and I had to shake myself, pulling myself upright as the three of us found our seats in the front row of the tent, much to my chagrin.

"Lizzie, the front row?" Temps cocked her head, obviously just and thrilled about the choice as I was.

"I want to be able to see." She squinted, pretending like she was an elderly woman or something. I couldn't stop the laugh, and we all sat down on the wooden bench, Lizzie in the middle, and our feet resting on a layer of straw that had been put down over the top of the parking lot's asphalt. We were in an unused property at the end of Water Street, and this was a common spot in town for traveling events to set up, the city renting the space to make a little money.

"Welcome, everyone!"

The overhead light in the tent went dark, a spotlight finding an empty spot inside the ring where I had to assume the infamous Ring Leader would appear.

"We are so glad that you have joined us for an evening of death-defying stunts and awe-inspiring tricks in our circus here at Illusion de Lumière! We kindly ask that you avoid flash photography as it interferes with our acrobats, and we don't want any accidents, now do we?"

The crowd answered with a resounding, "No!"

"Excellent! Then do sit back and relax, enjoy the show, and be sure to scream loud for our amazing performers as they test the limits of physics and reality!"

Deafening cheers roared out of the crowd, Lizzie putting her hands around her mouth to amplify her shout as Temps and I clapped quietly. The room went dark again, not a single light in sight, and a low, musicbox-like melody began to play from somewhere unseen.

It continued for several moments, the people inside the tent growing a little restless as the darkness persisted. Next to me, I could sense Lizzie shifting in her seat, and her hand patted around on the bench between us.

"Ms. Chamberlain?" I whispered. "Did you lose something?"

I squinted to see in the dark, and her fingers wrapped around the edge of the bench, squeezing.

"No, I...this is dumb, but the emotions and energy. It's *a lot*. I just needed to ground myself."

It occurred to me that I hadn't asked what their specialties or natural proclivities were yet. The stepsisters were not only new to the school, according to the dean, but also new to exploring magic at all. Many of the students at Night Grove came from families of practitioners, but these two, well, their guardians were mundane.

"You're psychic?"

Lizzie nodded, the music swirling louder as brighter notes and cymbals were added to it. "Yes. And empathic to a degree."

Swallowing, I understood why she was likely feeling overwhelmed by all the stimuli, but it was also a bit problematic to be seated so close to an empath—of any degree—when you were presently fighting back your own emotions. I needed to lock down my mental barriers all the more.

"Lizzie," Temps cut in, "are you okay?"

"I'm fine." She waved off the concern, barely visible as orange lights began to glow from somewhere behind stands across from us. "I want to enjoy the—"

A massive crash sounded from the cymbals, an explosion of light and sparks shooting out of the middle of the ring that made everyone jump. I reflexively grabbed for the bench, the shock igniting my hypervigilance. My hand landed on Lizzie's, but before I could apologize, the spotlight centered on the Ring Leader now standing where smoke was still billowing around the ground.

"Welcome, one and all, to the Illusion de Lumière circus!"

All eyes, even my own, were transfixed on the lengthy man standing in the center of the large ring, delineated from the rest of the tent by a short circle of red wood, the edges chipped and scuffed.

"In a time of such darkness," the Ring Leader continued, his voice deep but scratchy, like it was playing through an old radio, "we, the Children de Lumière, bring you the light!"

Gouts of flame erupted from both sides of the ring, fire breathers either kneeling on the ground or perched on wooden boxes, creating blazes that illuminated the ring. Subtle house light came on as the flames died down, and performers of various types came in from places hidden by the stands.

The Ring Leader wore a large black top hat, a bit dingy and worn, and carried a black cane, the head of which was decorated with a large, red knob. He sported the usual tailcoat and vest, with white detailing across the front accenting the oversized golden buttons that ran down the lapels and closed the vest.

"Feast your eyes, mortals, on the daring tricks of the Children de Lumière, and remember to *never* try this at home."

More fire burst from the breather's lips, and several acrobats leaped into the ring, flipping this way and that as a pair of performers swung back and forth from the trapeze that slowly descended into view. Each person doing tricks in the ring appeared to be a contortionist of some sort, and as a woman flew past on the trapeze, she gripped the bar with just a finger.

That's not possible.

Internal alarm bells sounded, but this was the point of a circus: to defy gravity and logic. I was sure that an invisible wire could account for the trick. All of this—the circus and carnival outside—was rigged. Nothing more than smoke and mirrors.

"No! No, you mustn't! I was only doing some peeping!"

A woman was led into the ring by a pair of clowns, their outfits so muted that the red hardly held any saturation at all. It was strange for such a public event, but everything inside the tent felt just a bit off. The grins stretched a bit too wide, the music was just a hair discordant, and the clothing wasn't shiny and new or even trying to be.

"Is this part of the show?" Temps asked, and I looked over to see the worry on her face.

I had to assume it was, but I couldn't blame her for being on edge. The woman was dressed in a similar clown's outfit, but hers was a skirt and tall boots. What felt off were the tears that streaked her makeup, the acting feeling a bit too genuine.

"You will face the Butcher!" The Ring Leader called out, using his cane to draw attention to the massive wheel that was being rolled out and into the center of the ring. "Punishment and repentance for the snooper!"

The acts were typical circus fare, from the fire-breathing to the trapeze, but the way the performers were doing it was odd.

There was an undeniable edge to the words, almost...religious. It was probably just a new gimmick to keep things interesting, but I had to admit that I wasn't a fan of that particular spin on things.

I was also hardly an impartial judge, considering my past.

As we all watched, the woman was strapped to the wheel by her wrists, ankles, and waist. She didn't struggle, not more than the act probably demanded, and I shrugged when Temps shot me a glance.

"I assume so. Though it does feel a little gruesome."

"Maybe they're just leaning into the spooky season thing," Lizzie added. "I mean, scary carnivals and shit are like a Halloween staple."

"That's fair." Temps wobbled her head in a roundabout nod, and the three of us turned back to the scene in front of us.

A larger figure stepped out of the shadows, and there was no doubt in my mind that this was The Butcher. He wore some of the traditional clown garb, including the makeup, which was streaky and sloppy, but he also had on a large butcher's bib and a belt of large knives.

Lizzie gestured out at the man. "Okay, yeah, that's some scary clown shit for sure."

The Ring Leader pointed with his cane again, now standing on a large box off to the side. "The Butcher!"

Everyone cheered. This had to be the knife-throwing portion of the show, and no one else seemed particularly concerned. I couldn't sense a large number of witches gathered in the tent either. A few sporadic pings here and there aside from the two near me. If there had been, it was possible more of them would have been picking up on the strange energy of the circus, but as it was, it seemed like only the girls and I were on edge.

As The Butcher stepped up in front of the wheel, it began to spin, and the woman held there appeared to cry silently, leaning into the act. The demented-looking clown pulled a knife from his belt and lobbed it at the wheel. It landed perfectly between he spread legs of the woman with a loud thunk.

More cheers from the crowd as the man demonstrated his impressive aim, and I watched intently as he took out two more blades and did the same, landing these in the space between the woman's arm and leg on either side of her.

"Pro eo qui nos corroboravit!"

"What the hell? What language is the Ring Leader even speaking?" Lizzie furrowed her brow, looking between me and Temps.

We both answered, "Latin."

"Oh, well, shit. Can you tell what he's saying?"

Temps looked to me, and I gestured for her to go ahead. "Something about for him who has given us power or something."

"Empowered us, but yes."

A crack of sparks shot off as The Butcher landed a knife right above the woman's head, this strike sinking into the wood all the way up to the hilt of the blade.

"Haec tibi gratiarum actione tribuimus, certiores facti ut donis nostris in nomine tuo utamur!"

"And that one was?"

"He said it too fast," Temps whispered, her brows knitted with obvious frustration.

"We give this unto you in thanks, with the conviction to use our gifts in your name." I looked at Temps, then Lizzie, my jaw clenched as the tension built inside me. "As far as performances go, I'd say he's laying it on real damn thick at this point."

A loud *thwack* boomed through the tent, and I shot my attention to the show to see that this last blade had struck the woman in the chest right above her heart. The crowd gasped, and the two clowns at the wheel quickly turned it around. The pointed end of the blade stuck out from the wood, dripping red. People began to scream and demand someone get help, but I was frozen in place as the wheel spun once more and the woman was nowhere in sight, no longer strapped to the wood.

Another crescendo of awed sounds emanated around us, and then an eruption of sparks from the center of the ring flashed, making me squint as the woman reappeared in the center, taking a bow with a massive grin on her face.

"Okay, damn. That was impressive as hell. I was worried there for a second." Lizzie sighed, and I could actually hear her release her breath in a nervous chuckle.

"Yeah, me too," Temps said softly.

But I couldn't pull my eyes away from the woman who stood in the center, taking her bows. The Ring Leader had walked up to her, taking her hand and spinning her about, presenting her to the adoring audience.

She was taller.

It wasn't much of a change, hardly noticeable, but this woman was just a tiny bit taller than the one who The Butcher's blade had impaled. A part of the trick? I didn't know, but it all felt... wrong.

"Thank you, our fantastic patrons! As we take this short intermission, we have exciting news! The winner of the backstage tour has ticket number 5691!"

From the ceiling of the tent, the trapeze artists swung down right above the man in one of the upper rows. A spotlight shone down on him, and he got up with a smile, waving at the people around him. The two trapeze performers reached for his hands, hovering him just an inch or two above the steps as they glided him down. They all landed in front of the Ring Leader, and the crowd hooted and hollered as he was joyfully escorted toward the back of the tent.

"Remain seated or get yourself a snack! The performers will be back in just fifteen minutes!"

As the announcement ended over the loudspeaker, I moved to stand up. Whatever was going on here, I wanted a damn look at it. I didn't trust this. Not one fucking bit, and—

"Ooh, if you're getting popcorn, grab me some more. I demolished mine." Lizzie held up her empty box of popcorn, the red and white striped cardboard wafting around that classic smell of butter and salt.

"I…" But I couldn't think of what to say.

The girls didn't have the same concern over this that I did, and if I left them here to investigate, I'd be leaving them unattended. If there was truly something sinister going on, I wasn't about to risk their safety.

Dammit. I want a look behind that fucking curtain. I shot a glance back at where I'd seen the man and performers disappear before returning my attention to Lizzie.

"Umm, sure. I'll be right back."

Taking the box, I stepped out into the aisle, and as much as I hated it, I went out the front of the tent to get popcorn instead of following my gut instinct. Still, maybe I was being ridiculous. PTSD came with hypervigilance and seeing enemies where there were none. It could very well be that my mental health condition was getting the best of me. Gods knew it wouldn't be the first time.

The rest of the show passed by rather quickly, each act leaning into the macabre with a final farewell from the Ring Leader proclaiming that he was so thrilled we'd all stopped by to begin the nightly celebrations of "spooky season."

Clearly, I had been overreacting.

"Holy crap, it's *so* late." Temps looked down at her phone before stuffing it back inside a small black purse in the same of a bat. "I'm going to fall asleep on my feet as we walk."

"I would absolutely carry you, but I'm not that strong, and I'm not spraining another ankle."

Lizzie eyed Temps before they both devolved into a fit of giggles.

91

I hated how adorable I found it, slightly jealous of how carefree their twenties were compared to mine.

"I'd be happy to walk you back to the dorms." They both shot up, eyebrows up to their hairlines as they gaped at me. "It's late at night, dark, and you two would be a target for anyone with nefarious intent."

Laughing, Lizzie hooked her arm through mine again, Temps walking around to my other side. "Offer accepted. I do not need to deal with a creep right now. Or ever."

"Thank you, Professor. That's really nice of you."

I nodded, trying to ignore the swell of something unnameable in my chest. "Of course. Happy to help."

Seven

INCONSPICUOUS CLUES ARE FOUND BY MANY SETS OF EYES

LIZZIE

My skin felt raw and alive as we walked out of the tent and past the rides. All of us had silently agreed that we'd be going right back to the dorms, and for once, I was actually thrilled about it. I felt strange, something about the carnival and what we saw with the knife thrower was infiltrating my blood like a cold virus. I was a little off, a little shaky, and more than a little confused by the signals that were coming from everywhere.

While we'd still be inside the tent, the intensity of the crowd's emotions and thoughts had made it difficult to think, but I'd also been picking up on some strange vibes from the performers. Sure, the need for attention, craving the applause, that was all normal. What'd been peculiar had been the way they oozed rapture, this almost holy feeling of being lifted up during prayer.

But it was a damned circus, so that was fucking weird.

As we walked out through the entrance, Temps clung to me on one side. Now, without the omnipresent pressure of the audience, I could sense how she was on edge, the performance having freaked her out. Oddly enough, Professor Harkert was giving off the same energy.

"Didn't like the spooky theme, Temps?" I glanced over at her, the sound of our footsteps on the sidewalk loud in the silent evening.

"I'm never particularly good at handling the horror things, sure, but that felt..."

"It felt off, is what." Harkert stared straight ahead, his eyes glued to the darkness in front of us as we walked.

Zeroing in on him, I could pick up on anger. He was angry about something to do with the circus, but he was keeping a tight lid on his thoughts, likely trained in how to keep a psychic out.

"It did, right?" Temps sounded so vindicated, and I couldn't help but smirk at her as we kept walking. "It was just a little much. Like, did they really need to go that hard on the horror? I'm still not sure how they even pulled that off. It seemed too quick to be a typical trick. Are they...well, damn, do you think they practice?"

I cocked my head, considering. "You know, that would track with the strange vibes they were putting out."

Harkert abruptly stopped in front of us, looking me dead in the eye and so intently that I swallowed hard.

"What vibes?"

"Umm," I narrowed my eyes at him, actually a bit shocked by how aggressive he was coming off, "it's kind of hard to explain. But it was like...Okay, have you been to a church or rally or ritual where everyone is just buzzing, like they're high on the energy of the event?"

Nodding, Harkert's jaw clenched, the muscles visibly straining as we stood beneath a street lamp.

"Well, it was like that."

"Something was definitely up with the performers. I could tell that—"

Crack!

A massive boom of thunder made us all jump, and within seconds, the sky opened up, pouring down on us like it had a point to prove.

I pulled Temps close, huddling into myself as we tried to rush under the awning of the building right by us.

"Shit!"

Temps pulled Harkert in after us, and the three of us stood there for a moment, eyeing the downpour that had come out of nowhere. A bolt of lightning lit up the sky behind the buildings across the cobblestone street, and thunder quickly followed it, rumbling low.

"We have to get back to the dorms. I'm not staying out on the street until the storm stops. It could be hours," my stepsister moaned, leaning forward to peer up into the night sky.

I waited for her to slip back under the awning. "Well, unless you have any better plans, that means we're running."

Harkert sighed, shaking his head. "That storm felt kind of sudden. I just pray it's not students fucking with the weather."

Turning down the corners of my mouth, I smirked at him. Our stuffy professor had just cursed about some students being annoying. I liked that on him.

"So we running for it then? We could get back to the dorms in like, what, five minutes?"

Temps rolled her eyes at me. "I hate this. Ugh, at least I wore boots."

"You'll both freeze to death if you let yourselves get drenched." Harkert took off his jacket, shoving it at Temps before unbuttoning his long-sleeve shirt to reveal a white tee underneath.

He thrust the shirt towards me and then gestured out into the rain. "After you."

With a laugh, I shrugged on his shirt, folding the halves over my chest. Temps did the same with the suit coat, and then we made eye contact for just a second before darting out into the rain and running straight toward our dorm. Harkert's footsteps sounded behind us, and I laughed as the rain came down in sheets, soaking me despite the kind gesture of our spellcasting professor.

"Looks like you'll be ready for a wet t-shirt contest, Harkert!"

I could hear him grumble even over the sound of the rain. Temps yelped as she stepped into a deeper puddle than the rest, cursing as another crack of lightning and thunder shook the sky.

"My sock! Ugh, so gross!"

Still chuckling and frankly having a fucking ball, I beelined it down an alley that I knew would cut toward campus a bit quicker.

"This way!"

Temps and Harkert followed me, and in a few minutes, we were standing at the front door of our dorm. We all caught our breath, Temps and me still giggling about how ridiculous we must all look. I pulled off Harkert's shirt, which did fuckall but was a nice thing to do, and handed it back.

"Thought that counts, right?"

Harkert took the soaked fabric, which dripped in a constant stream, and shook his head with a sarcastic chuckle.

"Well, I suppose." Temps gave back his coat, looking slightly drier than I did. "But you should both get inside and get warm. It's not good to stand out her freezing in the rain."

"You worried about us, teach?"

I knew I was pushing it, but the look on both Harkert's and Temps' faces was too good to miss out on. My dear stepsister looked so horrified, embarrassed that I would say such a thing, while our professor simply narrowed his eyes at me, his jaw muscles working again as his aura darkened. Goddamn, I liked it when he got all huffy, like he was excited to...*punish* me.

"Did it occur to you that if something happened to either of you that it would be my ass on the line?"

I shook my head, taking a step forward as I looked up into his glacial blue eyes. "Nah, you like us."

"Lizzie," Temps yanked on my arm, getting me to back up into her, and the feeling of her slick skin against mine was heavenly, "we need to go in. Thanks for walking us back, Professor."

"Of course, Ms. Montgomery." He cast a glance at her, and he couldn't hide the way his eyes tracked down Temps' body before swiveling over to mine.

Harkert swallowed hard, and I desperately wanted to get my buddies for the evening to give in to their "more entertaining" sides. The three of us together? That would be something magical, and I meant that in every sense of the word.

Words were on the tip of my tongue when I looked over at Temps. As she stood beside me, I got caught up in the way the raindrop slid down her skin, making little trails that followed gravity down to the gentle curves of her breasts.

Gods damn, she's gorgeous.

Clearing his throat, Harkert shook his head and took a step backward, nearly out of the cover of the trees and overhang from the dormitory. He glanced between both of us, and there was something about his soaked, dark locks. They hung in his face slightly, and he had to shake them out of the way.

"Uh, I'll be going." Harkert shivered, clearing his throat *again*, and then dropped his chin as he eyed my stepsister and me. "I expect to see you both bright and early for class tomorrow. No passes for late nights."

"So demanding," I teased. "You just *love* being the boss, don't you?"

My entire body heated under Harkert's stare. He fucking fumed, devouring me with his eyes even if he would never admit it. Temps yanked on my arm again, pulling open the door and then getting me inside behind her.

"Thank you for walking us back, Professor. I'll make sure we're both in class tomorrow. Promise."

He might have wanted to stop it, but Harkert smiled, breathing hard through his nose as thunder rolled through the sky overhead. We all stood there in a moment of silence, and then Harkert dropped his head in a combination of a nod and a bow, his stare flicking from Temps to me and then back.

"Thank you, Ms. Montgomery. You're a very go—" But he stopped himself, rolling his lips between his teeth as he blinked slowly. "I'll see you both in class."

With that, Harkert spun on his heel and sped off down the walkway. I wasn't sure how far his apartment was, but something told me that it was a much longer trip than the good professor would ever admit.

"Ugh, you're insufferable. Let's go."

Temps pulled me toward the stairs, and we headed up to our dorm. The thing was, I wasn't tired in the least. Not with a soaking wet Temps to still feast my eyes on.

By the time we got up to our dorm and inside, I was thoroughly freezing from being stuck in wet clothes. The adrenaline of running here was wearing off with each second, and I headed directly to my closet while Temps locked the door behind us.

Pulling off my top was like peeling the shell off an avocado, and I tossed the thing into my hamper with a resounding plop sound. My skirt and socks were next, and with each item of clothing I lost, I just got colder. The air hit my bare skin, sending goosebumps skittering across me from head to toe. Shivering, I fished around in my drawers for a pair of sleep shorts and a shirt.

All I could find was the thin long-sleeved sweater I'd had since middle school. It was wildly oversized then and now fits me about right, but it'd also been worn and washed enough times to make the thing feel like silk.

It even had Batman on it.

The shorts were a no-go, though, hiding somewhere just to be a dick. I gave up the search, grabbing a pair of thick, tall socks to provide that necessary warmth.

"Dammit. Ugh, Lizzie, would you help me with this?"

I spun around to see Temps struggling with the shirt I'd made her wear and chuckled. Padding over now that my socks were on, I helped her get the fabric up and over her head as it fought to remain stuck to her. Without thinking, I dropped my hands to the zipper of her skirt—well, my skirt—and wiggled the pull tab so that it didn't catch and actually came down. It was a finicky thing about wearing that thing that only I knew about.

"What are you..."

The question drifted off as I wrangled the zipper, and Temps was able to let the skirt hit the floor and step out of it.

"Zipper sticks."

She nodded over her shoulder at me, looking painfully aware of how exposed she was even with her back to me, and then whipped her head around toward the closet.

"Oh, thank you."

I didn't know what got into me, but as the glow of the moonlight peeked out from behind a storm cloud, I reached out, wanting to drag my fingers down Temps' back. Just before my fingers made contact, thought, a boom of thunder shook the room, and she jumped, wildly flailing as she fell forward into her clothes.

"Fuck, the storm is going to keep me up all night." She pushed out of her hanging clothing and yanked down a large sweater, pulling it on over her head. "If someone did mess with the weather, I kind of hate them right now."

"Hmm." It was all I could manage, my heart pounding as I hurried over to my bed and got in under the covers.

After a moment, Temps finished dressing, not wearing any shorts either, I might add, and rushed to her bed, practically diving inside. She peered over at me from her side of the room, the covers pulled up under her chin. In the dark, I could still see her enough to know that she was feeling off, something I didn't need my abilities to tell me.

"The carnival was weird, right?"

With a sigh, I shoved the blankets off and walked over to Temps' bed. "Scoot."

She moved closer to the wall so I could get in beside her, and I lay down with my head on the pillow, meeting her stare.

"Yeah, it was. I...I don't know, Temps. Maybe they like weird. Who am I to judge? Though..." But I had to be reading into this, so I shook my head, dropping the thought in favor of getting some sleep.

"What? You can't leave me hanging like that?"

Rolling my eyes, I chuckled quietly. *Like you do to me all the time?*

"Ugh, fine. It's just that I noticed something while we were there—a symbol I recognize from a necklace your mom has."

"A symbol?" Temps' brow furrowed as she visibly thought about what I was saying. "That one from the church thingy she's so into?"

I nodded. "Yeah. But I'm sure it's nothing. I mean, they probably both go to it right. She said the cult—"

"Lizzie!"

"Sorry, 'church' has a following, right?"

"Yes, they have locations and stuff across the country. At least according to her. It's not like I went and looked it up." Temps sagged, her eyes dropping to the space between us as she burrowed down into the bed. "She's been going a lot lately. I... Okay, it's stupid, but I don't really like it. It feels like one of those holier-than-thou places. And not very queer friendly."

I cocked a brow, tilting my head as I found her hand under the covers. "Queer friendly? That matter a lot to you?"

Yes, it was a leading question, but sue me.

"Of course! Everyone should be treated equally. Hell, you're bi, Lizzie. Why would I want my mother to be an asshole to a group of people at all, let alone one that includes you?"

I didn't sense even a spec of mistruth in Temps' words. She believed that wholeheartedly, according to her body language, aura, and everything else. But I couldn't tell if she was including herself in that group. Temps had never been much of a dater, and while we'd talked about me being bi, she'd always danced around the subject.

"Well, I appreciate your support, as a 'queer' and all."

"Oh, shut up." She playfully shoved me back, and as I rebounded back into the bed, I scooted up higher on the pillow, shoving my arm under her neck and pulling Temps in for a cuddle.

"I'm cold and couldn't find shorts. Keep me warm."

Temps didn't move for a second, but then snuggled deeper into my arms, resting her head on my chest.

"That makes two of us. Do we have a short-stealing gremlin?"

I laughed, which I knew jostled Temps, and closed my eyes, suddenly feeling much more relaxed and ready for bed.

"Well, if we do, we'll just have to come up with a spell or potion to get rid of it, because I need my damn shorts. I'm not about to get expelled because I couldn't find my clothes. It should be because I chose not to wear them."

Giggling, Temps shook her head against my chest, and then I felt her relax, her breathing slowing down as she drifted to sleep. I didn't rest until I knew she was out, soothed by the sound of her breath moving in and out like the ocean.

Eight

INCONVENIENT INTERRUPTIONS COME WHEN THEY CHOOSE, NOT YOU

TEMPS

"And in that way, a spell is simply a desire made manifest. It depends on the concentration, the innate connection with the witch, and the conditions to which reality is being stretched. Theoretically, yes. Anything is possible through the appropriate spell or potion. But like science tells us, energy does not burst into creation nor does it evaporate or die. It transmutes. So, the greater the magical working, the more energy must be transmuted. And just where do you think the spell gets the energy from?"

Professor Harkert scanned over the room, and I raised my hand quietly. The other students were feeling less than enthused this morning, and I had a feeling Lizzie and I weren't the only people who'd gone out last night.

"Ms. Montgomery." Harkert nodded at me, gesturing for me to answer.

"From the practitioner, or in the case of alchemy, from the practitioner and the ingredients."

The barest hint of a smile lifted the corner of Harkert's mouth, and Lizzie nudged me in the ribs playfully. Looking over at her briefly, memories of last night swirled in my head. I'd fallen asleep snuggling with her in my bed, and even when I woke up to roll over, I'd hauled her arm over me to keep us linked.

There was something about being next to her last night that had eased the discomfort I'd felt ever since leaving the carnival.

I still didn't know what was up with them, but I agreed with Lizzie that it felt off.

"Excellent, Ms. Montgomery. That's correct. The practitioner supplies the energy, so the greater the outcome, the greater the demand on the caster. Something to be cognizant of, wouldn't you say, Ms. Mitchell?"

The young woman from the first day of class was continuing to annoy Harkert, it seemed. I didn't blame him. She gave off the horrible vibes of someone looking to outsmart and outshine the professor. *Not a good look, honey.*

"I was merely positing the idea as a thought experiment. I certainly don't intend to—"

The door to the classroom opened, the loud creak startling everyone inside. The dean stood there, her expression dower and stern. Even more so than usual, it appeared, because even

Professor Harkert leaned back, eyeing her curiously as his brows furrowed.

"Ugh, thank gods. An interruption to end Blondie's fucking tirade. 'I was merely positing—' Ugh, next."

Lizzie complained as I tracked the dean as she cut straight into the room and went up to our professor, whispering with her head turned down and her back to the room. Harkert's expression was the only one I could see, and just as it dropped, Lizzie sat up straight in her chair, reaching for my hand and squeezing.

"Something's wrong."

I nodded, flicking her a glance before I refocused on the conversation at the front of the class. "Yeah. Something tells me we're about to have an early dismissal."

After another moment, chatter starting up all around Lizzie and me as we watched Harkert, Dean Owens stepped back, facing the class with her brows raised as Harkert stepped forward. He scanned over his student, his eyes lingering on me and my stepsister for a moment before he cleared his throat. He dropped his stare to the floor, then raised it quickly enough to address us.

"Class is dismissed for the day. Unfortunately, there has been a situation that I must assist the dean with. I will see you all tomorrow."

In a flurry of movement and chaos, the room emptied out, but I was glad to see that Lizzie was on the same page as me, remaining seated as all the other students left, likely to go start their nights early.

"Girls, you're free to go. If you have a question for Professor Harkert, you can—"

"What happened?" Lizzie cut in. "I can sense that you're both hella upset? I think we deserve to know."

I didn't usually love it when Lizzie lumped me in with her arguments, but she had a point this time. We did deserve to know because Harkert's expression was more severe than usual, and even I—a person with no empathic abilities—could tell that he was trying to remain calm when he was upset.

"Ms. Chamberlain, I can assure you that we have it well at hand. You're dismissed."

Lizzie scoffed and folded her arms, kicking her feet up on the chair in front of her.

"You should just tell her." Harkert offered, sighing as he came around his desk and narrowed his eyes at Lizzie. "She's stubborn."

She frowned. "Hey."

Standing up, I held a hand out for Lizzie and pulled her up so that we could both go stand down at the front with the professors. I could tell that for a moment Dean Owens believed I was going to take Lizzie out of the room, but I had no intention of leaving. Something was going on, and Lizzie was right. We needed to know about it.

"It's true, Lizzie. But in this case, it's useful. Please, Dean Owens, perhaps we could help. Four heads are better than two and all that."

The dean leveled me with a stare, but I didn't crumple or relent.

Maybe it was seeing the carnival and how gruesome even fake life could be, or maybe it was coming to this school and really seeing that I did have power and we could grow it here, but I was feeling damned confident right now.

"Ugh," the dean sighed, reaching up to pinch the bridge of her nose, the fabric of her tweed jacket stretching around her arm, "at this point, the school will take all the help it can get."

I nodded, keeping my expression neutral as I waited with Lizzie for her to reveal the big news. Lizzie still had her arms crossed, and I could see her leaning in a hair toward the dean as she squinted, trying to read the woman's aura.

"There has been a death. I have asked—"

"There's been a murder, Rebecca. Don't sugarcoat it if they're going to help, which, for the record, is a terrible idea."

Glaring slightly at Harkert, I felt Lizzie shift next to me, likely shooting her own glare at the man. But then I turned back to the dean, zeroing in on the distinction that Harkert had made.

"There was a murder? On campus?"

Dean Owens bobbed her head in a nod, her eyes pinned down to the wooden floorboards that creaked under our feet.

"I'm afraid so, though it wasn't directly on campus. At least that's not where...the body was found. Staff located it this morning during a sweep of the forest around the grounds. We've been increasing them since the previous spellcasting professor was *also* killed."

"You think it's related. You think the professor and this...girl are involved in something. Who would want to hurt them? Did they know each other?"

Glancing at Lizzie, Dean Owens worked to keep the annoyance off her face, her jaw muscles working as she chewed on the side of her lip.

"They were people involved with the school. Witches. That's all the connection we've been able to make so far. They were not in the same classes and didn't interact outside of school, at least according to people in their lives. But..." The dean straightened, pulling on her jacket to shove it back in place. "...that is why the school board is requesting Professor Harkert's assistance. He is quite skilled as an alchemist at deducing things from the residue left on a crime scene. We take care of the matters in-house, and do not need the mortals finding out about our world because of some awful turn of events."

"Was it one of them?" Lizzie didn't look away from the dean as she asked, her attention utterly focused on the pale-skinned woman who looked admittedly much more frazzled than she had when she first led us to our room.

"A human? I should think not." There was a nearly imperceptible twist to the dean's shoulders, her eyes tracking over to Harkert for scarcely a second. "There are...injuries on the body that look to be consistent with some sort of magic. Now, ladies, we need to get going. Time is of the essence, and—"

"Let us come. My sister has incredible powers of perception, and I am quite skilled with alchemy. I should like to act as the professor's second set of hands."

There was an extended pause, the professors exchanging looks with each other, then zeroing in on me and Lizzie again. I didn't falter, and of course, neither did she. We stood our ground, waiting for the dean to get this show on the road and lead us to where we were needed.

I'd never really thought of myself as the type of person to get involved with something like this, but there was a spark that lit up inside me at the prospect of seeing such an incredible use of alchemy in action. I'd been so obsessed with the subject for so long. This was my opportunity to learn, and by virtue, this was my chance to do some good with what I was able to do, and as corny as it might have sounded, I did want to help people.

Sure, I mostly wanted to survive my own life without getting myself into some mortifying situation that would leave me curled up in a ball on my bed, but beyond that, being a force for good sounded incredible.

"You want to be in there? T—Ms. Montgomery, what you're going to see will be brutal and nothing someone should *ever* have to deal with. You won't be able to go back to the place where you *didn't* know what a dead body looked like."

I knew what Harkert was saying, and it made sense. I'd never particularly wanted to see something like that, but this girl had been killed, and whoever or whatever had done it was still out there, based on what the professor and dean were saying. It could happen again.

It could happen to Lizzie.

No, if there were something that I could do to protect her, protect campus, I'd do it.

"I understand, Professor. But I would feel worse if I knew that I could have done something to prevent more deaths and didn't. I couldn't live with myself. I've been studying the signatures that magic leaves behind on a person for years in my spare time. I know a great deal about what can go hidden unless revealed by an alchemical solution. Please. As someone familiar with your work, allow me to assist you."

Harkert's eyes flared wide, and he stared down at me like he was finally putting two and two together.

Oh, yeah. I know you. You don't put your picture in the books, so I didn't before, but you're that Caleb Harkert. I got into alchemy because of your work.

"Wait," Lizzie pulled my shoulder so I'd look at her, "he's that book guy? The collection you've been growing for the past few years?" I just nodded. "Well, shit. Small world, huh?"

"You need to do exactly as I say." Harkert's voice made me look at him, and I held his eye contact, unwavering. "Understood?"

A single nod. "Yes."

"And I suppose Ms. Chamberlain is just going to *tag along*?" Dean Owens shot Lizzie a look.

"Where she goes, I go. Plus, you said it yourself. You'll take all the help you can, and I can read the body."

"What?" The dean's annoyed expression dropped into concerned surprise.

"Yeah, not a common trait, I guess. But I can…When my mom passed away. I'd seen…what happened when I touched her."

"You're a morrighan. I haven't seen…" Dean Owens shook her head, marveling at Lizzie, and my stomach tightened. I didn't like how she stared at her, an awe too close to jealousy. "…not in years. Well, this changes things. You will come, but as Professor Harkert said, there is no preparing you for what you are about to see. It will be gruesome. I cannot protect you both from that."

"We get it." Lizzie nodded as she scooped herself to face me, gesturing toward the door. "Time's a'wasting."

The dean cleared her throat, straightening her jacket again, and proceeded to the exit. "Right this way."

Nine

TAKE A PEEK BEHIND THE CURTAIN & SEE WHAT CANNOT BE UNSEEN

LIZZIE

Dean Owens led us to a room at the far end of a long hallway on the top level of the main building on campus. Harkert and Temps were behind me, chatting about some alchemy shit while I kept an eye on the dean. She'd gotten even more on edge when I mentioned being able to read the dead.

And that was saying something.

Ever since she'd walked into the classroom, I'd picked up so much tension in her aura that it felt like a rubber band ready to snap. It made sense to a degree, of course. I mean, there had been a murder of one of her students following the death of a professor, too. But her energy had been so frantic. Hell, it still was. Owens was blasting alarm bells like a damned neon sign, and it was giving me a headache.

Worse, it was so aggressive that it affected the motive and the clarity of her thoughts. I couldn't get a solid ear on what she was thinking. It was usually pretty easy if I were doing it to any non-magical person. Still, since I'd arrived at school, I was noticing that everyone had pretty solid blocks around their minds and emotions.

Some, like Harkert and Owens, were nearly impenetrable.

But that panic had been too strong for even the dean, who was probably packing a butt ton of power, and couldn't be hidden.

"Please do your best to avoid interrupting the members of the school board, Ms. Chamberlain."

I looked up at the dean as she pushed open a thick wooden door, revealing a large conference room of sorts. It had probably been a meeting chamber for witches ages ago, and now it was filled to the brim with stuffy old geezers in suits and robes. *Oh, how the mighty have fallen.*

"I'll do my best."

As the four of us stepped into the room, I was quick to peek around the space, looking for the body that we were going to examine. I didn't relish the idea of being caught off guard by it. I wanted to control when that bombshell dropped. Unfortunately, I couldn't see anything.

"Dean Owens, I don't recall instructing you to retrieve students along with Professor Harkert."

The voice pulled my attention across the room and behind the curve of a massive table in the shape of a ring. The empty center cleared the view for the intricate tilework on the floor, and in each of the chairs surrounding it, there was a person seated, eyeballing me and Temps like we'd stepped in dog shit on our way in.

The one who'd spoken was directly across from us and looked like something straight out of a TV show. He was probably in his fifties or so, dark hair streaked with gray, and scowled at us as he sat there in his black robe, his fingers tented in front of him.

Cocking a brow, he finally pulled his eyes off my stepsister and me, zeroing in on Dean Owens. "There had better be a fantastic explanation as to why two *students* are in the faculty meeting chambers."

She stepped forward, lowering her head in a semblance of a bow and regarded each of the twelve members before speaking.

"These students have offered their insight to aid in the investigation. Ms. Montgomery is a pupil of Professor Harkert's, has been studying under him for some time," Okay, that was a lie unless you counted reading his books, "and will act as his assistant. Ms. Chamberlain, on the other hand, well, you're looking at the first morrighan to set foot on campus in twenty-five years."

An odd zing cut through the room as the school board reacted to Owen's words. But what really stood out to me personally was the timeframe she'd mentioned. A morrighan had attended school twenty-five years ago. And at that time, my mother would have been about eighteen. She was the only other morrighan I knew of, the woman who'd prepared me for this magic before her own death.

Did Mom go to school here?

"Regardless of their apparent *talents*," Robe Asshole cut in, "they are students, and we do not need inexperience mucking up our investigation into these heinous crimes."

My hands squeezed into fists reflexively, and I wanted to tear across the room and kick this wanker right in the dick. As I fumed, I could sense Temps close in behind me, her hand finding my shoulder and offering a sympathetic squeeze.

"What would 'muck up' the investigation would be to turn away resources when this board is so desperate in need of them."

The entire room turned its attention to Professor Harkert. I turned over my left shoulder, watching him as he stepped up in front of the dean and leveled the head douchebag with a look. I could read the annoyance and superiority simmering in Harkert's blood, like he knew this man and didn't think very highly of him in the slightest. The guy behind the table felt exactly the same, and they were in a bit of a standoff as Harkert took off his glasses and began to wipe them off with a handkerchief from his pocket.

"A morrighan is wildly beneficial to this situation, and it's not like they're going on trees. Ms. Montgomery is my assistant, and I cannot do my work without her. So either pull your head out of your ass and let us get to work, or get comfortable with the idea of another body dropping soon."

Temps' mouth fell open as she stared at Harkert, and I just smiled. That had been damn fun to watch, and it certainly painted our mild-mannered professor in a very different, *very sexy* light.

I could watch that man tear the old bastard apart all damn day.

Dickless crumpled like a cheap suit, ducking his chin as he flustered in his chair. I could tell he was about to say something else when another member of the school board stood up from her seat and gestured toward a door on the left side of the room.

"Get us answers. Preventing more deaths is the only important thing here."

As she flicked her wrist, the double doors slid apart, revealing a room with a single table in the center and basically no decor, where this part of the room had been full of the stuff, from books to lamps to paintings all over the wall. On that table was the body. My stomach dropped as I instinctively reached for Temps' hand. She was right there for me, and I had to blink away the image of my mother lying in a coffin I knew she didn't want, as I'd been forced to go up to her like that and "say goodbye."

"Are you okay?" Temps looked back at me, but I only just noticed it as my eyes were glued to the sight in the other room.

"Y-Yeah. I'll be fine. Let's just do this."

Harkert appeared to be the only other person besides my stepsister to see my reaction, and when I met his stare, he gave me a slight nod, his eyes holding mine in a moment of silent communion. He'd seen dead bodies before, of course. I knew it from the moment he warned us in the classroom, and now, it was so painfully clear to me that they had been the bodies of people he loved.

We crossed the room, slipping into that other space that had been hidden, Dean Owens right behind us. The area around the body smelled strange, a pungent, almost sweet scent that I guessed was likely the herbs and concoctions keeping the flesh frozen in time. They couldn't have it decaying when we still needed to study it—or right in their office.

"Temperance," Harkert's voice blasted through my thoughts as I stared down at the person lying on the table, "the cart over there should have our supplies on it."

It was strange to hear him use her first name, but I knew he was trying to make like my stepsister was his assistant, and they'd be on a first-name basis if they'd been working together for a while, like the dean said. Hurrying over to the cart at the side of the room, Temps pulled it over to Harkert, doing her best to keep her attention on his until there was no choice left but to look at the dead body.

Together, Temps and I silently took in exactly what we were looking at.

It was a young woman, probably our age. She had dark hair with a blue streak in the front. Neither of us had spoken to her, but she lived in our dorm. I'd noticed her walking to class nearby when we were heading to spellcasting. That stung.

But worse were the criss-crossing slashes that littered her body. She was covered with a thin, white sheet, which gave her a modicum of privacy, but I could tell that the markings extended across her entire body because her arms were exposed, and the fabric didn't hide the red that hid beneath it.

Her skin was so damned pale, and on her forehead a symbol had been carved into her flesh. I had to assume that when they'd found her—whoever it had been—she'd been a ghastly sight. It would be hard to see the person behind all that blood. The girl was cleaned up now, much like how I'd seen bodies presented at the morgue in TV shows.

"Do we know what the symbol means?" My voice was scratchy when I spoke.

As I flicked my eyes up to the people around me, Temps met my stare. Her brow furrowed ever so slightly, but she didn't fall apart, using me as a bit of an anchor even though I was doing the same damned thing.

"No. We have people researching it, but it doesn't show up in any of our usual rituals or occult iconography."

Dean Owens crossed from behind me to stand near Temps, who was right by Harkert's side at the foot of the table. For everything I was starting to dislike about the woman, I had to admit that the look of sorrow on her face was at least believable right now.

"The butter of antimony, Temperance, and an alembic to dulcify with akahest and agrimony."

The sound of glass bottles clinking against each other echoed in the nearly empty room as Temps inspected the ingredients laid out in a tall, sectioned case on the cart. She pulled out three long tubes and then reached for the alembic, placing it over the burner and sparking it with the striker. Pouring the liquids inside, a fuming concoction slowly formed as the chemicals and herbs mingled together. It looks weird as hell, this putrid yellow color that morphed through the clear liquid, almost like ink. The agrimony was well known for revealing secrets, and as the other supplies coalesced into a thick smoke contained in the alembic, it sort of charred and turned the mixture black, with deep gray smoke wafting around in the vessel.

"Excellent. Now," Harkert held his hands over the smoke, "use your innate energy to manipulate the smoke from the alembic over the body, keep it slow and controlled, demanding the truth be revealed to you."

Temps nodded, her hands hovering in the air with Harkert's as they drew the smoke out of the vessel and over the girl's cold form. Owens and I watched it gradually work its way across her face all the way down to her toes. The smoke sank into her skin, lingering in the cuts and deep within her chest. I could sense the anticipation of the entire board as they looked on from their round table.

What a load. It was clear who was in charge there.

But there along the edges of the cuts and in a strange flicker that glowed inside the woman's ribcage, lighting her up from within but shorter than a blink, gold specs.

"What is that?"

Temps looked over a she manipulated the smoke to circle back around, Harkert's attention dropping to the glowing sediment forming on the injuries, especially the sigil carved into the woman's forehead. Dean Owens leaned over, getting a closer look at the almost glitter-like flecks that stuck to the slashes.

"That is proof this was not a human attack," Harkert spoke through gritted teeth, exhaling hard. "Magic residue. It's left over when a spell targets someone, but this is...nothing I've seen before. Spells track over the entire person, but these. It's like it's only where the instrument used to cut her touched her skin."

"And behind her ribs." Three pairs of eyes shot up to meet mine, and it hit me.

They couldn't see it.

"Oh, right." Leaning over the body, I focused on that tiny glimmer of something behind her ribs, reading it like I would emotions. "It's like...it doesn't like that you're nosing about. As if the lingering magic is pissed you're digging through its trash."

"This is a young woman, a student." Dean Owen sounded horrified. "Not *trash*."

I held up my hands in surrender. "Hey, not me. I'm just the interpreter. The stuff you can see clinging to her, it's *claimed* her. She belongs to whatever killed her. Her body, but more importantly," I breathed deep, tasting the malignance on my tongue, "her soul. It was torn from her."

"How in the hell—" Harkert shook his head, pointing at the dead woman's chest. "Can you see who did this?"

A shiver raked through me, and I did my best to stifle it. "I can't guarantee what I'll see, but...I'll try."

I hated this part. It felt like being the wrong kind of high while someone else was behind the wheel of your mind. But whoever had done this to her was one fucked up piece of shit. It wasn't like souls got torn from people on the regular. That was some heavy-duty shit.

Reaching out, I gingerly lowered my fingertips to the symbol on the woman's head, which was clearly important to whoever killed her. As soon as I made contact with her icy flesh, I was rocket hard by the wave of a vision, my head snapping back as I no longer saw the room around me.

Hazy images settled in my mind's eye like the mixture had in that alembic. The edges wavering like inky puddles, I focused on what the woman was seeing since I was looking out at the world from her perspective. The terror in her was so intense, making me nauseated and dizzy. Lights flickered around her, and as she'd turned her head to the side, unable to call out for the help she so desperately wanted, I saw faded red and white stripes.

"She was at the carnival. Or near it."

Another wave, and now I couldn't tell where she was. Only that there was a figure, all black and impossible to distinguish, standing above her with a knife. It was intricate, almost ceremonial, and the person above her smiled wide, wider, wider, and then too wide to be right, revealing sharp teeth as the hands began to glow gold.

I snapped out of it, back to the room around us, out of breathing and feeling like I was going to puke my guts out.

"Sharp teeth. Glowing hands. Ugh," I gagged on nothing, gripping my stomach, "and all wrong. It definitely wasn't some human."

"Dammit." Harkert slammed a fist down onto the table, making Temps jump. I wanted to tell him to knock it off, but I was too out of it, stumbling on my feet. After a moment, he looked over at me, and the anger on his face shifted to concern. "You look like you're going to fall over."

"Yeah," I waved a hand around, getting dizzier by the second, "that's the plan."

Before I hit the ground, strong arms caught me, pulling me upright. I couldn't really focus on anything else that was going on, dimly aware of a conversation being held right above my head.

"Lizzie!"

"We need to get her lying down. I have supplies in my office. Let's go."

And then I was moving, the world dark and fuzzy around me.

Ten

TIGHT CONFINES & A BIT OF SECRET LORE MAKE FOR STRANGE BEDFELLOWS

CALEB

Using my key, I opened up my office two floors down in the faculty building as Lizzie leaned against me, Temperance on her other side. She'd collapsed right after peering into the dead girl's last moments. I didn't have enough experience with a morrighan to know if that was common, but Temperance looked horrified.

"Help me lie her down on the couch." I let my keys dangle from the knob as the two of us walked Lizzie inside, setting her on the slim couch I had in the room, parked against the left wall. "Good. I'll get my supplies. Close the door so there isn't excess emotional stimulation."

Temperance didn't say anything, just rushed over to the door, yanked out my keys, and shut things up again. It was my job to get Lizzie the tonics she needed to right herself. That vision must have drained so much from her; if she didn't get regulated soon, she was going to drop into the space between and get stuck there.

"Hang in there, Lizzie. Harkert's getting stuff for you."

I glanced over my shoulder as I went to the thick, wooden cabinet behind my desk, pulling open the small doors and drawers to gather up everything I needed. Temperance sat on the couch near Lizzie, holding her hand as she peered down at her unconscious face. I needed to act quickly.

I yanked out the glass vials of bezor and magnesia, sniffing the bit of yarrow root and willowbark I had on hand to ensure it was still fresh. Dumping them all in a mortar that sat on the wood lip of this breakfront cabinet, I ground them with the pestle, using enough force to crush them all down quickly. The mixture began to subtly smoke from the effort put in, and I blindly reached for the moon water I knew was somewhere at my right.

"Come on," I whispered, finally grasping the bottle and pouring in a hefty amount until the solution was ready.

Bottling it up, I rushed it over to Lizzie. I scooped under her head, angling it back so that I could part her lips with the edge of my hand by pushing down on her chin. She opened, and I delicately poured a few drops of the liquid into her mouth, being sure to let them absorb before I poured more.

"What is that?" Temperance's voice was so quiet as she spoke, and I looked over at her, still cradling Lizzie's head.

"It's a grounding tonic essentially. It'll draw Lizzie's consciousness back to her body instead of the in between that's calling her. A side effect of gazing into a dead person, I'm afraid."

Her eyes glassy with unshed tears, Temperance squeezed Lizzie's hand. "How do you know about this?"

"I don't know as much as I'd like. I'm going off the limited knowledge I have and doing my best. The school taught me a fair bit about magic and spellcraft, but unfortunately, a morrighan is so rare that much of what I learned went used for so long. I'm trying to remember it all."

I dropped more of the tonic into Lizzie's mouth, watching the grayish-yellow mixture disappear on her tongue. The room sank into silence as Temperance and I waited. I could hear more rain pattering against my window, the ornate stained glass still quite thin and doing little to dull the noise. Wind howled, and I took off my glasses, setting them down on the coffee table in front of the couch as I adjusted my hold on Lizzie.

Her breath lifted her chest slowly, but it was picking up. Her color was getting better, too.

"Ugh!" Lizzie shot upright on the couch, nearly smashing her face into mine. "The fuck?! Where—Why does my mouth taste like shit?"

"You're okay!" Temperance launched herself into Lizzie's arms, a chuckle breaking through a sob.

Leaning back, I shuffled down the couch and then stood, giving the two of them some space. With a smile, I looked on as Temperance took Lizzie's face in her hands, shaking her head. The tension in my chest lessened, and I let out a sigh as Lizzie finally smiled back at her stepsister.

"Don't do that to me ever again. I didn't know what happened. You just dropped. Crumpled up like a flower or something."

Lizzie chuckled, dropping her forehead to Temperance's. "I'll do my best. Did you seriously wake me up with the world's worst-tasting shot, though?"

"I did not." Lizzie's eyes met mine as she looked past Temperance, resting her chin on her stepsister's shoulder. "It was a grounding tonic on crack, with a little desperation mixed in."

Sitting back, Lizzie smirked as Temperance joined her on the couch. I walked in line with it, resting back against the edge of my desk. This office was cramped, but at least the furniture was all solid wood and high-quality.

"Desperation, huh?" Crossing her arms over her chest, Lizzie stared up at me, not bothered by how Temperance rested her head on her shoulder.

"You would have felt the same had you seen Temperance's face. If I didn't bring you back, I'm fairly certain she would have killed me."

That made Lizzie's brows shoot up, and she turned to her stepsister, who was blushing bright pink under that warm tan skin of hers. The corner of Lizzie's mouth lifted, and she reached up to tuck a long brown curl behind Temperance's ear.

"Worried about me?"

"Don't look at me like that." Temperance playfully shooed Lizzie away. "Of course, I was worried."

They both eyed each other for a while, and suddenly, I felt like I was intruding on a private moment. I didn't think they realized it, however. Still, I cleared my throat and circled my desk, reaching into the lower drawer for that bottle of scotch and a rocks glass. Sitting down in the plush leather chair, I poured myself a few fingers' worth of the stuff and took a long sip.

"Mind sending a bit of that over here? I really need to get that taste out of my mouth."

Looking up, I rolled my eyes and restrained a laugh as Lizzie raised a hand, waiting until I nodded before she glided it through the air to herself. She took a sip from the bottle, making a face as she swallowed the strong liquor, and then offered it to Temperance.

"Really? Umm...oh, what the hell. Today sucked."

Closing her eyes, Temperance put the scotch to her lips and barely made it through a drink before she coughed and shoved it back toward Lizzie. That broke my resolved, and I laughed, shaking my head as Lizzie took one more drink and then set the bottle down on the table.

"We should discuss what happened today as well. Your vision implicates a serious magic user or users who were responsible for this killing. And unfortunately, what the dead didn't tell you was that there have, in fact, been several students and townsfolk going missing for the past week or so now. Just before the session started."

"Several?" Temperance's expression dropped, and she sat up straighter in her seat, looking between Lizzie and me.

"Yes. The profession I took over for, along with a groundskeeper and two other students. This attack puts the total up to four. That may sound small, but—"

"Any amount of dead people is too much." Lizzie eyed me, nodding along. "We hear you. So what else do we know about who's doing this?"

"Little, I'm afraid. The school has been targeted in the past by rivals or humans, but this is the first time that magic has been involved. Night Grove has not seen this many deaths before, either. In the past...when, umm," my voice catches as I remember how dark the world seemed when I was Lizzie and Temperance's age, the frenzied fervor of the bigoted crowd who thought they knew what this school was about, "there was a close-call as it were. Humans with rather narrow beliefs were getting louder and louder about their dislike of Night Grove. A couple who lived here in Rockport was killed, and that encouraged the school to take on greater precautions, and the less radical humans backed off."

Silence hung around the three of us, and then I heard the springs in the couch adjusting, looking up to see Lizzie staring me down with curiosity and concern.

"Your parents...they were your parents, weren't they?"

Sighing, I gulped down another mouthful of the scotch, dropping my face so that I saw only the open pages of the old book in front of me. I'd been reading up on transmutation because the circus display still didn't sit right with me.

The words peered up from the pages, taunting me with their vague explanations of how an injury could look real but not affect the person at all.

"Yes. They were." I was speaking before I even realized it, still focused on the book, the yellowing of the pages, and the scent of old paper and leather. "I was there the night they were killed.

Humans who thought we were monsters. I was a student here at the time, but I left shortly after. I couldn't...I couldn't face the constant reminders."

"I know what you mean." Finally pulling my attention away from the book, I glanced up at Temperance. "So much of my dad still lives in our old house. My mother has redecorated and moved on, but I can feel his essence lingering there, the scent of his aftershave permanently perfuming the air."

There was a quiet understanding between us, and I held Temperance's eyes, squeezing the bottle of scotch so hard that I was sure it would crack. Grief didn't just fade away. It simply became a part of your life, a new weight to carry around on your shoulders. It was always there; you just got used to the press of it.

"I know it's why my dad moved here from Salem. He's a doctor who couldn't save his wife. Eventually, he couldn't practice at the same hospital anymore. Then, it was moving to a new district. It wasn't until we got here a few years ago that he finally seemed better." Lizzie waves the scotch back over to her, taking a long pull before floating it back to me. "It doesn't feel different to me. I could sense Mom right up until she moved on. She's not here, and she wasn't in Salem either. Don't know about your dad, though."

She turned to Temperance, offering a mournful shrug. The two of them stared for a moment, gripping each other's hands and holding tight. I saw so much of myself in both of them, like they were halves of who I had been all those years ago.

Temperance was that book-smart, laser-focused part of me, obsessed with school and academia, with learning everything there was to know about alchemy. And Lizzie was the furious part of myself, the part angry with the entire world for letting me down. She was rash and impulsive because standing still felt like an invitation to Death. Moving was the only way to keep from breaking apart.

"Well, as you both can see, that's why this is so important. It's picking up steam faster than we can manage. We can't just keep watching people die."

"Okay, so what about the carnival?" Temperance sat forward on the edge of the couch, furrowing her brow as she swallowed. "We all know something isn't right there, yeah?"

Lizzie snorted, and I let out the breath that had refused to leave me during our little exchange. Sliding the book I'd been studying to the front of my desk, I rested my chin in my hand, my elbow leaning against the leather blotter that protected the wood surface.

"Indeed. I looked at this when I got in this morning. It talks about the level of magic required to create a convincing illusion of someone being harmed or changed. From everything it says, I *don't* think that's what happened last night."

"Wait, so that chick really...*died*?" Lizzie's brows were at her hairline, and Temperance scooted closer to her, threading her arm around her stepsister's.

"When I looked closed at the woman who appeared at the center of the ring. She was...slightly taller than the other one. I think the woman impaled by the blades was, in fact, another victim."

"The carnival is doing this? But how the hell would it get away with that? It travels all around. People are going to put two and two together and realize—"

"There's magic involved," I cut in. "I highly doubt they let their methods be discoverable at all. I lucked out last night, just catching the difference, and I've been practicing magic for twenty-some years."

Lizzie stood up, walking in front of my desk and planting her hands down on the surface so that she was right up in my face.

"Then we need to figure this shit out. What do we know about them?"

Gesturing toward my laptop on the corner of the desk, I cocked my head. "By all means, Ms. Chamberlain. If you can find something about them, please do."

She rolled her eyes at me, making my pulse flicker for a moment as Temperance joined us at the desk, laying her hand down on the pile of books I'd stacked up earlier.

"Fine. I'll Google. You both do the bookworm thing and see if you can find something in all these books of yours that looks like that symbol on the dead woman or this one."

Quickly, Lizzie scrawled an image on a spare pad of paper I had on my desk, stealing a pen from the mahogany desk organizer I had next to the books.

"My mom's necklace? The church thingy?" Temperance looked at Lizzie as if she'd lost her mind.

"Hey, I always thought it was more like a cult, and the vibes last night were all 'holy glory' and shit. They could totally be related."

"Holy glory?" I smirked, furrowing my brow as Lizzie took my computer and sat down with it on the edge of my desk.

"Yeah, like all those people who get off on praying and believe they're getting 'lifted up' by their god."

"That just sounds like religion, Lizzie."

"Which is all fucked sometimes, Temps."

Scoffing, I held up a hand. "Alright, back to your corners. Let's just see what we can find."

It was a handful of hours later that we all sat around my coffee table with a plethora of information and a bad fucking feeling about all this. The carnival did have a record of being around during some missing person reports, but there was no way to prove anything. From what Lizzie found, they were known for their macabre performances, and the symbol of that "church" was spotted on several of the performers in the photographs she'd managed to dig up.

The symbol itself—along with the one on the victim we'd seen— was tied to some ancient workings that were utterly alien to me. Temperance and I had found some obscure references to them in books that I'd had to call up from the depths of the archives and delivered to my office, which we passed off like an extra-credit assignment.

"This is odd. Have you looked at this?" Temperance lifted up onto her knees from sitting on the floor in front of the coffee table, pushing a book in my direction. "This isn't standard witchcraft stuff. The language is almost...religious. But there's a note in the margins, something handwritten by someone ages ago. Does that say what I think it says?"

I pulled the book to me, scanning over the faded writing. "His Holy Goodness, Barer of Light, nothing but...lies? I think that's what it says. Growing malevolence seeking to...Fucking hell, 'feast on the righteous.'"

Using air quotes around the last few words, just like the writing did, I glanced between Lizzie and Temperance before continuing.

"Golden light, powers exchanged, but not to god to It." Tilting my head as I set the text down, I raised my brows, chewing on my tongue for a moment. "Well, it looks like someone figured something out. Af if this is some sort of entity acting like a god, looking for worshippers, it's not unprecedented. It also tracks with the—"

"Cult vibes!" Lizzie said, her excitement laced with vindication. "I fucking told you!"

Unable to keep myself from laughing, I pulled my glasses off, setting them down on the table that was strewn with books and printouts that Lizzie had found. The sun was setting outside my stained glass windows, and the low lighting painted the room in soft hues of yellow and orange. I only had the lamp by the couch on, and it hit me how alone the three of us were in my office.

The entire campus was likely gone by now; surely, no faculty to come knocking. We'd also dispensed with the required uniform attire at this point. My jacket hung on the back of my desk chair, my sleeves rolled up to the elbows, and I'd loosened my tie when it was getting too fucking hard to concentrate. Both Lizzie and Temperance had ditched their school jackets, left haphazardly on my couch, and while Temperance's skirt was still the usual length, Lizzie had cut hers to hit at mid-thigh.

With her perched on the edge of the chair, her legs uncrossed, it was a test of fortitude not to glance down and follow the tantalizing warmth of her deep tan skin up to the shadowy juncture between her legs.

We'd also gone through like a third of that bottle of scotch.

What the fuck were you thinking, Caleb?

"Who fucking called it? I did." Lizzie stood up from the couch abruptly, strutting over to Temperance and leaning down into her face, so close I thought she might finally go for what they both clearly wanted—what I desperately wanted to see. "Who's amazing?"

No, you can't fucking go there.

Temperance rolled her eyes, the warm pink of a blushing coloring her cheeks. "You're amazing, Lizzie. I don't think I need to tell you that."

"No, but *damn*, do I love to hear it." She kissed the tip of Temperance's nose, smirking as she sashayed around us, proudly walking like she was some kind of peacock.

Lizzie's hips swished, and I was drawn to looking at her like my fucking life—or at least that of my cock—depended on it. My flesh was laced with lava, and I pulled my tight further away from my neck, feeling Temperance watching Lizzie as well, like a laser focused close to my skin.

Before I could think better of it, I stood up from my position on the couch, stepping in front of Lizzie to block her path. I couldn't tell which was strong in my blood fury or arousal.

"What the fuck do you think you're doing?"

It was an animal growl, and Lizzie stopped short before the shock on her face gave way to amusement.

Fucking *amusement.*

"Why's it matter? Something stuck up that cute ass of yours? Because we just cracked a fucking murder mystery, and you should be in a way better mood."

"Lizzie!" Temperance called from something beyond the bubble that existed between her stepsister and me. "Seriously? Are you *trying* to get us expelled?"

Suddenly, Temperance was there, and if the dim, burnt yellow glow of the lamp, the hair that fluttered around her face was as striking as a Degas. The backdrop of deep brown shelves and decades-old wallpaper sat behind the two of them, framing these exquisite women like a Renaissance painting. They were too damn beautiful. I didn't know what to fucking do with myself, and I needed out of this room. Out of this tight space, where I wasn't sure what I was about to do.

I rushed to the door, about to fling it open, when Lizzie interposed herself between me and the exit. She looked up at me, so much tinier than I was, and I could see the heavy up and down of her breath, sense the intensity burning through the air between us.

"No. I..." She flicked her eyes down, this miniature moment of insecurity. "I...I don't want you to go. Either of you."

Casting a brief look over my shoulder, Lizzie smiled ever so slightly. "You're damn good at keeping your cool, Professor. But not now. Not after the scotch has loosened you up a bit, and now there's no denying the waves coming off you. So, put your money where your mouth is."

Clenching my jaw hard enough to make the joint crack, I focused on the floor. "This isn't right, Elizabeth. I'm your professor. Temperance is your—"

"I'm well fucking aware of the labels, *teach*. The thing is," Lizzie blinked, looking up at me from under her lashes as she leaned back against the door, making the fabric of her blouse stretch across her breasts, "I don't fucking care."

Gods help me, every logical thought evaporated in that moment, leaving only the raw attraction I felt toward these admittedly impressive women.

And then my lips crashed down on Lizzie's.

Eleven

WHEN A LINE IS CROSSED, THERE'S NO GOING BACK

TEMPS

Professor Harkert was kissing Lizzie. I was standing across the room, my entire body feeling like it was going to burst into flames, and Professor Harkert was *kissing* Lizzie.

Holy shit, is this really happening?

I fought the urge to pinch myself, watching my stepsister and professor losing themselves to the feeling of roaming their hands over each other. I should have been horrified, turning tail and running out of this room faster than a blink.

But I wasn't.

Because I wanted to watch, no, I wanted to join. I'd been harboring these feelings for Lizzie since the moment I saw her, and she'd said that she wanted *both* of us to stay. Lizzie had said that she didn't care, and some part of me knew that had always been true. She flirted, and yes, she flirted with everyone, but there was no denying that how she operated with me and Harkert—*Caleb*—was different.

"You just couldn't help yourself, could you?" Caleb's voice was a low growl as he leaned back, his hand wrapped around the back of Lizzie's neck. "You had to go and be a little brat."

My eyes flared wide, but Lizzie just smirked, biting that damn lip of hers as she held eyes with our professor. She lifted her leg around Caleb's hip, that modified skirt of hers riding up. My pussy clamped around nothing, wet and aching for both of them.

There's no way you're denying you're bi now, Temps.

"Yes," Lizzie snarked. "I did. And something tells me *you're* a brat tamer."

Even from here, I could see how Caleb reeled back. He stumbled backward slightly, Lizzie following as she locked the door to his office. I was still frozen, unable to say anything as Caleb turned around, running a shaking hand through his hair.

"Dammit. *Dammit!*" Caleb crossed the room to his desk, standing behind it and facing the wall of bookshelves. "I should have guessed. We...we need to stop this. It was just a kiss. We can-we can move on. I'm your professor. We-We need to stop this."

Lizzie tracked Caleb to where he stood, running her hands up her back just as I realized that her telekinetic pull was yanking on my shirt. The move untucked it from my skirt, and I fought with the invisible force to keep it down.

"You were going to that sex club, weren't you?"

Caleb spun around, shock all over his face as he narrowed his eyes at Lizzie. "How do you know—It's not important. I can't do this."

It was a losing battle against Lizzie's powers, and I yelped as the button at the bottom of my shirt split apart.

"Ah! Lizzie!"

"Then maybe you just want, teach." She flashed me a grin before looking over her shoulder at Caleb. "Until you can't anymore."

She was walking toward me. I needed to stop this. I needed to be like Caleb and tell Lizze that—

"I've wanted to do this since the moment I laid eyes on you, Temperance."

In a flash, it seemed, Lizzie was in front of me, grabbing the collar of my shirt and pulling me toward her. Our breasts pressed against each other, and I ineffectively bit back a moan. Her mouth hovered over mine, the warmth of her breath caressing my face. My eyelids grew heavy, and I couldn't look away from the plump fullness of Lizzie's mouth. The tiny voice in my head was screaming, telling me to end this, to run away. But I was stuck to the spot, held by Lizzie's firm grip as she brushed her lips against me—featherlight and teasing.

"You're fucking mine, Temps. All godsdamn mine, and I won't wait a second longer. I've worked too damn hard to make sure I'm with you every step of the way, getting us the same room, applying to this school at all, and it's time you realize that you belong to me."

My mind reeled at the information, hearing that Lizzie had manipulated everything so that she could always be with me. It should have scared me, and maybe it did a little, but the rest of me was in awe. She'd done all this for *me*.

"But I might be willing to share if our third gets off his ass." Lizzie chuckled, bearly audible. "For now..."

And then she kissed me. I could taste scotch and magic on her lips, the warmth of her skin seeping into my being. Lizzie felt both right and wrong pressed against me, her hand wrapping around to the small of my back as she pulled me closer. We were so flush together, and then her knee shoved between my legs, slipping between them so that her thigh could brush against my core. I whimpered against her mouth, and Lizzie took the chance to slip her tongue past my lips. Our tongues collided, and wetness swelled, soaking my panties.

I was a horrible fucking person, but damn, I loved this.

Tongues dancing in an erotic courtship, we kissed and kissed until I could hardly breathe. Lizzie kept me pressed to her, one hand still at the small of my back while the other cupped my cheek. She dominated everything about me, and I felt so at home under her command like this. I'd always followed Lizzie wherever she led, and the truth was, I always would. She was my north star, the point I had to follow and damn me to hell, but I was so tired of fighting this.

Her caresses, rough and demanding, worked down my chin to my neck, both her hands now on my ass. Lizzie dropped her lips to my chest, using her magic to unbutton my shirt, the two halves hanging free while she worked her kisses down to the tops of my breasts.

"I've wanted this for so fucking long, Temps. Ugh, you taste *so good.*" I wanted her lips all over me. I wanted to touch her, do my own exploration. "My sweet little stepsister, I just knew there was a naughty girl beneath all those layers."

Holy hell, what Lizzie was saying was so outrageous. Still, she wasn't wrong. I'd touched myself to thoughts of her, watched her, wanted this, but tried to keep myself away for years now.

A low growl rumbled from a few feet away, and I remembered that we weren't alone. My skin burned with embarrassment. I was letting my stepsister kiss me and touch me, all while our professor watched. We were all going to hell for this, if it even existed. That was a human religion thing.

Crap, Temps. Get out of your head.

"See something you like," Lizzie pulled her mouth away from my skin, and I couldn't hold back he whine, "Caleb?"

"You're testing me, Lizzie." Glancing over at him, my stare still lidded because the sensations were intoxicating, I saw Caleb on the other side of his desk now, his arms flexed as he squeezed his hands into fists. "Do you have any idea how much trouble we could get in?"

Laughing against my flesh as Lizzie lowered her mouth to me again, it was a moment before she answered him. A moment she spent finding the hard nub of my nipple through the thin material of my bra and playfully biting down. I squeaked, bowing back as Lizzie held me up, stopping me from falling.

"Do you have any idea how wet our sweet Temps is? Because I'm about to find out for myself."

"Godsdamn it."

Mortification flared through me as hot as the sun as I heard the sound of hurried steps across the wood floor, the heels of Caleb's dress shoes clicking softly. The scent of dark amber and scotch wafted through the air towards me, and then icy cold hit my skin a Lizzie's mouth was pulled away. I could keep in the whine, and forcing myself to look up, I watched as Caleb gripped Lizzie by the throat, smashing his lips against her mouth before he leveled his hungry gaze on me.

"You have one chance, Temperance. One. Say something now, or I swear to gods, I'll—"

"Kiss me."

The words were out before I could even think them through. But I didn't care. I wanted him. I'd wanted the feel of his hands on my flesh when I saw him at the bonfire, and even the thought of letting him touch me in front of the crowd right then and there was enough to have me clamping around nothing.

Empty. Too empty. I want...oh gods.

Still holding Lizzie, Caleb used his other hand to yank me against his mouth. He was fiery and aggressive, even more than Lizzie, and I melted under the scorching heat of his lips. Caleb's tongue shoved into my mouth, seeking out more from me, and I gave everything I could, relinquishing myself to the dominant claim of his kiss.

I felt drunk. Drunk on the exquisite feelings of arousal and need singing through my blood. I'd never felt anything this profound in my life, and the satisfaction at finally getting what I wanted was as potent as a drug. I wanted to be good for them, to show my Lizzie, my Professor, that I would give them whatever they wanted.

It was so wrong, so clearly insane. Lizzie was my stepsister, Caleb my teacher. This went against so many fucking rules. I was bad, naughty, a sinner.

À la folie, as they say.

The world around us was a distant memory as Caleb gripped my throat, tightening his hold just enough so that my breathing was constricted, but not gone. I'd never had this done to me. Hell, I'd never kissed anyone before today, which was entirely because I was saving it for Lizzie. And now, I got the both of them.

Then suddenly, I felt something at my back, quickly realizing it was Lizzie. Her thin fingers found the edge of my skirt, lifting it up until I felt the chill of the air on my ass, on the damp fabric of my panties. Her lips found my ear before she playfully nibbled on the lobe, Caleb's kiss leaving me breathless. I arched against him as Lizzie's fingers dusted over my seam, wishing I could cry out, but Caleb ate up the sound.

His free hand found my breast, fingers reaching inside the fabric of my bra. Then in one swift yank, he tore the thing off me. The bra was done for, and I yelped, exposed to both of them as my skin burned. My nipples hardened all the more, aching from the cool air and the need to be touched.

Still holding my throat, Caleb pulled back, looking down at me. "Fucking hell, Temps. You're fucking stunning. Such sweet little tits just begging to be abused."

Fuuuck. This is really happening—ho-ly shit.

"Take off her panties." Caleb didn't break eye contact with me as he pulled me closer to him. "Leave the skirt. And don't you dare think I want you holding out on me, *Ms. Chamberlain*."

Hearing him boss Lizzie around, calling her Ms. Chamberlain like that, it was wild, and my body buzzed all the harder. Her fingers found the top of my underwear, and Lizzie hooked her fingers in them, slowly dragging them down my legs. I was bare beneath my skirt now. My *pussy* was bare, and they were going to *do things* to it, to me.

"Mmm," I whimpered, unable to find my words.

"Such sweet, little sounds you make, Ms. Montgomery." Caleb shot a look at Lizzie behind me, holding out his hand, and then my panties were hanging from his fingers, making me blush furiously. "And how pretty you look when you're so embarrassed for me."

Caleb put the fabric to his face, sucking in a deep breath as he drew in the scent of sex from my wet panties. My eyes flared wide as Lizzie chuckled darkly behind me, her fingers winding up through my hair and fisting it.

"Fuuuck." Caleb groaned, his eyes rolling back as he squeezed my throat tighter for a moment. "So *fucking* good."

"You should know what you're missing out on," Lizzie whispered in my ear, and before I could even begin to comprehend what she meant, her own panties were pressed to my face.

Sin. Sin and sex and everything I've ever wanted.

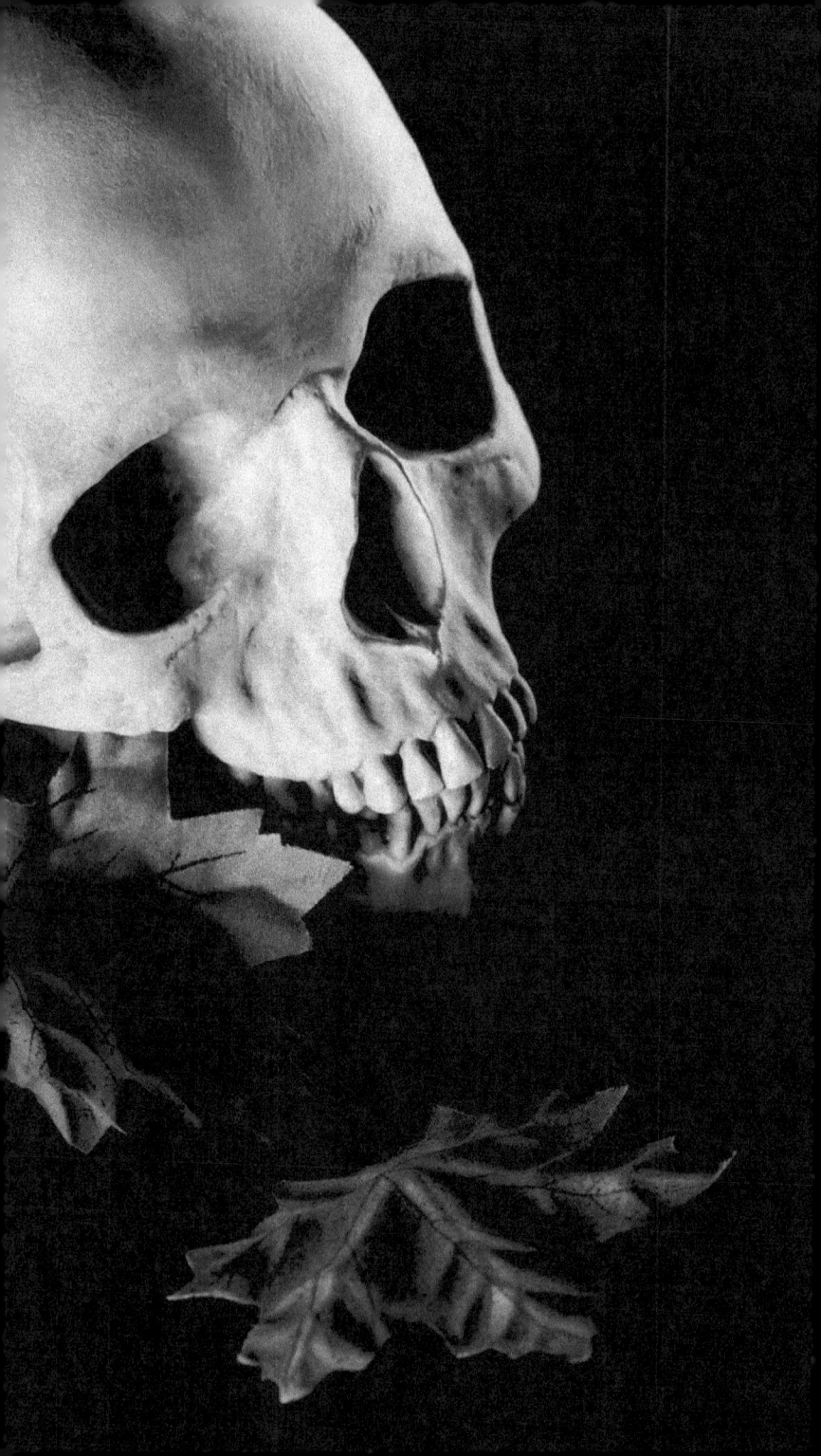

Twelve

AND SO YOU SLIP INTO THE DARK, NE'ER TO BE THE SAME

CALEB

If it weren't for the searing ache in my straining erection, the scents that infected my senses, I would have thought I was dreaming. But there was no dream I could conjure up that would even touch the wicked acts unfolding before me. Temperance whimpered, her eyes fluttering shut as Lizzie pressed her panties to her nose. We were in far too deep now. There was no denying how depraved we were, and miles away, there was a part of me that cared.

But right here and now, there were only these incredible women and what I was going to do to them.

The sun was entirely behind the buildings outside my window now, making my office a dark, intimate bubble. The moment was just as fragile and marvelous, Lizzie and Temperance softly

Their warm tan and brown skin was silky smooth where I touched them, Temperance's throat still in my grip as Lizzie came around to stand in front of me. She stared up at me as she chewed on her lip, and I pulled her in for another feverish kiss, Temperance's panties sliding over my sleeve to my wrist. I reached between Lizzie's legs as she wrapped her arms around my neck, sliding my fingers through her slick seam.

"So very wet for me." I stuffed my fingers deeper inside Lizzie, feeling Temperance squirm in my grip as I did. "Oh, don't you worry, Ms. Montgomery. You'll have your turn soon enough."

Lizzie squeaked, hissing as I sank deep into her cunt, her brow furrowing as she instinctively pulled her hips back.

"It's no use trying to avoid me, Ms. Chamberlain. You're going to take everything I give you."

Her eyes flicked up to mine, a tiny note of apprehension there. One that I should have been much more concerned about, but it only made my cock jump, pressing against my zipper.

"I'm...Oh fuck," Lizzie's head fell back as I pumped in and out, squeezing Temperance's neck and walking her closer to me, "I'm a virgin."

The air left my lungs like I'd been punched. "What?"

Nodding, Lizzie ground herself down on my fingers. "You're the first. And Temps."

I shot Temperance a look, and she nodded, her blush reaching epic proportions now. "Yes. Me too."

They're both fucking virgins. *Fucking hell. I should stop. We need to end this before it gets any further. I—*

"Oh, *Professor*," Lizzie moaned, her eyes fluttering, "you're fingers are so thick. It feels so *goooood*."

My erection wept, precum smearing on the inside of my pants. I couldn't bring myself to stop, to pull my fingers out of Lizzie's tight pussy. It was so damn good. She was right, and there was no going back now.

Yanking Temperance to my side, I kissed her hard, fucking her stepsister with my fingers, her arousal dripping across my hand. Temperance mewled as I squeezed down on the sides of her throat, her small hands coming up to my wrist and holding on tight. But she didn't pull me away. *Good girl.*

For a brief moment, I realized how many protocols I was tossing at the wayside. There was the student-professor problem, yes. But there was also the fact that we hadn't discussed hard lines, reds, yellows, and greens. Nothing I would usually do when setting up a dynamic. But this was just too feverish, too desperate, and unhinged.

I'm breaking so many rules. What's one more?

My dark core flared, slipping my fingers free of Lizzie as I got Temperance to take a step backward. Turning my attention to Lizzie, I narrowed my eyes on her, licking my fingers clean as she gaped at me.

"Get down on your knees. Now."

A flash of defiance lit Lizzie's eyes, and she started to lower, but *very* slowly.

"Malicious compliance, huh? Fine." I shoved her head down, making her hit the floor. Lizzie grunted low as her knees hit the wood, and then I took her wrists in one hand, Temperance's panties still looped over my arm. "Hold them up, or I'll spank you until you scream."

Lizzie's eyes flared, her mouth dropping open slightly. But she raised her arms, holding her wrists level with each other. Now I was going to need two hands. I looked to Temperance, smirking.

"I'm going to let go, and you're going to stay right there."

She nodded in a series of quick little bobs, gazing up at me like I was some type of god. And hot damn, wasn't that just incredible.

That's right, little witch. I'm your only god now.

"Good girl."

I focused on Lizzie as I let go of Temperance. I took the panties that hung around my wrist and looped one of the holes around one of Lizzie's wrists. Winding the fabric up so that it was tight, I forced the other loop around Lizzie's other wrist, creating a beautiful makeshift bind. As Lizzie dropped her wrists, her eyes pinned to mine, I reached for her chin, pulling her mouth open.

A string of saliva stretched between her lips, and I smirked. "Stay."

In a bit of a surprise she did, and I reached for my belt, dragging the leather through the buckle and then down my zipper. Lizzie's stare dropped, and I took a step forward before reaching back and shoving my hand between Temperance's thighs, pulling her toward me by cupping her ass.

"Oh!" She stumbled to me, and I dragged my hand slowly to her pussy, her skin so damn slick.

"This is all mine, Ms. Montgomery." Lowering my eyes to Lizzie, I smirked ever wider. "And hers. But right now, Ms. Chamberlain needs to get my cock out and suck like her life depends on it."

Try as she might, Lizzie couldn't keep the grin from consuming her stare, the corner of her mouth lifting. She glided her hands up the front of my thighs, converging at my downed zipper. Reaching in with one hand, Lizzie freed my erection through the hole, gripping the base tightly. She'd been staring at me the entire time, and now that her eyes dropped, I was soaring on cloud nine as her eyes widened.

"Holy shit."

My cock kicked in her grip as she held me tight, no doubt marveling at the rows of gleaming beads that went down the underside. I'd got one at first and had enjoyed it so much that I went for the full ladder.

"I didn't tell you to look, Ms. Chamberlain. And your sweet *sister* is waiting for you to get started so I can stuff her pussy full of my fingers like I did for you."

A shuddering breath left her, Lizzie's eyelids fluttering, and then she leaned up onto her knees, her lips hovering over the head of my dick. Shyly, Lizzie extended her tongue, licking up the bead of precum that gleamed on my skin. The moment the heat of her tongue hit me, I groaned, gliding my finger across Temperance's seam without going in.

Snatching Lizzie's wrists by the panties that held them, I held her arms up toward my shoulder. "Suck."

Moaning, she craned toward my shaft. Both women—*my*

students—were about a foot smaller than I was, making so many positions possible. Lizzie hung from the hold on her wrists, wrapping her full lips around my cock. The warmth was exquisite, and she took more of me before bobbing her head up and down, sucking me hard.

"Ugh, good girl," I praised, and I looked to Temperance, watching her face as I pressed one finger between her folds and circled her clit. She was so wet for me—for *us*. I moved in circles, making Temperance tremble as she dropped her head to my arm, clinging to it as her legs wobbled.

The sound of Lizzie's gulps was music to my damn ears, and Temperance sang along with the melody, moaning and whimpering as I worked her clit faster. When she whined, pressing her face into my arm, I slid one finger into her pussy and then another. It made her shoot her head up, peering up at me with pink cheeks and watery eyes.

"It's so much."

Temperance's voice was so breathy, this sweet, high-pitched croon, and I smirked at her, filled to the brim with dark need and sinful arousal.

"Sweet little virgin cunt can barely take my fingers?" I chuckled, utterly lost to the intoxicating pull of these exquisite beings. "How are you going to take my cock, little flower?"

"Uhh..."

Her eyes rolling shut, Temperance's head dropped back as she rubbed against my hand, rocking her hips as I slid in and out. I turned to Lizzie, squeezing her wrists as I held them, her mouth completely wrapped around my shaft as she swallowed me down.

"Does the brat like her treat?" I huffed as she sucked her way up, popping off the head of my cock with a loud smack.

She swallowed, flicking her eyes up to me. "Yes. But is that all you got?"

I chuckled. "You really do like to push my buttons, don't you?"

Smiling, Lizzie held my stare, dragging her tongue up the underside of my shaft, paying attention to each bar under the skin.

"Get up."

Pulling on Lizzie, I make sure she doesn't take her sweet time, hooking into Temp's G-spot to make her squeak before sliding my fingers free. They went straight into her mouth as she tried to catch her breath, and I pulled on her jaw to get her moving toward my desk.

When the three of us get there, I direct Temperance to the mahogany until it hits the back of her thighs.

"Up. Put that ass right on my desk, little flower, and make sure your skirt isn't in my way."

Temperance gawked at me for a moment but then reached for her skirt and inched the fabric up to her hips. Lifting a leg, she settled on the desk, papers we'd been looking at crumpling up under her ass. She flinched at the sound, her face screwing up as she let go of her skirt.

"Sorry."

I shook my head, taking her chin in my hand and kissing her. "None of that. Put your arms behind your back."

She did as told, and I watched as Lizzie went around to the other side of my desk, moving my chair out of the way so that she could lean over it and smear kisses along Temperance's throat. I drank in the sight of them, pulling off my tie and winding it around one hand as I relished the way Lizzie found Temperance's breast and toyed with her nipple.

"Lizzie," Temperance moaned.

"I've wanted to do this for so long, Temps. I've been *dying* to touch you. My sweet, innocent girl. If I'd met you any other way, I swear I wouldn't have hesitated."

Stepping up to the desk, I lowered my mouth to the other side of Temperance's neck, licking across her skin as Lizzie continued to play with her. With our girl so distracted, I wound my tie around her wrists where they were stacked together, making sure she'd have to keep her arms behind her. Lizzie noticed what I was doing, looping the loose ends of the tie between Temperance's palms as a tiny cushion.

We both pulled back from her simultaneously, and Temperance swayed forward, lust-lidded eyes and shallow breath. Moving her skirt up to her hips, I got my first peek at her cunt. Wetness smeared across her thighs, so much that it sullied the papers she was sitting on.

"You made a mess all over our important research." Temperance's face was a mask of horror, her cheeks glowing with a hot pink blush beneath the tan. "Lizzie, what would you like to do to her as punishment?"

The brat's eyes gleamed as she beamed at me, clearly ecstatic to carry out more of her wicked fantasies. Like that, her attention went to Temperance, kissing her fiercely before getting her stepsister to lie down on her side. Comfort wasn't much of a concern right now, but I noted the pressure on Temperance's shoulder and kept it in mind.

Crawling onto my desk, Lizzie turned Temperance's face up, lifting her leg over her head. "Eat up, Temps. I want to be the first taste you know."

My dick kicked, and I stroked as Lizzie flexibly lowered her pussy to Temperance's mouth. Lizzie's eyes rolled back as she closed them, holding herself open as her stepsister lapped at her with her tongue. A shocked moan fluttered out of Temperance, but it was abundantly clear that she loved this.

"Such a naughty, little slut, flower. Acting all innocent, but you're devouring that pussy like your life depends on it."

Lizzie's fingers speared through Temperance's hair, grinding herself on her mouth. "My filthy girl. Ugh, fuck yes. Don't stop."

Smirking, I hoisted Temperance's leg up, smoothing my cock through her folds. I coated my shaft in her slick, slapping it against her clit. She cried out into Lizzie's cunt, and I inched the head of my dick into her, swirling it inside her. Temperance squeezed with her leg, Lizzie's grip keeping her mouth pressed to her stepsister's pussy.

I pressed in a little further, working in and out. "So fucking tight, little virgin. And you're going to give it all to me. Sweet little sinner. So pretty, so damn tempting, aren't you? A walking ticket to hell."

Sinking in further, Temperance's pussy stretched around my cock, half of me inside her now. She whimpered against Lizzie's slippery skin, and another back and forth got me further. A muffled wail left her, and I knew I'd need another way to keep her quiet when Lizzie moved.

Just then, Lizzie reached down for her pussy, leaning back from Temperance as she stuffed her fingers inside roughly and then furiously rubbed her clit.

"Fuck, fuck, fuck." Lizzie moaned—a delicious crack of sound—her pussy poised at Temperance's face. "Keep your mouth open."

My hunger soared, knowing what the clever brat was up to. And just as another curse left Lizzie's mouth, I trust all the way home inside Temperance's cunt. She gasped as Lizzie came, squiring into Temperance's mouth, and my cock surged, my own orgasm burning through my shaft. The filthy sight powered on as Lizzie swiped across her clit, and Temperance mumbled curses as I picked up the pace, fucking her hard.

"Caleb!" My name, leaving Temperance's mouth, lit me up, but we couldn't afford to be heard.

I fisted some of the papers on my desk, wet from Lizzie's cum, and stuffed a crumpled piece into Temperance's mouth.

Smirking, I thrust up quick and sharp. "There's the naughty sinner. Such a bad girl enjoying her punishment so much."

She whimpered, biting down on the paper as I pistoned my hips, thrusting hard enough to make her slide up on the desk. Lizzie sucked in heavy breaths, leaning forward to lick across Temperance's cheek.

RE Johnson

I wanted her pussy on my fingers.

"Get down here." Pulling on Lizzie, I got her to stand next to me, shoving between her legs and ramming my fingers inside her. She clamped down around me as I fucked her stepsister, Temperance's tight cunt clenching down around me like a vice. I grunted low, rocketing my hips up hard, and then pulled Temperance back down to the edge of the desk with one hand.

"Oh fuck, fuck, fuck, fuck!"

Wetness gushed around my fingers as I hooked them into Lizzie's G-spot. Wiping them free, I flicked over her clit, making Lizzie squirt again all over my floor.

"Mmmm," Temperance mewled, nodding her head vigorously. "Mmm, mmm, mmm."

Her pussy fluttered around my shaft as she came, and I was so damn close. It felt too fucking good, her no longer virgin cunt milking my cock like it was desperate for me to breed her.

Not yet. Not yet.

Riding through the waves of Temperance's orgasm, I swirled my fingers idly inside Lizzie. I slowed down until I pulled all the way out. As both women struggled for breath, I hoisted Temperance's legs up onto the desk, getting her to the side and untying her arms. Lizzie was next, and I lifted her easily, plopping her down in front of me and hooking my arms under her legs so I could pull her ass right to the edge as she lay back.

"Brat's turn. And you have been so bad." I flicked at her cut skirt, smacking across her pussy next. "Flirting with your professor. You're just begging to go to the pit. But who cares if the ride is so fun, eh?"

Lizzie whimpered beneath me, flinching as I smacked her clit one, twice. "Yes, oh gods, please. *Please* fuck me."

My cock poised at her entrance, I grasped her throat, letting one leg fall as I thrust forward. I slid in, her pussy slick and need, cum smeared all over the insides of her thighs.

"Ugh!" Lizzie flung a fist to her mouth, biting down on her knuckles.

"Ms. Montgomery, why don't you give Lizzie something to do with that sinful mouth?"

I looked over to her, holding out my hand. She took it, and I pulled her forward, my blissed-out, dainty Temperance, so disheveled and corrupted. Gods, it was beautiful. Moving her to her knees, her back to me, I threw one on the other side of Lizzie's head, getting Temperance settled over her stepsister's face.

"What was it you said, brat?" I thrust hard, bouncing Lizzie and sinking in a little bit further. "Eat up."

Lizzie reached up with both hands, grabbing onto Temperance's ass. She immediately went to work, going by Temperance squeal, still muffled by paper. I closed my eyes, reveling in the sounds as I fucked Lizzie, my next thrust bottoming out. She clenched, crying out into Temperance's pussy.

"That's it, little brat. Make her come. May our little sinner come, and I'll breed this virgin cunt."

A wave of euphoria hit me, and my mind reeled. It was like the pleasure I felt doubled, tripled. I could sense so much more, the reverberating feeling of the sensations creating a...feedback loop.

"Oh, you little whore. That's damn clever." I grasped Lizzie's hips with both hands, anchoring as I moved faster—*harder*. "Devious little thing. Ugh, fuck yes. We're nothing but depraved heretics, and I fucking love it."

It was the most intoxicating sensation I'd ever known, and I completely lost myself to it. Fucking Lizzie with abandon as she ate Temperance out. I could *feel* how good it felt, I could sense both of them right on the edge of climax, tongue swirling, cock spearing.

Holy hell, I'll never get enough of this. I'm...I'm so fucking done for.

Lizzie surged around me, moaning sharply as she rubbed her lips briskly across Temperance's pussy. Temperance had both her hands in Lizzie's hair, and she threw her head back, crying out with a mouthful of cum-soaked paper. It was more than enough to knock Lizzie over the edge, that burning need so bright in her veins and delectable through this connection. She pulsed, milking my cock, and I didn't hold back this time, emptying myself deep into her cunt.

Ropes of cum spurted out of me, my dick twitching hard as my fucking soul left my body for a second. The euphoria was so damned profound, and I was spinning, every drop squeezed from me. The dark, wicked part of me peaked, and I slipped back, watching my cum drip out of Lizzie's pussy.

And then I shoved it back in.

Everything slowed, heavy breathing filling the room, and we all just *recovered* for a moment. Reality crystallizing around me, making a sharp contrast of panic sweep over me.

You fucked your students. You fucked your two virgin stepsister students. Fuuuuck.

Thirteen

THE WHEEL OF THE YEAR TURNS ONWARD & TIME IS OF THE ESSENCE

LIZZIE

I'd gotten an IUD in college just in case some creep pulled some shit, and I was so fucking glad I had it right now because I was pretty damn sure without it, Caleb would have *actually* bred me. Not that I was mad, far from it. That had been the single hottest thing in my entire life, better than the fantasies, and holy shit, I *finally* got to kiss Temps.

Got to *fuck* Temps.

It'd been a few minutes, and we'd all gotten dressed again, as best as we could anyway. Temps' bra was fucked, the buttons on her shirt. I gave her mine, willing to just throw on my uniform jacket and call it a day. Caleb, which was definitely how I was going to be thinking about him now, sat behind his desk, his stare distant as he rubbed his fingers across his lips.

"So," I broke the silence, "we should probably get back to the dorm. But hey, there's apparently a killer on the loose. Think you could walk us?"

Temps walked over to me with a nod, hardly able to make eye contact, but Caleb didn't answer. Walking over, I waved my hand in front of his face.

"Hey, walk us to the dorm, yeah?"

"Oh, umm, sure." He stood up from the chair roughly, pulling down on his jacket to straighten it.

Caleb gestured toward the door, clearing his throat. I eyed him for a moment, but then shrugged, letting it be for now. Grabbing my bag and Temps'—which was way heavier than mine—I joined her at the door, and she pulled it open, looking down either side of the hallway before stepping out.

The walk was a silent one. I didn't like how both Caleb *and* Temps were clearly feeling ways about what had just happened. That was incredible, and yeah, I wouldn't be walking comfortably for a while thanks to that pierced, monster cock he was rocking, but I had zero regrets.

Why did they?

We arrived at the dorm quickly enough, and before Caleb could skadaddle, I pulled on his sleeve, getting him to turn back around.

"Hey, I really do think we need to figure out what else is going on with the carnival. I didn't, umm, well, I wasn't able to look at everything before we had our fun. Would you come up so that

I can finish going through it with both of you? I don't want to have to repeat everything later."

Okay, as far as excuses went, mine was a solid six out of ten. But hey, I was doing the best I could with limited resources.

"Lizzie, I—"

"Caleb, she's right. I found another book, too, and I *know* there's something important in there. What if we go to the library, though? It's open late with professor supervision, correct?"

Well, shit. That was a better argument than I thought.

"The library, yes. Alright. That's fine. If you truly think there's something important, it would be stupid to delay things. Besides," he checked his watch, pushing back the sleeve of his tweed jacket, "it's only quarter to seven. It's not that late."

"Alright," I perked up, bouncing on my feet as I strode in the direction of the library, which we'd yet to visit, "let's go."

The library was absolutely massive, with dark wood columns of books that stretched up into the enormous vaulted ceilings. Several floors ringed the room, ladders going up to the higher shelves, and staircases leading to the other floors. It smelled like old paper, that vanilla musk scent that I always associated with Temps.

And now Caleb.

The books all looked ancient, lit gently by glowing lamps on the tables strewn across the wide wood floors and sconces secured to the wall in various places. There were stained glass windows, larger and more ornate than the ones in Caleb's office, and I smiled as Temps gasped and spun around like Belle in *Beauty and the Beast*.

Standing near an iron staircase that spiraled up to the second floor, Temps put her hand on her chest as she gripped it and leaned out. She was pulling a "Singing in the Rain."

"This place is marvelous! Oh my gods, I never want to leave."

Chuckling, Caleb rolled his eyes playfully before wandering closer and holding a finger up to his lips.

"Shh. This *is* a library."

Temps brows shot up, and she clapped a hand over her mouth. "Sorry."

I walked over to her, slinging my arm over her shoulder, which still made her blush after everything we'd just done.

"I actually get it, Temps. This library is a stunner. Did you see those ladders? You could ride them just like in the movies."

She laughed, looking up at them. "I couldn't do that. I mean, they're like school property and probably centuries old. I wouldn't dream of—"

"If we have time, Temperance. But I think we should get to the research first."

RE Johnson

Doing her best to contain the squeal, Temps nodded happily, and we all walked over to the nearest table, setting out our stuff to get started. I glanced around, my eyes drawn to the varying shades of brown and black and even green occasionally from the spines of the books. They were all leatherbound, and the entire room was very weighty and grounded, a solid foundation infused with knowledge.

I'd seen pictures of the Trinity Library in Dublin, and it had nothing on this place.

"Alright, I'll go get a few other tomes I want to look at. Temperance, why don't you go through the book you mentioned, and Lizzie, and you can check on those files about the carnival?"

Temps and I exchanged glances, fighting the urge to laugh. I met Caleb's eyes and nodded. "So bossy."

Turning pink, Caleb actually blushed slightly, and if he weren't glaring at me, it'd be the cutest damn thing. He clenched his jaw, turning decisively on his heel and taking off toward the stacks. I pulled out my laptop from my bag, and Temps put her book on the table, angling the light to hit the pages.

And then time melted into something strange as we all went into research mode, something I definitely didn't do often. Still, clicking away on the computer as I dug through records about the carnival didn't feel nearly as hard as it would have been to try reading all those cryptic books.

"Okay, this is something. I got a name. Jebediah Paine. Junior. His dad was some big preacher guy in the Appalachian area before he vanished during a sermon. No one knows what exactly happened to him, but the son, Jeb Jr., had a rather rocky life with his mother before she passed, and it looks like he started the carnival as soon as he turned eighteen. That was fourteen years ago."

"Jebedian Paine, why does that name sound familiar?" Caleb furrowed his brow, staring into the middle distance as he held his fingers between the pages of the book he was reading.

"Probably because he made the news. After his death, a bunch of people came forward and accused him of molesting them when they were kids. The cops dug around the house since it was empty, Junior having abandoned it, and they found bodies, too."

"Oh my gods. Bodies? That's awful." Temps reeled back, looking sick to her stomach.

"Yup, that's it. Fuck, I remember the news report on that asshole. I was traveling then. That was six years after I lost my parents." I reached across the table, squeezing Caleb's hand. He smiled and shrugged, refocusing. "What else does it say about Junior in this case?"

Turning back to the screen, I read off the rest of what I'd found in the public criminal records. "The carnival has had its fair share of complaints. People have accused them of stealing, abduction, but nothing has ever been found, so it didn't go anywhere. If you cross-reference their tour dates with missing persons reports, though, it gets pretty fishy. They're definitely up to something."

"Holy shit." Temperance cut in.

"I mean, it's something, but—" I glanced over at her, and Temps was looking down at a book. "Oh, you're reading. Great."

"Sorry, but I can't believe what I just found. I was trying to see if there was anything about the Paines in the ancestry records the school keeps."

"And is there?" Caleb asked, beating me to the question.

"No. They're not in this. But...I am. At least my family, going back decades, and Lizzie, your mom went to school here."

"What?" Shoving my computer out of the way, I looked at where Temps was pointing. "Holy shit."

"See! She *was* a student. The other morrighan."

My brain swirled, so many feelings coming up from the past that I didn't know what to do with them. My mother went to school here. She'd probably told me about it at some point when I was little, and I couldn't remember. My mom. And I was following in her footsteps.

A tear slipped down my face, and I hurried to wipe it away. Temps took my hands, and I let myself be anchored to the present through her touch.

"What, umm," I had to clear my throat, "what does it say about your family?"

"Lizzie, do you need a minute. I can—"

"It's fine." I offered her a tight smile. "I need the distraction."

Temps nodded. "Okay. Well, my family goes back to witches and shamans from the earliest days of America. It looks like the line has been dormant until me. No one from my family has gone to school here since another woman named Temperance, of all things, and that was in the 15th century, when Europe was just starting to colonize."

"Her name was Temperance?" I looked down at the page, seeing the asterisk near her name. "Wow. What's with the asterisk, though?"

"Usually, that means there's more information. She is probably referenced in a different text." Caleb tilted his head at us when we looked up at him.

"Goody, more homework." I moaned, rolling my eyes to the sound of dual chuckles.

Temps elbowed me. "But look, it found her mother, too. A woman named Bethany Ashdown. That's where it begins, I guess. So cool. And weird, but cool."

"Bethany Ashdown?" Caleb leaned forward, his brows up to his hairline. "That's not—Holy shit, indeed. That woman was responsible for the idea of a magic school. That's essentially our founder. Her most famous quote is, 'I do this not for me, but for Temperance. To be as tempered as steel, in her mother's name.'"

"Wait, so she *wasn't* Temperance's mother?" Temps shook her head, trying to process as I fell back in my chair.

Talk about information overload.

"She raised her yes, but the 'legend', as it were—the rumor, myth, what have you that Bethany herself circulated—was that her birth mother was a witch from a realm of Eternal Winter. Someone called 'Wren,' according to Bethany. There's not much about her, though. Unfortunately, there are just a few clippings from Bethany's diary and an old news report of sorts from that same era, which stated, 'Merchant Trumaine found dead. Slave, Wren, likely to blame.'"

"Gods, the fuck was going on back then?" I furrowed my brow as I slumped in my chair, the physical drain of running on all cylinders all day catching up with me.

"You're welcome to research more about your ancestors," Caleb said, standing up from his seat at the table as he closed the book in front of him and began to clean off his glasses. "I need to return to my apartment, though. I will continue to look over the things I can from there."

"Well, here take mine," I slid the book I'd been reading across the table toward his stack, "cuz it didn't make much sense to me anyway."

"Unfortunately, books are not permitted to leave the library. You'll have to come back."

"Everyone is really making this homework shit drag on, huh?" I shrugged, looking over at Temps, who'd started to pack up. "Alright."

It didn't take us long to gather stuff up and put it back on the claims desk to be filed away later. Caleb and Temps could hardly look at each other, or me, and I stared between them, waiting for someone to just grow a spine already.

"I will see you both in class tomorrow." Caleb nodded, his posture stiff as a damn board. "And we say leave all talk about what occurred in the past. It's better for all of us to move on."

"Speak for yourself, teach."

I was going for the tease, but Caleb was obviously worked up, so after that, I just let the guy wander off. He'd be back. Yeah, we'd see him in class tomorrow, but I *knew* we weren't done. And when I looked at Temps, watching her follow him with her eyes, I had a feeling she knew it, too.

Fourteen

FALSITIES FOLLOW THOSE WHO BLINDLY TREAD, WHERE TRUTH GRANTS FREEDOM, NO MATTER HOW FORBIDDING

TEMPS

After we split ways with Caleb, I could tell that Lizzie had a lot to say about what happened. She'd never been one to beat around the bush or sugarcoat her words. Lizzie was blunt and forward. Honestly, it was what I loved so much about her, because I could never seem to find that strength myself.

Gods, we all had sex. In Caleb's office.

I was still reeling from that one, but I didn't necessarily feel the same way Caleb clearly did. I knew it was wild and extremely against the rules, but I'd enjoyed myself in ways I never dreamed possible. Alone and untouched was how I assumed I'd be spending the rest of my day. Having experienced it now, it was impossible to deny that I liked it on this side of the fence a lot more.

Grass really is greener over here.

Lizzie hung back at the door this time, locking things up now that we were back in the dorm room. It was warm and cozy inside, an enormous difference from the chilly, damp air that swirled in constant torrents of wind outside. I went to turn on the overhead light, but then stopped, not wanting to force the space into such bright light right now.

Instead, I turned on the small lamp by my bed, the Edison bulb glowing softly. Lizzie took the hint, flicking her fingers to get the candles we'd placed strategically through the room to light. It stayed dim and so very warm in the room, and I slung off my bag, setting it by the foot of my bed as I kicked off my shoes.

I went to my closet, reaching in for a new shirt since I was still wearing Lizzie's. Immediately, I was aware of how I was going commando, realizing how ridiculous we both must look. Turning over my shoulder to look, I saw Lizzie pulling off her second boot, the jacket Caleb gave her tossed to the side. She stood there in her cut-off skirt and bra, planting a heel on each sock to pull it off.

She's so beautiful.

Working open the buttons on the shirt, I watched her as she reached around to the zipper of her skirt, pulling it down and letting the fabric drop to the floor. She was still wearing panties, but they were thin, white lace, and even in the dim light, I could see the silky warmth of her brown skin beneath the fabric.

"I can feel you watching me, Temps."

I froze, zinging upright as my fingers fell away from the buttons, leaving the shirt half on, half off. Lizzie turned around, smirking, and *daaamn*. I was going to melt under that look. She sauntered over, getting right up in front of me so that I was trapped between her arms and the closet door behind me. Tracing her fingers delicately up my arm, Lizzie watched the progression of her touch, pushing my sleeve down, until her finger was beneath my chin, tilting my head up.

"If you're going to look at me *like that*," she lowered her lips to my shoulder, kissing the skin, "then I get to touch you *like this*."

"Lizzie," I moaned on a shaky exhale, the feeling of her lips moving up to my neck making my entire body buzz, "I...I don't want to go back to what it was before."

She leaned back with a smile, her eyes sparkling. "I don't either. I want all three of us, but if Caleb is going to be a stick in the mud...I need you, Temps. I have since the moment I laid eyes on you. You're my oxygen, my water when I'm dying of thirst."

More of the white fabric covering me fell away, revealing my breasts once again. I knew that Lizzie had seen me, but there was something to the intimacy of this moment, how slow and concentrated it was. I was on fire, the tight buds of my nipples straining. Lizzie cupped my cheek, kissing me as she got rid of the shirt altogether. Then her fingers moved to my lower back, pulling down the zipper of my skirt.

I reached for the clasp of her bra, undoing it and gradually peeling the straps down her arms. As my skirt dropped, so did Lizzie's bra. A grin lit up her face as she devoured me with her eyes, her fingers sliding underneath the waistband of her panties. I knew I was blushing furiously, but I didn't want this to stop. I wanted Lizzie all for myself for a while.

"Help me." Lizzie gestured down with her head, and I slid my fingers under her panties alongside hers.

We formed together so perfectly, and I helped to push the lace down until it hit the floor, gazing up at her from my knees. Smiling, Lizzie pulled me up to stand using her finger under my chin again. She smoothed her lips across mine, humming this satisfied sound as she reached around me and took two handfuls of my ass.

"You're so fucking pretty, Temps." She flicked her tongue over my lip before nuzzling into my neck and caressing, biting playfully.

"Fuuuck, Lizzie." My knees were wobbly. "You feel so good against me. You're so...so sexy and bold. I've always admired that about you."

"Admired?" She chuckled, pulling back to cock a brow at me. "And here I thought it annoyed you."

"Well..." We both snorted a laugh, naked and comfortable in each other's presence for the first time like this. "Sorry, sorry. I do mean it, though. You're yourself. All the time and confidently. I don't know how to do that. You drag me into things and that scares the shit out of me, but ninety percent of the time I end up so damn glad that you did."

Smoothing her hand down the side of my face, Lizzie used her other hand to scoop me up to her, laying us flat against each other. She was so warm, so soft and supple against my body, and every inch of me heated, *wanted*.

"That's my job, Temps, to bring excitement to your life." Dipping forward, I silently begged for the touch of her lips, and

Lizzie obliged, kissing me and sweeping her tongue across the seam of my lips.

I eagerly let her in, and then Lizzie was backing us up until my legs hit my mattress. We worked together, unwilling to stop our kiss, and got into the bed, Lizzie on top of me, straddling my lap. I could feel how wet she was, and my brain short-circuited for a moment, my pussy clenching.

"Let me touch you, baby girl."

Lizzie began to slide her hands down from where she held my face, going achingly slow until she brushed her thumbs across my nipple and I squeaked.

"I'm like a month younger than you are," I murmured against her mouth.

"True." She dragged her thumbs in slow circles, twisting my nipples just enough for them to pinch slightly. "And you're my *sweet* baby girl."

"Not that 'sweet' now, am I?"

Laughing against my lips, having this conversation like this, felt incredible. It was us, Lizzie and Temps, just like we had always been, but it was that and more, making it eons better.

"You have been a little *corrupted*, haven't you?" Lowering her head, Lizzie sucked on the skin of my neck, teasing with her teeth. "And damn was that pretty to watch."

My eyes rolled closed, and I arched against her. But I wanted more. I *needed* it. Reaching between us, I gently searched for her pussy, sliding my finger across the seam when my hand was pressed between us. Lizzie groaned against my touch, instinctively moving her hips back and forth. I let her set the pace, focusing on manipulating the sensitive bud of her clit.

As she straightened, a gorgeous whimper leaving her, Lizzie pinched down on my nipples harder. I gasped but leaned into it, pressing my lips to her sternum before gradually working my way over to her nipple and pulling it into my mouth with a suck.

Lizzie rocked her hips on my hands, and I slipped a finger inside her as I used my thumb to put pressure on her clit. Holy hell, she was warm and slick and perfect. I added another finger, doing what I had done to myself when I was alone and hooking into the magic spot at the top. More of that wet warmth pooled around my fingers, and I glided my fingers in and out.

"Temps...oh fuck, baby girl." I pulled my mouth off her delicious skin to look up at her, marveling at how gorgeous Lizzie looked when she was experiencing pleasure. "I'm going to—Ugh!"

Coming on my fingers, I worked Lizzie until she was heaving for breath, my skin wearing her arousal. With a quick bite of her nipple, I gently slid my fingers free. She watched me as I did, taking my hand as soon as she could and putting my fingers in my mouth. I licked the taste of her off my skin, unable to stop looking at her and how magnificent she was.

When I was done, Lizzie pushed me back toward the pillow, shimmying down until she could throw my legs over her shoulders, her face between my thighs.

"I've *dreamed* about this Temps. I've wanted you so badly it *hurt*."

Taking her face in my hands, I held her eyes. "Me too. I'm sorry for not getting to you sooner. With my mom and everything—"

"Let's not ruin this with talk of shitty parents." She kissed the inside of my thigh, sending sparks down my spine. "I'm just thrilled to have you now. My brilliant, alchemist's assistant, research-pro witch. You're incredible, Temps."

"You are, too, Lizzie. *My* brave, outspoken, doesn't take shit from anyone, *morrighan* witch. I...I love you."

Lizzie's eyes flared wide for a moment, but immediately softened, her smile going proud and devious all at once.

"And here I was holding back on the L word." She chuckled, shifting in closer to my throbbing pussy. "I love you, too, Temps. Now, the next words out of your mouth better be 'I'm coming.' Or I'm going to spank your fine ass."

I went to laugh, but it was abruptly cut off as Lizzie's mouth found my seam, her tongue sliding through my folds and swirling around my clit. I arched against her, gripping the sheets until my knuckles ached. She alternated between delicate flicks and hard sucks, driving me right to the edge. I was already so damn close, so worked up from everything else, and then her finger pressed into me.

"Ugh!"

Lizzie reached up with her other hand, grabbing my breast and gripping tight. Then another finger slid in as she pulled back enough to whisper, "Shh, baby girl. You'll wake the entire dorm."

It took everything I had, including chewing on my knuckles, to be quiet as Lizzie pumped her fingers in and out of my pussy, finding my G-spot and pressing hard as she lightly sucked on my clit. I was barreling toward release, on the precipice of flying off into the cosmos. Flinging my hand to the side, I reached for Lizzie's hand on my breast, spearing my fingers through hers so I could hold it.

"I'm...I'm...I'm..."

She released my clit with a loud pop, and I peeked down to see her looking up at me. With a smile, Lizzie crawled up my body, still moving her fingers inside me, and then her lips were on mine. I could taste myself on her tongue as she increased speed, yanking her fingers free to rub briskly over my clit. I cried out into her mouth, still holding her hand as I wrapped my arm around her neck.

"Come for me, Temps."

"Lizzie, ugh," I buried my face into the crook of her neck. "*Lizzie*."

And with that, I shattered, coming so hard I actually saw stars. It powered through me for several moments, and then the two of us were just lying there in the bed. I was curled up into Lizzie's arms on my side, her chin resting on my head. She held me against her, and I felt so safe and seen in her arms.

Like magic.

"Now, I'd like to start tomorrow with something a little

different." Caleb's voice boomed through the classroom, and we all took note, straightening in our chairs, except for Lizzie, of course.

"What I'm about to discuss with you might be a little unsettling, but I believe understanding the basics of spellcasting comes with understanding whether or not you're being lied to. Not by someone but my 'magic.'"

Caleb used air quotes on the last word, and both Lizzie and I looked at each other. My brain pinged with what we'd talked about yesterday, the false idol and supposed "god," and I had to assume that our professor was doing his best to prepare all the students for what could very well be on the horizon. Lizzie nodded back at me when I pointed at my notebook and drew a picture of the cult symbol we'd found. She definitely agreed with me.

Still, I had to wonder if Caleb would get in trouble for changing the lesson plan or bringing up something that might have been over the students' heads.

Like he'll get in trouble for fucking us?

Jumping slightly, I snapped my attention back to Lizzie. *Are you in my head?*

She smiled at me, shrugging. *It's a lot easier now that we fucked. You're not pushing me out like usual. But I can go if—*

Ugh, no. It's fine. Just warn me, Lizzie. I almost choked on my spit.

Oh no. I'd much rather you choke on my spit.

Lizzie, gross. I rolled my eyes, gesturing back at Caleb. *Focus.*

"Fighting false magics starts with being aware of them. You need to be able to clock a spell, twist, or curse before it's coming at you. Please go to section fifteen in your books. Look for figure eleven-A and read from there for tomorrow's assignment. Class is dismissed."

The students funneled out of the classroom, and again, Lizzie and I stayed behind, sitting in our chairs and waiting to speak until the room was totally empty. When it was, I was the first to speak up.

"So what was that about? Are you trying to clue in the students about something or—"

"I found something last night when I went back to my apartment. I have a book on false magics that I've been hanging onto for years, and since I couldn't look at the books from the library, I thought, what the hell."

Lizzie leaned forward on her elbows, resting her chin on her hand. "So what'd you find? Because something tells me that the section in our spellcasting 101 book you assigned, ain't going to cut it when it comes to whatever is killing these people."

"Always so direct." Caleb grinned, his stare narrowing on Lizzie in a suggestive way that I watched him visibly fight back. For once, I was with Lizzie on something. Caleb just needed to let that society stuff go. I was actually happy, for the first time in years, maybe ever, and I wanted him to feel the same.

I wanted *him*.

"Well, I did find something interesting. I'd like to show you rather than risk talking about it here. I confirmed my suspicions in a book at the library. If you both have a free period, we can go there now. I'd feel more comfortable discussing it where a sanctuary spell has been laid out."

"A sanctuary spell? And why are we not 'risking it?'"

Rubbing Lizzie's arm, I raised my brow at her, offering a small, hopefully helpful smile. "Lizzie, maybe we should just talk about it there?"

"Ugh," Lizzie rolled her eyes as she stood up from her chair, and I quickly moved to follow, "fine."

"I assure you, Lizzie. It's best we move with discretion. I'm more concerned about the killings than I was even last night. There's so much to fill you both in on."

"Duuude," Lizzie laughed, pulling me along as she stuffed her arm through mine, "phrasing."

"What?" Caleb looked so confused, and I couldn't help but laugh a we left the classroom. We walked companionably, the campus busy as ever this morning, and I glanced overhead at the dark gray clouds that blocked more of the sun.

"Is it ever clear out?"

Caleb looked up, smirking as he chuckled low. "No, not really. We get *a lot* of rain. Though during the summer, we will get the occasional sunny afternoon when the grounds finally need a break from all the 'gloom.'"

"The grounds? As in the school decides the weather?" I raised my brows at him, halting for a moment, which unfortunately made Lizzie stumble, her water bottle flying out of her bag.

"Dammit, Temps!"

"Sorry!" I called out, waving as she rushed behind a bush to fetch the thing. "But seriously? Does the school *building* decide the weather?"

Laughing louder now, Caleb sighed as he nodded once, reaching out to the stone pillar of an archway nearby that hung over this walkway.

"It does. Gets finicky, too. However, it doesn't affect the town. So keep that in mind if you're going back and forth." Caleb glanced around me, his brow down over his mesmerizing blue eyes. "Where'd Lizzie go off to?"

"She dropped her water bottle." I turned around, looking at the bush where she'd scampered off and still not seeing her emerge. "But it shouldn't take that long. Hold on. Maybe she's peeing."

"Behind a bush?"

"You never know with Lizzie."

Shrugging with a laugh, I smiled as I hurried over to the small thicket of bushes at the edge of the arch and called out for Lizzie.

"Lizzie! Dude, what are you doing? We need to go!"

She didn't answer at first, and then, as I pushed through a small gap between the stone of the arch and the stone of another dorm room's bricks, I found her standing with her back to me, not moving.

"Lizzie? Lizzie, what's up?" She still wasn't answering me, and I approached, reaching out to grab her shoulder and force her to spin around. "Elizabeth, talk to me."

I knew she hated her full name, so I figured that would snap her out of it, but nothing. "Come on. This is getting freaky. I—"

But as I looked from my stepsister to the ground in front of us, I knew why she'd stopped, why she hadn't said anything, and a scream tore from my throat before I could even think to do it.

There on the brown earth—orange and yellow leaves flattened to the mud underneath them and dusted over the top of them too—were two bodies. From what I could tell, they were both students, lying there as white as death and more. It was a young man and a woman, and their eyes had been burned from their sockets.

Fifteen

WHAT CANNOT BE NAMED CAN STILL CAUSE PAIN

CALEB

Gods damn it, this is exactly what I've been so fucking nervous about. Because I let them get involved with this, two more lives have been traumatized because of this bullshit.

"Do you want water or anything?" It was a stupid question, but Lizzie and Temperance had been sitting on the couch in my office for a few minutes now, once the cops released us from the scene, and I didn't know what else to do to help them through this.

They'd been the first to stumble upon two more dead bodies, these far more gruesome than the last. The sigils were still carved into the flesh, but now, something had been done to literally burn their eyes out of their sockets. It was brutal and not something I'd ever heard about in all my time studying witchcraft and alchemy.

Witches could be capable of horrible violence just like anyone else, but the magic used to do *that* was unheard of.

"No." Temps shook her head, her stare pinned down to her lap as she held Lizzie's hand.

They'd worn their uniforms to class like always, and I'd been half expecting to see them missing items before I remembered that Night Grove provided you with more than just one set for fuck's sake. I was perched against my desk, leaning back against it as I gripped the edge, likely turning my knuckles white, but I didn't bother to look down.

Someone in town is channeling the wrong aspects of magic, using powers they shouldn't have access to to kill people.

Focusing on the stitches in my shoes, tracking them around the toe and back, I tried to center myself in all this. Finding the bodies had been horrendous, but seeing the look on Lizzie's face, on Temperance's, that had nearly destroyed me. I could feel how I was hanging on by a thread, the temptation to drown my dark thoughts in a bottle of scotch peaking.

"Oh, I meant to give you this."

I looked up, and Temperance was digging in her bag. She pulled out my jacket from yesterday, and a flash of heat speared through me. Lizzie looked up, her expression unusually blank.

"Oh, right. Thanks for, umm, letting me wear it."

My chest felt like it was going to crack open. This wasn't the Lizzie I was used to seeing, and despite how much I knew it was wrong, how much I knew I should deny it and pull myself away, I pushed off the desk and walked over to her, crouching down

at her side because I wanted to see that light in her eyes again—
desperately.

"Hey," I reached up, wrapping my hand around both of hers
where they hung over her knees, "I'm right here. If you need
anything, just tell me."

Looking over to Temperance, I leaned so that I could get my free
hand on hers, too. "That was...no one should have to see shit like
that. And trust me, I get how it feels."

Temperance looked up with a subtle smile, one corner of her
mouth tilting up. "Thanks, Caleb. I just...I don't want that to
happen to anyone else."

I should have told her not to call me that, that we needed to keep
things professional, but who the fuck was I kidding? Last night,
I'd dived into the books because all I could think about was
marching right back over to their dorm room and spending the
night with them. These women in front of me had gotten past
all my defenses, all my walls, and I wasn't sure I wanted to build
them back up again.

At least not for them.

"You think we can?" Lizzie's voice was just above a whisper. "Do
you *truly* think we can do something to stop this?"

Beneath my fingers, I could feel her trembling. "Yes, but...not
without more than just us. That's what I'm afraid of, anyway. I
told you I did some digging last night, and...what I found wasn't
good."

Temperance scooted closer to Lizzie, and they both looked up
at me. Where some might have expected to see terror or grief,

I was beginning to really know these women, and I wasn't surprised in the slightest to see them both meeting my eyes with fury locked in theirs. What was happening on campus was a corruption, malice made malignant by a force older than we could comprehend, and they were rising up to meet it because that's just who they were.

I fell all the harder for them in that moment.

"Go on. We're ready to hear it." Temperance nodded once, reaching into Lizzie's lap where I held her hands and joining in with a squeeze.

Nodding back, I offered a smile—damn impressed by their resolve—and then stood up, going to my desk to retrieve the photocopies I'd made, which was also against school policy.

"There have been similar occurrences to what's happening now throughout witch history. From what I found," I passed the two of them the sheets, "it appears like the name of the cult and the exact workings or beliefs change, but beneath all that, it's always the same. A cult of humans gains powers, they like it, and from what I can parse out, they—however many and whoever they might be this time around—retain those powers by sacrificing people to their 'god.'"

Lizzie and Temperance scanned over the pages I handed them, their brows up and their eyes wide as the information funneled in.

"Now, I have to guess at some of this, but I imagine they're luring people in somehow. I can't imagine many people signing up to be a sacrifice nowadays. My best bet is that it's done under the guise of salvation or redemption. Think those fringe Christian organizations and the like. I also have to assume that since those are becoming harder and harder to manage effectively that their tactics may have changed."

Perking up with a look of such intrigue etched into her brow that I worried Lizzie would give herself a headache, she asked, "Would these assholes be fond of using things like cults to do all this? Like Manson and stuff like that?"

"Yes, I believe so. The point of this...*being*, as you can see, it gains power through sacrifice. It doesn't care how you get the person there, and it will give you power in return. Not as much of course, but enough to be intoxicating."

"Lizzie," Temperance turned toward her, brows knitted as she chewed on her lip, "the symbol that you think you saw. The one that looked like the necklace my mom's been wearing. They're this weird Christian group, and it's like my mother isn't even the same person now."

I shook my head, sitting on the coffee table in front of Temperance. "What do you mean?"

"She's been going to this mysterious church group of hers. And look, my mother has never been the most 'woke' of people, but it's so much worse now. I...Part of the reason for never saying anything to you," Temperance turned to Lizzie, pain behind her eyes, "was because I felt like she'd actually do something crazy if she found out I was bi. She's been plenty vocal about not liking that 'side of you.' And it's gotten super trad-wife and weird."

"Trad wife?" I cocked a brow, staring between both of them before they chuckled, and I realized that this reference was just going to fly over my head. "Forget it. It does sound like there's something there. Do you think you could ask her about it without it being awkward?"

"I could try, I suppose. Awkward if kind of a given with my mother and me."

"I would. It couldn't hurt, right? And we need to gather as much information about this entity as possible, *covertly*. It'll be that much harder to learn what we need if it knows we're onto it. From the texts, this is a paranoid being that makes everyone else do its dirty work, and it *does not like* being exposed."

"I saw something."

Lizzie's voice cut through the room, knife-sharp as she spoke so clearly and without holding back. I could sense the air around her change, and I remembered just when the sirens had closed in after calling the police that she'd knelt down and put the back of her hands on each of the victims. She hadn't collapsed this time, but it made sense to me now that she'd been processing this entire time.

"What did you see, Lizzie?" Temperance ran a hand up and down her back, eyes fixed on Lizzie so intently.

"Lights on a string, glowing yellow and red. Faded colors in a blur. But...it reminds me of the carnival. We knew something wasn't right there. What if it's this thing? This malevolent being of the past. What if *that's* how the performers are able to do what they're doing?"

"It certainly doesn't bode well, and it seems like far too much of a coincidence. We picked up on their magic during the show, and now, the clues from your vision are leading us to them."

"But what about the church connection?" Temperance shot me a look, getting figety on the couch as the light outside dimmed, a thick cloud blotting out more of the sun.

"I don't know." I shook my head, hanging it as the feelings of overwhelm and dread swirled. "I just...It could be both, for all I know. I haven't directly dealt with any of this before now. We might need to split our focus among the three of us. I can learn more from the school board about the murders and any others that have occurred in the past. Lizzie can peep in on the carvinal, and Temperance, you can speak with your mother."

"Split the party? Have you ever played D&D? That's a terrible idea."

"You *have* played D&D?" Lizzie poked Temperance in the side with her elbow as the two of them glared playfully at each other.

"That shouldn't surprise you. I'm a huge nerd."

Smiling, Lizzie leaned in and pulled Temperance under her arm, kissing her head. "True."

My spine tingled watching them, this sense of something I didn't want to name because I knew it would crush me; I knew what came with it. Clearing my throat, I stood up off the coffee table, but Lizzie was quick to grab my hand, preventing me from walking across the room. She had a way of doing that.

"Uh-uh. Don't do that. Don't run." Those deep brows eyes seared into my soul, perceiving everything I was, inside and out. "It's a thing. I'll give that to you. But with what's going on, with what we've seen, I'm going to tell you right now that I want this. Temps wants this. Apparently, life is real fucking short, Caleb. So, make it count."

Temperance snorted beside Lizzie, ducking her head so that I wouldn't see her laugh. It did no good, of course. Still, I was more focused on what Lizzie had said, and the churning in my gut that told me all this wasn't going away any time soon. They were missing puzzle pieces I never imagined I'd find, lost to the horrors of my past.

And if I wasn't careful, I knew I'd lose them to the horrors of my present.

I sighed, sitting back down on the table. "What's just a bit more important right now is that we figure out exactly what we're dealing with. We can't prepare a sealing ritual unless we know what it is we're shoving back in the box."

"Fair enough. But after…"

Lizzie grinned, and gods help me, I couldn't keep myself from smiling right back. "Ugh, anyway. To stack bad on top of bad, we risk giving away what we know if they seek out help from the school board because this particular evil loves manipulating people so much. Those brainwashed followers could be anywhere, anyone, and they won't hesitate to kill in the name of their false god."

"So," Lizzie raised her brow, tilting her head onto Temperance's shoulder, "what the fuck can we do then?"

"There may be one way to get the upper hand, to secure more power." I walked over to my desk quickly, snagging the last photocopy of the library book I shouldn't have been copying and holding it up in front of them. "Soul weaving."

Temperance and Lizzie exchanged looks, both straightening with their brows raised, speaking simultaneously, "What the fuck is that?"

Sixteen

THREADS THROUGH HOLES, REEDS WOVEN IN TIME, CREATING DUALITY FROM WHAT WAS MINE

LIZZIE

Caleb stifled a grin as he shook his head, looking between Temps and me as the joined words hung in the air. He sucked in a deep breath, meeting us at the couch again with another photocopy in his hands. He laid it on the small coffee table, pointing to a line near the bottom of the left-hand page.

"Soul weaving. This is from one of the books at the library that I couldn't take out. Hell, I shouldn't have been copying it either, but desperate times. Anyway, it's an ancient practice that I know a little about. I've been curious about the mechanics for a while now, even doing some research when I was abroad."

"Ancient is good, or does that mean this could go tits up real easy?" I asked, cocking my head as I scanned over the words on the photocopy.

"Potentially both." Caleb sighed, pulling off his glasses and polishing the glass on the fabric of his tweed jacket. "It's rarely done. Always has been. But from what I understand, it was more common in the past when witches and practitioners weren't as concerned about what spirits they might be letting in. Thankfully, we've gotten more cautious over the years."

"It lets in spirits? Isn't that a big no-no?" Temperance's brow was furrowed way down over her eyes as she fiddled nervously with the hem of her skirt.

"Usually, yes." Caleb slid his glasses back in place, pointing down at the passage again. "You'll see that it warns that you may not always have control over the spirit you soul weave to. But it does increase power, and depending on the potency of the spirit or being, the power achieved could be drastically changed. Many in the past, more reckless witches who were greedy and too intoxicated by the promise of more, didn't view the incoming spirit as a person or entity but as a thing to be used. The results of the course could often be a toss-up as a result. You either got your powers and stayed who you were, or the incoming spirit took over."

My pulse skittered under my skin as I realized what that could mean. "Wait, so the soul weaving could leave the person as... someone else?"

"Potentially. There are a handful of reports that detail someone using a typical spirit, but it could be done with a willing elder being or deity as well. That was much more uncommon, but in either case, it would be possible for the spirit invoked in the soul weaving to take over the host body, to change what the person was altogether."

"And you think that's a good idea?" Temps shook her head, her brows up to her hairline as she visibly protested against the notion. "And here I thought Lizzie was the unhinged one."

I couldn't help but laugh, reaching over and stroking Temps' arm. "Aww, thanks, babe."

"I'm being serious. All this sounds wildly unpredictable and dangerous. How could you guarantee that we wouldn't just be left with a situation ten times worse than the one we have now?"

"I couldn't, Temperance. That's usually the case with higher magics. But if a deity, one of the elder gods of the World of Below or hell, even a forest protector, agreed to be part of the soul weaving by answering the call, they could give us the power necessary to fight off the thing using the carnival for its own purposes. I think it's worth that risk."

Shoving up from the couch, Temps stepped past the coffee table and paced around Caleb's office. I could tell how on edge she was, the raw ringing of her aura a tone of apprehension and fear. She genuinely worried about losing me or Caleb to the soul weaving, and I could even pick up on her torn desire to be the one to do it if it came down to that, and knowing that she shouldn't because she wouldn't be strong enough to take it with her history of heart problems.

I stood up, following her to the area in front of the window. The gloomy sky was even darker now, almost as if it had picked up on the tension in the room. A low, gentle rumble of thunder echoed, and in just a few seconds, little raindrops began to patter against the windowpane.

"Temps, this is a conversation right now. Try to center yourself."
I ran my hands up and down her arms, trying to send out as
much soothing energy as I could. "None of this was going to be
easy. There were always going to be hard choices that required
sacrifice. But those students...what we saw...We can't let this
continue. You know that."

Bobbing her head, Temps leaned forward, resting her head on
my shoulder as she came in for a hug. I wrapped my arms around
her, breathing in that scent of old paper and vanilla. She slipped
her arms under mine, her thumb smoothing over the spot
between my shoulder blades. After a moment, she looked up at
me.

"I hate this. And I know you're right. Ugh," she turned toward
Caleb, "what else? Something tells me that wasn't the only
bomb drop."

Caleb stood up from his seat on the coffee table, walking over
to us. As he stood there, right next to our shoulders where they
touched, I glided one hand around his side to his back. Temps
was quick to do the same, joining him in our little huddle even as
he rolled his eyes.

There was a moment of silence, one where I was sure Caleb
would get spooked and pull away, but then he lifted his hand to
Temps' shoulder, holding it there as he locked eyes with her.

"It's permanent." His stare swiveled to mine, his free hand
finding the small of my back. "Whatever version of me you
ended up with, that's how it would stay."

"*You*? And who says it has to be you?" I cocked my head, reeling
back with an air of indignation.

"You honestly think I would let one of you two do it? You're both young; there's so much of your story ahead of you. I'm the grizzled old professor. If anyone is going to have their book cut short, it should be me."

"You make it sound like death is another option on this 'choose your own adventure.'" Temps aura flickered, going dim when I brought that up, and I looked over quickly as I squeezed her with the hand on her hip.

"It is." Caleb nodded, his expression dropping all the more. "The deity could replace me altogether, or I might not be a strong enough vessel to contain it, and it could destroy me."

"That's *not* worth the risk, Caleb." Temps stamped her foot down, her expression desperate as she turned toward him and put both of her hands on his face, me at her back. "We care about you. There's something here, something between us all that none of us can deny, and I'm not throwing that away when I just got my hands on it."

Expression softening, Caleb took her hands and put them on his chest, holding them there.

"Temperance—"

"We need to try and deal with this on our own without the soul weaving. At least try. If we can't, if it's made abundantly clear that we're outmatched, then...well, then we'll have no choice, and I won't be pissy about it."

Sighing, Caleb dropped his head, bringing Temps' knuckles to his lips before looking at her again. I ran my hand up and down her back, chewing on my lip as I shot a glance at the photocopy and then back at them.

"What do you suggest? How are we supposed to get into the carnival to confirm our suspicions and make it out alive? You are brand new to the craft, and I'm an alchemist, not a combat witch. I...I...care about what happens to you both. If something were to go wrong—"

"So we get items and potions we need to blend in, provide us with a quiet entry and exit. If we go during the day, we'll have that on our side as well. The carnival runs nearly all night. They'll be exhausted if we go first thing in the morning."

Caleb shrugged, tilting his head down. "That's not terrible. I might be able to come up with some things we could bring with us to keep them drowsy."

"Alright," I clapped Temps on the shoulder, squeezing tight as I came around her side and standing so that I could grip both of them, "we have a plan. Mostly. We need to get some supplies, those good old drowsy potions, and I'm going to show our girl here how to fight the old-fashioned way. You grow up around a bunch of creeps and you get good at knowing which spots to jab."

Temps laughed, Caleb shaking his head as he eyed me with a smirk. "I'm not sure if I should be terrified or...extremely turned on."

I gave a laugh back, throwing my head back. When I looked at them both again, I bobbed my head in a nod, turning down the corners of my mouth, feeling very satisfied with myself.

"Well, you know that saying that's been making the rounds on social for a while. 'Women? Women. But also, women...'" I paused for effect, pumping my eyebrows. "'...who can kill you.'"

"Where do you hear that stuff?" Temps giggled, this look of mild disgust hitting her as she shook her head.

"Eh, social media is a wild place, babe."

"I think I'm glad to be too old for that shit." Caleb narrowed his eyes at me, smiling before he squeezed both Temps' and my shoulders. "But that sounds as good as anything else right now. Teach Temperance your stuff, and I'll be sure to gather what we need to be as discreet as possible when we go to the carnival. Meet back at the gate tomorrow morning, like five. And if we don't like what we see, the soul weaving."

He made sure to look Temps directly in the eye for that last part. I didn't love the idea of losing Caleb for good either, whether it be through death or because some ancient fuck took his place, but I had to admit, even if only to myself, that we did need more power.

Caleb was right. We were new at this. Temps and I didn't have the skills, and for all of his muscles, fighting something like an unnameable evil was going to take a lot more than punching. I just hoped that our little trip would convince Temps of that.

"Fuuuck, that's *so* early," I turned up the moan as I spoke, really laying it on thick.

'You'll be fine, Lizzie." Temps smiled at me before looking down at the floor with a sigh. "But we should go. Hanging out in here for too long again might get noticed this time."

"Indeed." Caleb stepped back, walking casually to the door, which he opened for us with a grin. "I'll see you both in the morning then."

Temps was the first to get moving, and I was surprised when she stopped in front of Caleb and leaned up onto her toes to deliver a soft peck on his cheek. It was so quick, and there was no one milling about in the halls, so we were fine, but to know that Temps was willing to risk a little spoke volumes.

"If anything changes, call one of us. Or text. Do you have our numbers on file?"

Caleb nodded with a sly grin. "I may have combed the records last night for them. Just in case."

Blushing slightly, Temps nodded and slipped past, her footsteps echoing as they filled the quiet with a steady beat. As I walked up to Caleb, I thought about the student we'd found. Those charred sockets would haunt me for a long fucking time, and I knew that Caleb had seen his parents killed in front of him. How he was walking around with all that was a testament, and I knew he didn't see it that way.

As I reached him, I stopped, looking up into those expressive, deep blue eyes of his, reaching up for his cheek.

"The fact that you're helping us with this, the school with this, says a lot about you. Even if some of the other stuff is twisting in your head, I hope you realize that you're a good person. You could have turned tail and run when all this started, and you didn't. Don't forget that."

His eyes widened, his lips parting slightly, and I pushed up onto my tiptoes to kiss him—too quick for my liking if I was honest.

"See ya in the morning, teach."

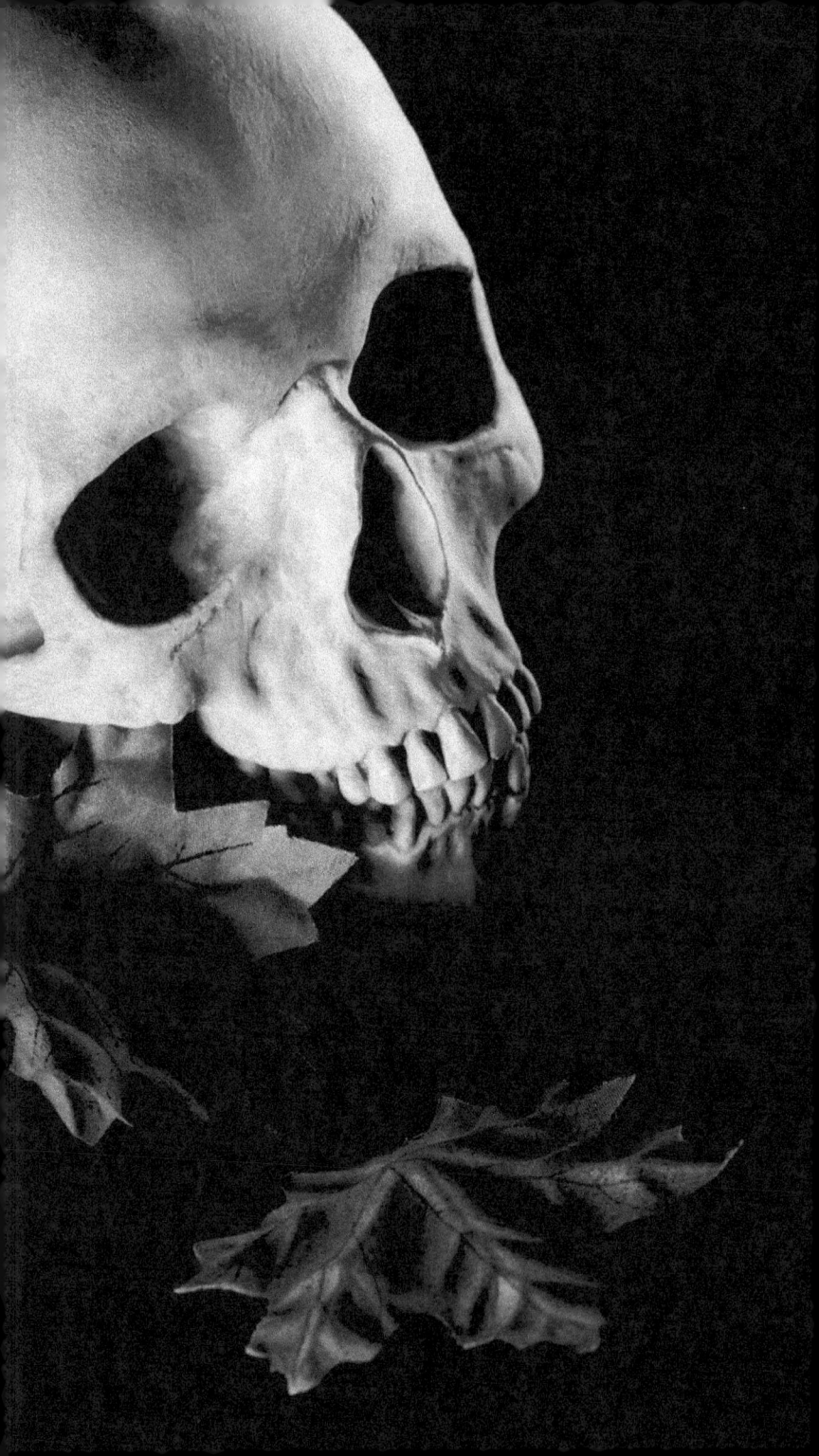

Seventeen

WHEN LOST LAMBS STUMBLE INTO THE DARK, REALITY WARPS & THE BLACK BITES BACK

TEMPS

At the front gate of the school, I saw Caleb waiting, noticing immediately that he wasn't sporting the typical tweed jacket and slacks. If it weren't for what we were about to do, I would have likely been a drooling mess taking in all that leather.

Yes, your hot professor is wearing actual leather. Gods help me.

Lizzie chuckled next to me, nudging me in the ribs with her elbow as she nodded. I tracked how her eyes went to Caleb's ass in his jeans before sliding up to the black motorcycle jacket he was wearing. She wagged her brows at me, and I rolled my eyes, feeling like an idiot since we were about to sneak into a carnival that some evil cult could very well run.

He was yummy before, Lizzie said in my head, *and now it's even better.*

Would you pipe down in here? I'm trying to concentrate.

Laughing, Lizzie pulled me along as we hurried up to Caleb, who spun around, his stare going straight to our clothes.

"That's what you wore to infiltrate the carnival?" I looked down, considering my boots, skinny jeans, and black fuzzy sweater. Lizzie was hardly better, in sleek black leggings, a black tant, and what barely passed as an excuse for a jacket since it was cropped to circle up over her boobs, only covering her arms.

I mean, at least it *was* black.

"Says the guy in a black leather jacket, who I've never seen on a bike once to merit it." Lizzie really was quite adept at being a bit of a brat, and I stifled a giggle as she faced off with Caleb, his jaw muscles working as he stared down at her.

"Just because you haven't *seen* me ride, doesn't mean I don't."

We both stopped short at that one, glancing between each other in a bit of pleasant shock.

"Hot damn, Caleb." Lizzie nodded, sidling up to him and yanking the zipper up on his jacket. "That's pretty sexy."

A low growl of sorts rumbled out of him, and I blushed, trading my weight between my feet as I gestured at the gate with my elbow since I was unwilling to take my cold hands out of my pockets. It was another chilly fall day here, orange and yellow leaves trampled flat on the ground beneath my feet.

"On a less appealing note," Caleb shook himself, pulling out his cell and showing Lizzie and me the screen, "I spoke with Dean Owens, and she says that these missing people in town—a few over the past few weeks—also had strange symbols carved into them. The local cops aren't spreading that news around, of course. But it looks like the Illusion de Lumière Carnival has been busy."

I scanned over the headlines as Caleb scrolled down on his phone. There were five. Five people from Rockport had gone missing. Nothing had been found yet, but it looked like the families were still calling on anyone to volunteer information.

Fucking hell. They're family is probably dead, and they can't even properly grieve.

Conversation faltered at that, but then Lizzie brought a hand down on my shoulder, making me jump slightly.

"Welp, we should go. Time's a'wasting right?"

Caleb cleared his throat, nodding back at me as he waved a hand over the gate's lock. "Yes, it is. I can't fit three of us on the bike, so we can just walk. I don't think a car would be smart."

"I agree." Lizzie hopped through the fence, starting off at a quick pace. "And I am buzzing on five cups of coffee. So let's do this."

"So what does this do again?" Lizzie asked, the three of us hunkering down just around a corner from the dormant carnival.

The place looked so odd without all the lights and people, the tarps of the tent flapping in the breeze. It wasn't as overcast here in town, and I was glad for the fact that meant rain was unlikely. The only thing worse than trying to sneak into a potential deadly circus was doing it in the rain.

"You throw them, and a chemical reaction will powder the herbal concoction, putting whoever breathes it in to sleep. It'll only last about thirty minutes, however."

"A damiana-based recipe?" I looked over at Caleb, studying the faintly yellow liquid, bits of metallic chunks floating around with a miniscule layer of bubbles around each piece.

"Yes." He nodded back at me. Caleb was perched on the balls of his feet, wearing combat boots instead of his usual leather loafers. "With a bit of chamomile and salt peter to essentially create an—"

"Aerosol. That's brilliant. I suppose it reacts well with the usual suspension in the clear layer of—"

"Temps," Lizzie eyed me, then our professor, "Caleb, I feel weird being the one to do this, but focus, please. We're about to break into a fucking carnival."

The nerd-joy of talking alchemy with a leading purveyor of the craft died in my chest, making me cringe back as I refocused on the task at hand. Caleb nodded, covertly squeezing my fingers that I had planted on the ground to help me keep my balance.

"So there's one for each of us. Hopefully, we won't have to use them." Caleb reached into his inner pocket, pulling out another vile, this one long and slender, filled with a gleaming silver liquid. "I only had time for one of these, so it's a last resort, for sure. This is a pretty intense poison. It'll cause coughing, skin irritation, nausea, eye pain, the works. Same drill. You throw it. Definitely stay far away from the landing spot, too. It'll linger for a few moments. Since we have one, I was going to hold onto it, but I can give it to one of you if you think that's better."

I smiled at Caleb, adjusting slightly in my crouch because my knees were beginning to ache. "I'm going to be honest with you. I can't throw for shit, so don't give it to me."

Lizzie snorted under her breath as Caleb grinned. "She's not wrong. I always beat her at darts. But hang onto it. I dig through your pockets if need be."

"I'd expect nothing less, Lizzie. Alright," Caleb faced the carnival, dark and quiet as the wind howled, "I don't think it's smart to walk up to the front gate. I think we need to circle around back."

I nodded, Lizzie mirroring me as we both said, "Agreed."

Moving as silently as we could, the three of us took the long way around the lot where the carnival sat, looming like a haunted house or something. A thin trail of ropes stretched between tiny wooden posts, which someone had hammered into the grass just beyond the cement structure. It cordoned off the carnival grounds, ringing the tent at the very back. I'd never been this quiet in my life, and I feared even sighing loudly.

"Let's go into the tent directly," Caleb whispered, and my attention snagged on the way his curls tumbled in the breeze. "I have a feeling whatever information we can find will be in the back, where the performers were taking that supposed winner."

"Supposed?" I kept my voice low, watching Lizzie fiddle with the rope tie on the little stake next to us.

"With everything we suspect, I highly doubt being sacrificed for power is some sort of winning, don't you?"

"Right." I nodded, and Caleb and I waited for Lizzie to finish untying the rope so that we could slip underneath and then beneath the back flap of the tent. My mind went back to the articles Caleb had found and the confirmation from the school that they were also victims of whatever evil was infecting the carnival.

The night we'd watched the show, the circus had selected a winner from the crowd, and I was sure that Caleb believed it had been a sacrifice chosen at random. I couldn't argue with that. Still, it turned my stomach to think that these people had been going out for a fun evening, thinking that they won some prize, and then winding up dead, with ancient sigils carved into their flesh.

"If we're lucky," Caleb held up the top line of rope for Lizzie to crawl under and then me, "the Ring Leader will just be some twisted witch and we can bind his powers on the spot."

I dragged my shoe across the grass as I slipped underneath the rope, puffing up the dried pieces and sending them scattering into the wind.

"And if we're not. If this is a case of soul weaving gone wrong or some corrupt asshole working for a fantasy-style big bad?"

Caleb slunk under the rope next, moving to the tent and lifting open the panel only slightly so we could all slip inside.

"Then we run. We get back to safe ground at the campus and

regroup. Because the three of us aren't enough to deal with more than that."

Inside the tent, the ring and stands lay in front of us, the seating curving away from us on either side. We'd slipped in behind the seats, and through the rows and cross-sections of wood, I could see the empty ring, that short red trim surrounding it as the dusty earth in the center sat vacant. The room where Caleb had seen the Ring Lead taking the winner was directly across from us, and we rounded the tent toward it.

It went without saying between us that there was no talking now, and I did what I could to keep my breathing even and quiet. As we pushed through another set of hanging tarps, which created a door of sorts between the back area and the main floor, the air temperature dropped precipitously. It was pitch black as we all slunk inside, and my lungs protested sucking in the frigid air.

"Fucking hell, it's cold. The fuck is that about?" Lizzie kept her voice low, and I patted around in the dark for her, wanting to hold her hand.

"Has to be something to do with—Oof," Caleb grunted, stopping short just in front of me, from what I could tell. It was impossible to see in the lightless expanse, and all I could do was wave my hands through the air, desperately seeking Lizzie or Caleb.

"What the hell is this? Temps are you *that* cold?"

Lizzie's voice came from the side of me, and I turned in that direction, stupidly holding up my hands like I might feel her, but I was nowhere near her.

"I'm not over there."

"Alright, this is getting ridiculous. I'll summon a bit of light. Just give me some space." Caleb sounded annoyed as hell, even through his whisper.

"I'm nowhere near you, teach. Do your thing."

"You're not—Ugh, never mind. I'm done with this."

Then, from my other side, in a gradual move that slowly bathed the area around us in light, Caleb summoned a small glowing orb of burnt orange, offering much-needed illumination. Still, it was such a change that I had to blink several times, turning away from the dim light and looking up at what I assumed was the tent wall now in front of me, since it moved back and forth if I touched it.

"What the—Temps, don't!" Lizzie whispered-shouted, her voice urgent. "Don't look up!"

But it was too late. I was already blinking open my eyes when she called out, pulling my hand back from the shifting fabric. Squinting, I tried to make sense of what I was seeing. It couldn't be what I thought it was, but as the fuzzy sheen over my eyes disappeared, they were still there. What I knew were...feet.

My head tipped back as I followed them up, a scream bubbling to the surface right as Lizzie's hand clamped down over my mouth.

A body. Except, no. Several of them. I spun this way and that, Lizzie unable to stop me even as she held her palm to my lips. They were all around us, hung up by meat hooks that violently poked through the soft spots beneath their shoulders. So many.

Too many.

Arms sealed around me, pushing me close to Lizzie as I realized it was Caleb surrounding us. He pulled our heads into his chest, trying to erase the damage that had already been done. Tears dripped free, smearing over the fabric of Caleb's jacket, and nausea crawled up the back of my throat, threatening to make me vomit all over him.

"I'm so sorry. Dammit, this isn't what I wanted. We should go back. This is too much to—"

"Welcome, folks, to the Illusion de Lumière Carnival. We weren't planning on visitors this morning, but since you've come all this way, why not take a *good. **Long. Look.*** At all we have to offer."

The scratchy voice came from somewhere unseen, echoing through the room around us like the place was made of stone, not tarp. I leaned back from Caleb, Lizzie doing the same, and we searched around the room for any sign of the Ring Leader or his little circus minions. Aside from the horror, swinging corpses on display like some prized hog, I couldn't make out anything in the shadows behind the way we'd come in or the singular door that led out.

Voices, mumbling and muted, came from every direction at once as I looked around, but they were indistinct, a quiet din that sounded so much like it would if there were a crowd gathered in the "big top." The faded white and red stripes around us shifted quicker, an invisible wind testing their limits, and the music from the other night played, slightly discordant and hollow like it was coming from an old music box.

"Fuck. This isn't safe. We need to get out of here." Caleb

grabbed my wrist, doing the same to Lizzie, and hauled us toward the threshold where we'd come in.

We landed hard against the shadows that were too deep to be natural. Slamming his fist against the black, Caleb spoke an incantation beneath his breath, trying to break the charm that blocked this exit. But it wouldn't budge.

"Come on now, folks. Don't be spoilsports!" The radio-like announcement knife through the air, stinging in my head and ears, and I finally tracked it to an ancient speaker affixed to the upper corner of the room near the fabric ceiling. "Go for a little walk. Such *fun* awaits."

"I can't ghost us back to the campus until I can see the sky." Caleb seethed, and I could see how hard he was working to keep himself from just tearing into the tent with his bare hands. "We need to get through this until I can get even a glimpse at clouds."

Lizzie nodded, and it was then that I remembered we were all still together. Something was worming through my head. It was almost like Lizzie's telepathy, but it felt wrong—intrusive and cold and manipulative. Suddenly, my legs felt shaky, and I whipped out a hand to steady myself, both Lizzie and Caleb coming up under my arms.

"Can you feel that? My head...is...ugh."

Scanning around us, Caleb hoisted me onto his shoulder. "We need to move. It'll be worse if you stay in one place."

"Why do you seem fine? Jerk." I almost felt drunk, covering my mouth with a gasp as soon as the words left me.

"I'm trained to block this shit out, Temperance." He sounded annoyed, his brows scrunching up as he glared at me.

Well, he can fuck off then.

Moving to shove myself off Caleb, I slapped wildly through the air, as uncoordinated as me on my fifth beer. Lizzie was at my side then, appearing like she popped in out of the shadows, and I jumped back. Her hands went to the side of my face, her middle fingers touching my temples, and I tried to swat at her.

"Temps, come back to me. Don't let the pull get to you. Come on."

Warmth buzzed through my skin. Something solidified, and I corrected myself in a snap, pain zinging through my brain as I gripped the bridge of my nose. It was as if I'd rushed through the process of being hungover and then all right again.

"Fuck. What was that? I...Oh gods," I shook my head as I faced Caleb, "I didn't mean to say that."

"It's alright," Caleb soothed, his eyes now sympathetic where before I saw irritation. "It's the tent. There's a lingering effect. The details aren't important. We just need to move. Come on. And keep an eye out for a window or door or anything."

Turning, Caleb pushed forward toward the only other exit out of this room, and Lizzie looped her arm through mine as we hurried to follow behind him. Like before, we had to shove our way through an almost visceral layer of shadow, and when we came out on the other side, I smacked into something cold and solid at my right.

"Jesus fuck, seriously?" Lizzie dropped my arm, patting the air in front of her as if she were testing to see if she'd smash into nothing as well.

I looked around, realizing what had happened. "A house of mirrors? Dammit, I hate these!"

The room was dark, all the passageways—false or not—showing rows and rows of matching frames that led off into the dark. The mirrors themselves were dusty and splotched, aged from possibly decades of use. Around them, those frames that reflected all around us were red and white, bulbous curves that looked like harmless circles or skulls piled on top of each other, depending on how you look at them.

Straight bars of white light criss-crossed over the ceiling, illuminating the mirrors to create the infinite hallway effect. The floors were black, as were the undersides of the arches that framed the mirrors. I saw unending versions of myself reflected back at me, mirroring my movements perfectly.

Except for the smiles.

I wasn't smiling. Why the fuck would I? But the chain of Temps were all grinning at me, mad glee in their eyes as the three of us stepped into another trap. When I looked at the reflections of Caleb and Lizzie, it was the same, but they both turned this way and that, trying to figure out the path forward.

"Wait!" I called out, moving to Caleb to grab the sleeve of his leather jacket. "Stop turning. I can't keep track of you when you keep moving."

But as I groped wildly for him, my knuckles hit glass—a reflection. I turned around, set on going back toward Lizzie, but as I took off in the direction I'd come from, or at least what I believed to be the right path, I got another handful of steps and ran into a mirror again.

I was alone. I'd lost them.

"Caleb! Lizzie!" Frantically turning around, I tried to peer through the halls of reflections for any sign of them. "Where are you?!"

"Temps!"

The sound came from behind me, and maybe a bit to the right? I held a hand out in front of me, pressing it to the cold surface I knew was glass and not the way forward. I kept running it along the edge until my fingers could hook around the edge of the frame and turned, following the path that I prayed led out of here and not just right back where I'd come from.

Using my sense of touch, I kept going until I hit another mirror, forced to turn left when every instinct in me was saying to turn right. For a moment, I paused, keeping my fingers on the mirror as I looked over my shoulder and then back ahead.

Am I going the right way? Dammit. Where are they?

The endless versions of myself all grinned at me, their eyes too wide, the smiles stretching too far. This was bad. I needed to find Lizzie and Caleb and get the fuck out of here. Movement to my left caught my eye, the flash of what I thought was Caleb's jacket. I went toward it, keeping my fingers to the glass but skipping the open passing to my right and moving straight ahead, where I saw the back of Caleb's jacket more clearly.

But how was I seeing him from behind if he was supposed to be somewhere in front of me, and I'd yet to pass him?

Physics wasn't my strong suit, and they weren't lining up no matter how I rearranged my thoughts. So, I shook it away, still hurrying forward toward Caleb's reflection. He was so close, just up ahead, but when I reached him, I touched glass again. Spinning around, Caleb had to be someone who was nearby to reflect like this, but I came face to face with that odd smile pinned on my professor's face this time.

"You're not Caleb."

"Aren't I?" The voice sounded like it was coming out of a speaker. "Or is it that one?"

Mirror Caleb pointed, and I turned to see the row of infinite arms doing the same, their backs to me. How was this possible? One of the reflections, several down the line from me, turned this way, breaking form from the others. It stepped into the black space between Caleb's reflections and mine, seizing one of them and yanking on the wrist that both did and didn't belong to me.

It *hurt*.

I was taken down to a knee, staring at my wrist as indentations appeared in my flesh, icy tendrils skittering up my arm. It burned and froze, my skin feeling like it was going to crack as the pressure reached my bone. As I huffed out a breath, crying out and fighting against the hold, my breath turned white in the air around me.

"Temperance!"

Yanking my head up toward the voice, I searched the dark furiously as tears dribbled down my cheeks. My bone was going to snap, the pressure rising, and from down the endless tunnel of shadow, Caleb came into focus.

He launched himself toward me, and I held up my free arm, shielding myself as I screamed. "Don't break my arm! Stop!"

Sweat collected on my forehead and the back of my neck, and then hands hauled me to my feet before one settled over my wrist, mumbling some Latin I didn't have the awareness to understand right now. The pain stopped, though, and I desperately scanned the area around me, landing on the Caleb that stood before me.

"Are you real?"

"I'm real." Caleb nodded, his eyebrow bleeding over his left eye. "Have you seen Lizzie?"

I shook my head, a sob tearing free as I cradled my arm against my chest. "No. I was trying to tell you not to turn around, and then I was just alone. Please don't leave me again."

The words came out like the terrified plea they were, and Caleb furrowed his brow, his lips parting gently as he pulled me to his chest, smoothing his hand down the back of my head.

"I won't. Fuck, I'm so sorry, Temperance. We never should have come here. We weren't prepared."

"It was my idea. I was just...I was so nervous about the soul weaving, and—"

"We can talk about it later." Caleb held my shoulders as he looked down at me, then eyed the tunnels of shadow around us. "We need to find Lizzie."

All I could do was nod. But then I heard it—a scream.

It was just on the other side of the glass, and without thinking, I flung myself toward it, pounding my fists on the frozen surface.

"Lizzie!" *Pound, pound, pound.* "Lizzie!"

Caleb grabbed my shoulder, putting me behind him even as I fought to get back to the glass. But he was damn strong, and I had to watch as he held up his hand to the mirror, meeting his smirking reflection in the eye as the image began to waver and shake.

"I'm done with this shit." The vibrations rumbled enough so I felt them in the floor, staring in disbelief as the air in front of Caleb's hand appeared to ripple with invisible force. "Lizzie, if you can hear me, stand back from the glass!"

The thundering wobble of the mirror crescendoed, so loud that I had to cover my ears, and then the glass in front of Caleb shattered, pieces flying in all directions as he turned and huddled over me, protecting me from the shrapnel. For all the noise, the room was suddenly quiet, and little shards of mirror tumbled off me as I hurried to look at the empty space where Caleb had broken through the maze.

Lizzie was lying on the floor. I rushed to her, glass crunching beneath my feet and then digging into my knees as I knelt by her.

"Lizzie." I shook her gently, sliding my hand under her head. "Lizzie, come on."

But she wasn't answering, tiny cuts on her face as she lay in my lap, unmoving. Caleb was there in a blink, putting his fingers to Lizzie's neck and checking for a pulse. My stomach was a useless jumble of knots as I shook my head.

She can't be dead. She can't.

"Unconscious, but we need to get out of here. Hold on." Caleb's word offered some relief, but Lizzie was still out, and how the hell were we going to get out of the tent when it was obviously some extraplanar realm?

Pointing up at the ceiling, Caleb sent those vibrations up, up, up. His leather jacket was marred with little slices on the back, and his other hand was bleeding now, the tiny red trail leaking down the side of his palm. There were too many lights up there, too much glass. If he broke through again, we'd be torn to shreds.

"Caleb, I don't...the glass..."

"Grab my hand and hold the fuck on." He focused like a laser on the room until it tore and cracked like the mirror wall, a curtain of broken fragments hurtling down toward us. But just behind, clear as day, if not very big, was a view of the sky.

And just like that, he whisked out of there, me clinging to his bloody hand and my unconscious girlfriend.

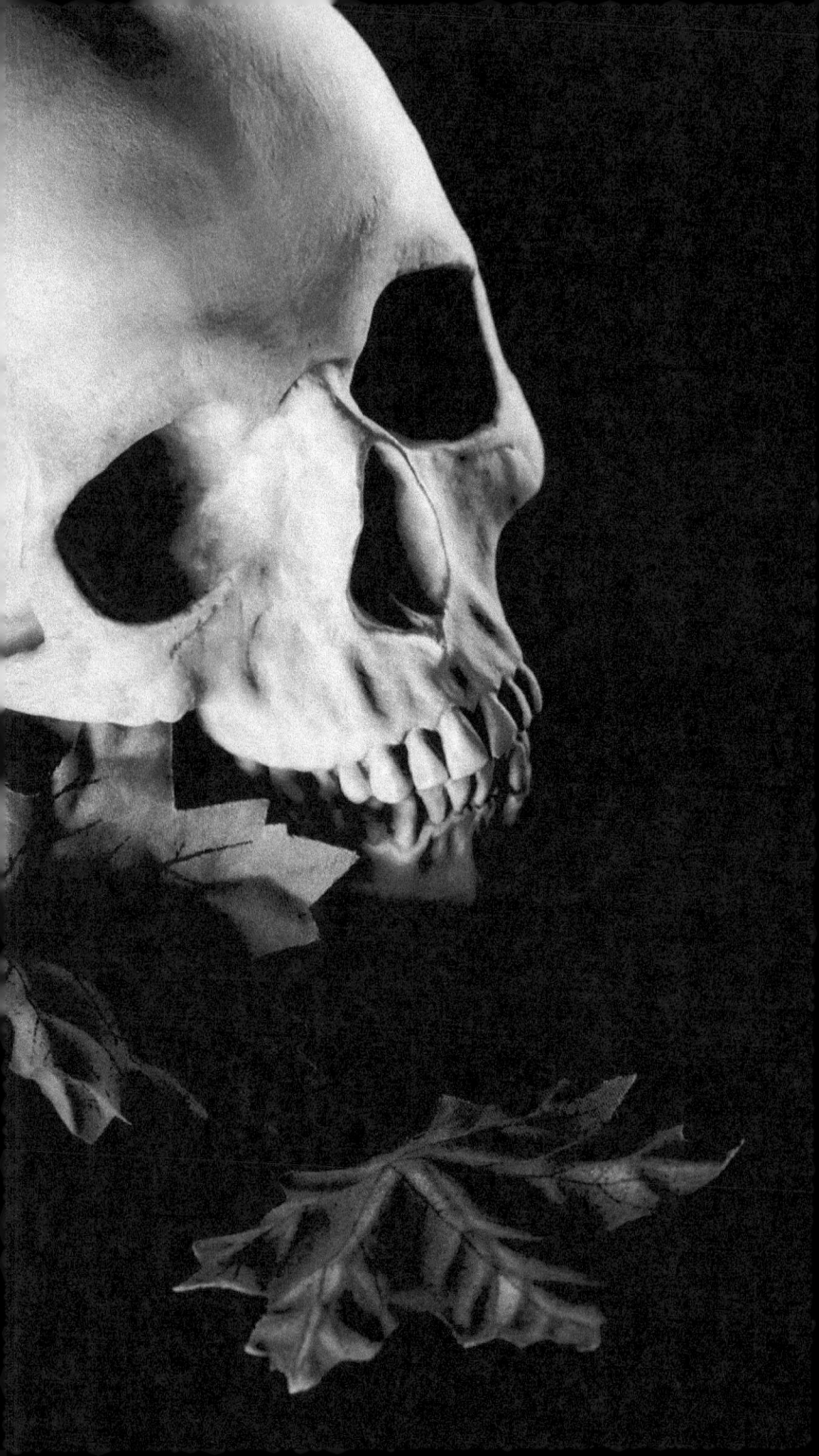

Eighteen

And In The Time Of Darkness Rises A Soul Made Two, Bound & Everlasting

Caleb

We landed back in my office, Temperance and Lizzie spilling out across the floor as I hit it hard with my knees. It had hardly been the most precise bit of magic I'd ever done. I was still ringing like a damned tuning fork as I braced myself on my hands and knees, breathing as if I were sucking in tar. The world around me wobbled, only dim fragments of what I was seeing making any sense.

Yes, I knew we'd made it back to my office, but my skin, my being, still felt off. I wasn't sure if I was going to vomit or pass out. I had no time for either.

Hauling myself across the floor, I searched for where Lizzie had landed, with Temperance no doubt holding her tight. My eyes burned as they tried to focus, and as they did, I found gray flecks marring my vision. The debris from the ceiling and mirrors must have scratched my glasses. I could think about that later. Right now, I needed to stabilize Lizzie.

"Caleb, do something."

On cue, Temperance's voice oriented me, and I shifted to the left, pulling off my glasses and shoving them away so that I could try to inspect Lizzie. More and more clarity as the seconds went on, and I immediately noticed that her color was off. Lizzie looked too pale, and I touched her forehead with the back of my hand. Clammy and feverish. That was a sign of illusion magic, something that had gotten inside her head and caused enough damage to knock her unconscious.

"Well, what's happening?" Temperance sounded so desperate, terrified. "What the fuck is wrong, Caleb?"

"I'm not sure. The mental manipulation of the tent. I think this is something similar. We need to call back her essence, get Lizzie firmly back in the realm of the living. Like before."

"On it."

Temperance got up and ran to get the supplies, my brain only processing the sounds of her moving, because now that I was taking in more of what Lizzie looked like, I was crumbling. She was hurt, with cuts on her skin, smeared blood. Bright red blood. A flash of my mother's face superimposed over Lizzie's, and I choked back a scream.

No, no, no. This isn't happening again.

But the wood floors were gone, replaced by a muted gray carpet.

The coffee table and couch were not the ones from my office, but those that sat in my old house. The ones that had been splattered with blood when those men had slit my parents' throats.

My hands shook as I tried to wipe it away, get it off her face. "No, no. Too much. There's too much. I can't..."

Nausea pulsed in my guts as the world spun. I heard the door breaking in again. My parents were telling me to run, but I couldn't get away. And then there again in their grips—my mother and father's pleading eyes, wet with tears. I could hear it, the way that man had told me he was going to butcher them. We were witches, foul, heinous creatures to him, and his little fucking friends were going to kill them. I was going to watch them die—right now.

"Caleb!" Something was shaking me, and I blinked, looking over to see Temperance kneeling on the floor next to me, jars and flasks around us. "I know this is a lot, but I need you to fucking focus, okay?"

I stared at her, glancing back at Lizzie and still seeing ghosts hovering at the corners. "I'm not sure if—"

"I am. Come on, Caleb. Do this. Don't let Lizzie—She *needs* you." Temperance took my hand and put a small glass container against my palm. "I'll do what I can, but you have to tell me the steps."

Nodding, I gripped the jar tighter, grounding myself to the moment with the feeling of that glass against my skin. I was here. I was in the office. Lizzie needed me. I was here, in the office, and Lizzie needed me.

"Okay. Umm, unstopper that. We need the base solution. And

get a bit of Lizzie's hair to really anchor the magic."

Temperance worked quickly, and we blended and heated the ingredients for the tonic faster than I thought possible. The truth was, we made a damn good team. With the mixture ready, we each took one of Lizzie's hands, and I started the Latin incantation to draw her back to us. Temperance spoke the words after me until our voices mingled, creating a melody that wove through the air in gold threads. We were a choir of intent, calling to our girl and offering up everything we had to ground her in the present.

My body ached, my shoulders drooping as the spell claimed energy I wasn't sure I even had, but it embroidered itself into intricate knots that settled over Lizzie, this version of the working so much more intense than before. It solidified, sealing around her as Temperance and I finished the words.

Silence hung in the air as we waited for something, anything. I watched the frozen form, eyeing Lizzie's chest for a sign of that first solid breath. She was still so cold, that damned tent wanting to keep the dark magic hooked inside her.

"Come on, Lizzie," I growled, conjuring up more energy from nowhere, shoving it into the tapestry of gold that wavered in and out of reality above her. "Come on! Come back to us!"

One, two, three seconds passed...

"Gah!" Lizzie bolted upright, swinging wildly.

Jolting back, I clutched my shirt as Temperance launched herself forward into Lizzie's arms. She clung to her, wrapping her arms around her neck and burying her face in Lizzie's mussed-up curls that'd come undone from her usual braid.

I could breathe a bit easier now, but a weight settled on my chest. We'd gone in there, and Lizzie had almost died. Hell, we all had. I'd waited to use the resonance spell when I should have just blasted that fucking tent from the get-go. And we weren't any closer to putting a stop to the carnival either.

"I thought I lost you." Temperance's voice was muffled, but then Lizzie pulled her back, smiling through the exhaustion at her.

"Me too. That, umm, sucked ass." Lizzie bobbed her head tiredly, breathing hard as her eyelids drooped. "I don't think we were ready for that."

"No. We weren't."

Two sets of eyes hit me as I sat on the floor, my arms draped over my knees. I stared blankly at the fancy mahogany trim, the stained glass window with a clear view of the campus beneath the ornate colors. The rain from earlier had stopped, but it was still so grim, so gloomy outside, and part of me wondered if that was because of me. I certainly wouldn't be surprised if I trailed a black cloud permanently overhead, a porryah that infected the world around him.

"I nearly got you killed."

The words were already out when I glanced back at the girls. They both narrowed their eyes at me, Temperance leaning back from hanging on to Lizzie. She slid her hand across the floorboards until her fingertips met mine, sliding between the digits and holding my hand.

"You got us out of there. And you *did* say we should get more power. This isn't your fault. If anything," Temperance sighed, "I shouldn't have been so afraid of the soul weaving. Sometimes, there *are* more important things than your own happiness. Right?"

I cloaked myself in impenetrable armor since the moment I walked out of the police station those twenty years ago. After I'd lost my parents, I vowed never to let anyone that close to me again. It wasn't worth the pain, because invariably they'd all leave me one way or another. I kept my exchanges with people superficial and scarce.

And yet from the moment I saw these two women before me, I knew something big had happened. Hell, I knew everything had changed completely.

"Sometimes, Temps." I smiled, my vision shimmering as my eyes burned. "But not always. I...I get your reticence to perform the ritual. I won't give up what we have here either. I won't. I don't think I could. I never planned for this, but you two have become the most important people in my life. I won't lose you."

I could feel the wetness on my face, but I just didn't give a shit anymore. I'd believed all my tears were used up the night of my parents' funeral, but I'd found new ones, and I couldn't hold them back.

Lizzie's brows rose as this look of something akin to awe washed over her beautiful face. She looked to Temperance, and they both turned back to me, crawling across the floor until they surrounded me, one of them straddling either leg as I collapsed back against the edge of the coffee table. I couldn't hold it all in, the span of emotions and thoughts that powered through me—furious and dedicated as a freight train.

So, I just broke down.

What was truly the shock of the season was that there were actually people there to support me through it. Yes, I'd had a handful of people in the past who would be there on the hard days, but something no one talks about is that as you age, friendships and relationships just change. Some will stand the test of time, some won't. I knew I cut myself off from people, but I'd be lying if I said some people had really fought to be around me.

Becoming an island was damn easy, actually.

Time stretched for a while, an amorphous thing that passed by without fanfare or spectacle. So, after the worst of it was over, I looked up into two gorgeous sets of eyes and found the strength to nod.

"There's nothing that makes the grief go away," Temperance said, cupping my cheek as she perched on my right knee. "It's always there, but it can be more manageable when you're not alone. And you're *not* alone, Caleb."

"And we will never understand how horrible it was to see what you did. We won't. But we've both lost a parent, too. That's a hole that becomes a part of the fabric. You'll always notice it. But Temps is right. We're here. Yes, there's the mind-blowing sex we had the other day, but hell, I actually like hanging with you. And when you talk about alchemy? Ugh, you and Temps like up like fucking Bunsen burners."

Laughter erupted from my chest, cleansing fire that burned away some of the lingering darkness.

"I like being around you both, too. And I'd prefer it if I didn't have to add you to the list of people I've lost. So..."

"Soul weaving." Temps nodded, gripping my hand. "Alright. How do we do it?"

"Well," I shuffled slightly, jostling the girls as I pressed away from the coffee table that dug into my spine, "we'll need to visit the library for the appropriate tome and then proceed to the cemetery behind campus. Holy ground is required for the ritual according to the text I've already read. And since books are allowed to leave the library—and there's an enchantment in place—we'll have to be crafty."

"Good, more breaking and entering. And now with theft." Lizzie nudged Temps with her elbow as her stepsister complained.

"Eh, I think I have an idea for this one."

Lizzie's eyes twinkled with mischief, and I made a face, narrowing my eyes at her as I pointed just an inch or so from her nose.

"Why do I get the feeling that if it weren't for our relationship, you'd be my problem student?"

Keaning forward, Lizzie kissed my finger before pushing off me, making my thigh muscle stretch in a sharp tweak.

"Because you're very smart. Now, shut up and follow me."

"You're absolutely insane! That was your idea!" Temperance

screamed out over her shoulder as the three of us ran away from the library, clinging to our stolen book in a repetitive, high-stakes version of hot potato.

"Hey," Lizzie called out, catching the book as I tossed it gently to her, disorienting the animated lock and chain that was coming after it, "it's not very nice of you to throw around the word 'insane,' you know. I would have thought you knew better."

"Lizzie!" Temperance sprinted for the gate of the cemetery, all of us praying to Hekate that the fucking holy ground would dispel the charm—at least while we were on it. "I'm going to murder you!"

The heavy, slightly rusty chained knocked me in the head as it tried to swing around toward Lizzie, and I glared in her direction.

"Seconded!"

She rushed forward, her laugh trailing behind her as she leaped for the open gate Temperance had propped open. As her body flew past the threshold, the chain stopped midair, circling before a moment before zooming past me, nearly smashing into my face, I might add, and heading back toward the library. Lizzie looked up from the damp, leaf-strewn ground with a smirk.

"Ha, told you it'd work."

Without the hot pursuit, I slowed down, catching my breath as I walked up to the cemetery gate and stepped in. Temperance shut it behind me, turning toward Lizzie as she folded her arms. I leered down at our naughty little morrighan, mirroring Temperance's arm cross.

"You're going to pay for that, brat."

Looking up at me from the ground, Lizzie let her leg fall to the side, revealing the sight of her bright white panties beneath her skirt as she continued to grin up at me, a cat who'd gotten the cream.

"Promise?"

I rolled my eyes, stepping forward to offer her a hand up. "Yes. As a matter of fact, I do. But we have work to do."

The mood sobered at the mention of the soul weaving. We still weren't sure how this was going to go. We agreed that we needed to take the spell slowly, remain focused, and end it if things looked like they were turning south. We even had the dean's cell on standby, consequences be damned.

Temperance and Lizzie stood in front of me for a moment, both of them gripping my forearms. They held my stare, a silent promise, and then we split up so that we could set up the ritual circle.

It took several minutes, but quietly and intently, the three of us had found the oldest grave in the cemetery, belonging to Bethany herself, and circled the site in protective salt and herbs. Temperance got copal and palo santo burning in a squat cauldron, circling from north to south three times to solidify the sacred space. Lizzie channeled the elements, bringing offerings of incense, seashells, stag bones, and a burning candle to each cardinal point.

"Excellent. Now, we start. It's best if you stay beyond the inner ring of quartz and amaranth. That will focus the spirit onto me." Reaching for the buttons of my shirt, I began to undo them, stripping it off to mark myself with the ague root solution. It should minimize the chance of an unwelcome spirit taking advantage of the soul weaving. "Begin the chant."

It was impossible to be oblivious to the nervous energy both Temeprance and Lizzie exuded. I knew they were both terrified that something would go wrong. I didn't want to admit it, but I was, too. Sure, we'd studied the text in the library while we could, but there was only so much we could prepare for. At some point, we were just going to have to try this and hope for the best.

A leap of faith. Ugh, fucking cliche.

Lizzie ensured the borders of the circle were stable, walking the salt line, and then handed the book to me as she and Temperance chanted the ancient words into the night air. We'd been in the library for some time, the moon now rising over the trees. It cast the graveyard in an eerie glow, a stark contrast of grays and whites from each of the centuries-old gravestones.

Magic picked up behind the words, making Temperance and Lizzie's voices ring with purpose, melodic and haunting. They spoke in a long-forgotten language of the first witches, a relative of Gaelic. As the rising energy began to reach its peak, the two of them stood to my left and right, holding their hands up to the starlight sky.

I looked up, calling on whatever benevolent deity had seen fit to bring these incredible women into my life, finding the name I needed to call out.

"Hear me!" I threw my arms up, giving myself over to the resonant vibrations. "World of Below, I summon to me your fated partner to my soul. We beseech you! Your last earthly bond is required."

Something took hold of me, power surging in my veins as I felt something from deep within the core of the earth rise up to meet me. It had been there all this time, whispering at the edges, pulling me toward this moment, this soul weaving that would change our three interwoven fates.

"I feel you," my voice traveled through the wind, dusting over Bethany's grave marker and around Temperance and Lizzie. "World of Below! You have claimed your Winter Witch. You have found your Queen of the Shadowed Summer Sun! You have brought home your Queen of the Cauldron & Endless Forest! It is time now for Harbinger, Black Wolf of Three Faces. His mates stand before the edge of the realms, ready to claim and be claimed, to embrace the stands of fate, held safe by the Horned Queen. A great evil, one that has long touched this world, grows stronger. The time has come to seal it away for good!"

I could hardly understand the words sprouting from my mouth, but I knew they were true. I could sense both Lizzie and Temperance eyeing me with anxious confusion, but this was it. This was what everything had been leading toward all this time.

The earth shook, rumbling with enough force to send us all to our knees. Before me, it cracked open, a fissure that glowed orange and red, liquid fire bubbling beneath it.

"Ah!" I heard Lizzie yelp somewhere distant, my stare trapped on the gateway in front of me.

A massive black paw shot up from the depths, enormous claws sinking into the earth at my knees.

"Oh my g—"

Rooooaaaaarrr!

The noise was everywhere, even in my head, and I gripped my skull. The world I knew was gone, a curtain of black surrounding my consciousness. Then I heard it. No, not it. Him.

I have waited so long for you, little sage. You have called, and I have come, as it is ordained in the writing of the earth itself. I accept your call, mate. We will face this malice that has plagued our realms for these long eons. I need only to hear your affirmation. Let me in.

Overwhelming anxiety welled inside me. This could be a trap. This could be some setup from the very thing we were fighting. But as I searched the presence in my mind, all I could feel was a profound sense of something I'd lacked for so long.

Home.

Sucking in a breath of pungent air, the smell of molten rock and ancient dirt, hallowed by the protections of witches long-since gone, I closed my eyes, turning inward.

Yes.

Reality snapped. I felt myself hoisted up from the ground as a torrent of wind swirled around me. He came inside, entering the very fabric of my soul and weaving through the gaps and leaving me more complete than I'd ever been. Some part of me recognized him, but as I landed, I was no longer in control of my body, this entity taking over.

"Caleb!"

From within, I felt him move my head, staring at Temperance through my eyes. "Not quite. But he is listening. And he will be returned to you when I've at last claimed you both, *my mates*."

Nineteen

WOVEN BY TWO, THE WOLF WILL CLAIM BY FULL MOON'S LIGHT

LIZZIE

I wasn't sure what the hell I was looking at, except for the fact that I strongly believed that hell might actually be involved. The fucking earth had opened, and a giant, three-headed wolf had climbed out of a fiery pit of sorts. Three godsdamn heads, something straight out of mythology, goodest boy for dear old Hades, and it'd just popped out of the ground like mother fucking daisy.

But it was the part where the hound had disappeared into Caleb's body that really through me for a loop, and that was saying something.

"Is that the fucking soul weaving?!"

My voice barely carried with the wind that circled the sacred space we'd set up for the ritual. Temperance stood across the way from me, and she shrugged, looking back down at Caleb as he knelt in that inner circle. When he spoke to her, it was off, a second voice rumbling over his, darker, deeper. Before I could say more, I watched her reel back as Caleb shot up, his hands in claws at his sides as he sniffed the air near her.

What the...?

"So long. I have waited eons and more. Reborn to my Mother Queen, and still I waited. And now you are finally here." Caleb turned over his shoulder, his eyes glowing yellow. "Both of you, and the sage who watches from within."

"Sage, what do you—oh gods." Temperance's hand shot up to her mouth, covering it as she peered forward at Caleb. "You're not Caleb. Is he alright?! I swear if you hurt him—"

Quicker than humanly possible, Caleb—or whoever this was—leaped forward, crossing the border of the inner circle and landing right at Temps' feet. He growled, the sound wolfish and terrifying, and dragged a clawed finger up the side of her arm. I was already moving, trying to be quiet as I got closer, and the being puppeting Caleb's body spoke.

"It's rather adorable that you think you can threaten me." He chuckled, and there was a heady darkness behind it that had my mind going fuzzy. "Still, I'd have my mate no other way. And rest assured, little witch, your sage is just fine. Enjoying the view and the taste of my hunger that fills our blood."

"Our?" The word was out before I could stop it, and the being shifted to face me, this gradual fluid motion that was as graceful as it was frightening.

"Yes, morrighan, 'our.'"

The face I knew was Caleb's shifted as the wind picked up, the moon overhead resonating with more pale yellow light. I could do nothing more than watch as fur, black as the deepest shadows, spread out over his body, and fangs descended into her mouth, his claws lengthening as he stretched taller. Caleb's clothes were torn to fucking shreds, falling away from a body even more muscular than his had been and all covered in that midnight fur. His brown curls deepened in color, falling to his shoulders now.

"Holy fuck." I had to crane back to keep my eyes pinned on his, so much more yellow now and glowing fiercely. Temps ran to my side, crashing against me as she gripped my hand. "Am I looking at a fucking werewolf?"

"I...I don't know. W-Who are you?" My girl's voice shook, and I brought her closer to me. I'd keep her safe from any asshole looking to fuck with her, no matter what shell it wore.

Still, I wasn't getting terrorizer vibes from this guy, whoever he was. I couldn't sense that bloodlust I got from every inch of the carnival. There was hunger, pure and raw, and it *was* for us. The heat of it licked my skin, making me shudder as the wolf-like creature towered over us, sniffing the air.

We should be running. Why are we running?

"You may call me Cerberus." I swallowed hard, feeling Temps wobble on her feet next to me. "And it is time we finally sealed our bond. I will not wait another moment."

Sealed our bond? What the hell did he mean by that? As I stood there with Temps, Cerberus lowered that fanged muzzle toward us, and I put her behind me, doing what I could to shield her. That intoxicating chuckle rippled through the air again, my eyes fluttering as the sound hit me. I bloomed with warmth as Temps squeaked behind me, and I could sense the growing heat inside her like I had when we were in Caleb's office.

The signal rebounded, circling over and over between the three of us. Well, four, sort of. With this connection, I could pick out the hum of Caleb's aura humming inside the wolven body in front of us. The feedback loop rang like a tuning fork struck with another, and it hit me that amid the undeniable fear, there was almost blistering arousal.

I was fucking dripping.

With that inhuman speed again, Cerberus ducked low, stuffing his nose between my legs. I yelped, my brows shooting up to my hairline as I pitched back against Temps. She barely caught me as the enormous creature, at least eight feet tall when he stood on those wolf-like feet, breathed in. His exhale sent a wave of hot air across my core, melting through the fabric of my panties since my skirt wasn't doing me any favors.

"What the fuck? What are you doing?" I eyed Cerberus, his massive, clawed hands planted in the earth, and he inhaled the scent of me. Temps still kept me from falling, but then the wolf was lifting my leg over his nose and doing the same investigation of her, his nose disappearing beneath the longer fabric of Temps' untrimmed skirt.

"I can scent your arousal, witches. So thick and reverent." My cheeks heated, and I exchanged a look with Temps, who was blushing just as hard as I was. "I will have these horrid coverings off you."

Claws hooked into the waistband of my skirt, spearing a hole straight through the fabric at my hip. They ran down, slicing it clean open and taking one side of my panties along with it. The useless garment fell to the ground, and Temps' joined it in a flash.

"The hell?! You can't just—" But my stepsister's words died as Cerberus nuzzled into her again, cutting through the remaining side of her panties and tossing them behind him.

I was frozen in place as I watched him with her. Temps held my stare, her pupils blown wide as Cerberus licked a massive tongue up the inside of her thigh and right to her pussy. This was wild. How this was even happening was absolutely beyond me. We'd performed the soul weaving, successfully it seemed, and Caleb wasn't dead or gone, at least according to the wolf god animating him right now.

But it wasn't just that. I could sense him. I could sense a fucking lot right now, and holy hell, this ancient being was so ravenous for Temps and me that, regardless of how "insane" it might make me, I was ready to see just what he could do.

Cerberus felt strange and familiar all at once, and there was no denying the appeal of being fucked in a cemetery by a muscular werewolf with a tongue that long.

"Oh, gods..." Temps' eyes rolled back, her balance faltering as Cerberus trailed that pink tongue up to her pussy.

He let her pitch back, snatching her right leg and hoisting it up by the ankle. Temps was split wide, and even though Cerberus' enormous body blocked most of it, I could *feel* the pleasure worm through her as he tasted her. My pussy clamped down, all of me aching to know what that would be like.

"Ambrosia, little witch." Cerberus set Temps down, a cushion of autumn leaves under her, and he fisted the front of her button-down shirt. In a flash, he tore through the cotton and her bra beneath, exposing her breasts as she let out a surprised cry.

At this rate, we were going through uniforms faster than a painter who worked in explosives.

"There you are, my Temperance, lineage of the Winter Witch herself. You and our devious morrighan will scream for me this night."

"I..." Temps lie on the earth, gravestones scattered without pattern just behind her, and the wind howled low again. "He's really in there? Caleb?"

Chuckling, Cerberus lowered down, hovering his mouth over her ear, but when he whispered, it was still loud enough for me to hear, and this voice I recognized immediately.

"I'm here, Temperance. And I want to feel you fuck our elder god. I want to feel him claim you both."

The apprehension circling Temps' aura evaporated in a puff of white breath from her lips, and she dug her fingers into the ground, looking up at the wolven form of our sweet professor. Her eyes reached mine over Cerberus' shoulder, and I finally remembered that I could move, that I could get to her and have my own taste while our new buddy joined in.

Starting for her, I got about a step away before a massive tail swept around me. It gripped me tight, yanking me off the ground and holding me so that I dangled head down above Temps. As far as I knew, wolves lacked a prehensile tail, so this was an interesting treat.

"Morrighan," I turned slightly in the air as Cerberus faced me to look at him, "I had almost thought you would be stuck to that spot and silly enough to just watch."

Wetness glimmered on his dark lips and the fur around them, and I shook my head. "Absolutely not."

A wide, fanged grin split his face, illuminated by the corn-yellow moon that swelled in the sky as if pulled closer to us. His claws found my shirt, easily tearing through the flimsy white button-down. I wasn't wearing my school-issued jacket, always one to run a little hot, and Cerberus cocked a brow when he saw there was no bra for him to get through either.

"You are the devious one. I see our sage's memories, the way you tease and taunt."

My pulse roared in my ears, the blood rushing to my head nearly too much to take, and then Cerberus lowered me to the ground beside Temps. She looked over at me before her eyes slid down my face to my neck and then breasts. I roamed my stare right back at her, drinking in the sight of her slight breasts revealed by her shredded top. Temps nipples were so hard, mine too, and the chilled air made goosebumps ripple across her skin.

"Touch me," she whispered low, her eyes begging.

Reaching out, I ran the pads of my fingers over her collarbone, then down, down, down, dusting them over her pert nipple. Temps hissed in a breath, and warmth funneled around us as above us, our massive wolf breathed hard.

"Take her in your mouth, little morrighan."

No one had to tell me to get a taste of Temps twice, so I happily leaned up onto my elbow, which sank little into the damp earth, lowering my lips to that tasty little bud at the tip of her breast. I sucked it between my teeth, teasing before I licked a long circle around it, making her arch up from the ground.

The sound of the leaves crinkling bracketed her soft moan, and a heavy rumble reverberated out of Cerberus. Fur dusted my bare thigh as he lowered his hips, a hard bulge pressing against me. Fuck, I was wet. I was desperate to feel him, to take the massive prize he was no doubt packing.

"That's perfect. Our sweet witch moves so beautifully, her pleasure seeping into the very earth from her dripping cunt."

Daaamn. Cerberus certainly had a way with words.

"Lizzie, ugh." Temps rolled her hips up, her body clearly begging for more. "*Please...*"

I reached between her slick thighs just as a ravenous growl erupted from our wolf. Parting her folds, I used my middle finger to circle around her clit. Temps' hips bucked, and I bit her nipple playfully, continuing to work her up with gentle pats of my finger and teasing her entrance.

Cerberus rubbed against my thigh, then the warmth vanished, and I was seconds from checking for him when my leg was craned upward, and the flat of his huge tongue found my pussy.

He swirled it against my clit, so dextrous and wide. That glorious werewolf tongue was so big that it covered me from clit to asshole, wet warmth spreading through me as I dripped with need. I suckled on Temp harder, sinking one finger and then two into her tight pussy as Cerberus slid the tip of his tongue to my entrance.

"Fuck, Lizzie, yes…" Temps moved up and down, fucking my fingers, and I squeezed around Cerberus' tongue as he began to press in.

Gods, it was just so thick, gradually filling me up, stretching me, and in the back of my mind, I was extremely grateful for the warm-up. If this was just what he could do with his mouth, his cock might actually break me.

But what a way to go.

"So…close…" Moving in shorter, faster jerks, Temps clenched around my fingers. She needed exactly what I did, though, so I slowed if only to slip a third finger inside her, swirling them until she was mewling and so wet that I could add a fourth. She was going to take my entire hand, readying her sweet cunt for our beast-boy's cock.

Yes, devious morrighan, stretch her cunt for me, ready our witch.

Cerberus spoke in my head, and the surprise almost had me faltering. I was used to being the one to initiate that kind of conversation. But damn, was it the way to go since his tongue was currently working me like a fucking champ, pressing against my G-spot so that wetness pooled inside me.

I was gentle and slow as I worked my fingers in and out of Temps' pussy, using every bit of slick arousal to make her stretch comfortably around my fist.

"Ugh!" Temps smashed her balled up hands down as I sank inside. She was warm and perfect and fluttering around me as she rode that edge, ready to tip over.

Pleasure perfumed the air around us as everything built up. I was right there with my girl, riding a damn werewolf tongue that was going to have me squirting all over. Temps gripped my arm, digging her nails into me as she rocked her hips, taking my fist so well.

"Right there, right there! Don't...stop...I—Fuck!"

She orgasmed hard, clenching around my wrist. It was bliss, and I roared out my own release as Cerberus rammed his tongue home, hitting my cervix. I gushed, pulsing against him as I ground my hips down against his mouth, squeezing his fur between my fingers.

A moment and then two, and then he was leaning back as I glided my hand free. I was struggling for breath, lying on Temps' chest as it rushed up and down, when I glanced down at this ancient being that had transformed Caleb into something incredible. He smiled at me, his fangs gleaming, and my heart stuttered, another spike of fear that only heightened my arousal.

Leaning back on his knees, Cerberus reached down, rubbing across that impressive bulge. I sat up, shifting so Temps could see our towering hunk of a sex god, because as far as I was concerned, this incredible being—this ancient elder deity summoned through a soul-weaving and sharing a body with our hot as fuck professor—definitely held dominion over carnal activities.

His glowing eyes tracked Temps and me, feasting on us, and from beneath the midnight fur extended something that I was *not* fucking prepared for.

I have to be dreaming. That can't be fucking real, except...

"There's...two of them," Temps managed to stutter out, my eyes glued to the twin cocks that stood out proudly from Cerberus' hips as he stroked them, utterly speechless.

With a smirk, he thrust forward into his fist, precum dripping from the rosy tips of his shafts. "There are two of us within the form, are there not?"

Well, that's fucking handy.

Twenty

To Give Of Yourself, Bound In The Sacred Circle

TEMPS

Caleb had transformed into this remarkable werewolf-like form, the creature Cerberus at the wheel as it were, but not for one second had I expected there to be *two* cocks.

My body had done things in the past, however long it'd been, that I didn't think it was capable of. Taking Lizzie's hand had been an utterly wild experience, and now I was more grateful than I think I ever had been in my life because if I was going to take even *one* of the monstrous appendages in front of me, I had certainly needed to be *warmed up*.

"I...I..."

I was a stammering mess, and Lizzie wasn't talking at all, which I was pretty sure was a first since I met her. All either of us could do was stare down at the long, thick shafts that Cerberus stroked, the glistening tips so pink, curving slightly upward. His massive hand could easily handle both of them, and he stroked, a sinful chuckle rumbling out from behind those powerful fangs.

"Perhaps a taste will convince you of reality."

What? Did he say—

But then Cerberus palmed the back of my head, doing the same to Lizzie, visible in my peripheral vision, and pulled me forward. I stumbled onto my knees, the cool earth smoothly around them as the damp soil absorbed my weight. Leaves clung to my hair, my clothes were destroyed, and it hit me how unhinged we all must look right now.

Hell, even the location. We were doing this in an ancient cemetery, in a sacred circle we'd just made, and the earth rumbled beneath me, this whelling sensation of the spirits in tune with this halllowed ground stirring.

And that was saying nothing for the giant wolfman lining up his cocks with my stepsister's and my mouth.

A dark sheathe slipped back further as Cerberus rolled his fist down his shaft, lining it up with my lips. There was no possible world in which I took that entire thing, and still, I craved a taste—curiosity and lust mounting. I could feel Lizzie's magic heightening the experience, too. It'd come online when we had started, feeding off each other like it had during our first time. The ethereal plane hovered just out of reach around us, too, this thinning of the veil as a spell of a different type wove between our bodies, binding and uniting in strands of gold.

I've heard of sex magic, but this is...

Glancing over at Lizzie, she winked at me, sliding her hand up Cerberus' opposite thigh until she squeezed the base of the shaft on her side, unable to close her fingers completely around it. I watched with rapt awe as she took the head between her lips, sucking on it before opening her mouth to drag her tongue along the ridge at the bottom.

A growling groan shook Cerberus' chest, and I refocused on the glistening tip near my mouth. It was slimmer than the rest and rosy, and I leaned forward, gently reaching with my tongue. The moment I touched the precum that leaked down his skin, my eyes flared wide, rocked by the taste of him.

It was incredible, this sweet, spicy taste that my brain struggled to comprehend. It was like burnt flowers and cream, candied pomegranate and smoke. I licked him up like I was starving for my last meal on earth, stretching my mouth as wide as I could so that I might fill my throat with his taste.

"My hungry, little heathens." The pinpricks of claws nudged at my scalp as Cerberus held me, swallowing his cock, while he undoubtedly did the same to Lizzie. "You will both take my knots so perfectly."

I wasn't a stranger to werewolf porn and romance novels. I knew exactly what he meant when Cerberus said knot, and my pussy clamped down on nothing in response. I couldn't deny how badly I wanted to try that, to be so filled up, especially knowing that Lizzie would be right there with me, enjoying it all side by side.

When the pressure on my head disappeared, tears streaming down my face for how deep I'd taken Cerberus' shaft, I looked up at our elder god, seeing that flicker of Caleb behind his glowing yellow eyes. He was there behind all this, experiencing it with us. What on earth could it be like to feel and see through this monstrous form?

Cerberus gripped my cheek, pulling my lip down as he loomed a shadow of the night over me. Lizzie still sucked the other head as he took hold of the one near me, rubbing it along the exposed inner skin of my lip. *That taste*. I was going to fucking burst if I didn't take him soon.

In fact, my body was on fire, and the need inside me was overpowering. It almost hurt, this squeezing deep in my core. I bent over, my hand going to my lower belly. Cerberus knelt in the soil in front of us as the feelings spiraled higher, slick arousal pooling inside me before trailing down my inner thighs.

"Whoa, Lizzie, is that...are you doing that?"

Glancing over at her, she shook her head, her skin rosy and misty with sweat as she stared out with lidded eyes. She looked how I felt: drunk or high or both. Everything inside me *ached*, demanding that Cerberus knot me, the ground shaking harder beneath us.

"No. I..." She looked up at Cerberus, who smirked down at us both. "You?"

"Yes, little morrighan." He stroked her cheek before turning his luminous gaze on me. "Your bodies respond to your mate, heating from within, demanding my seed."

What is my life right now?

I shook my head, staunchly in camp, "I don't give a fuck." I wanted him. I wanted Lizzie. I wanted them both, and Caleb, wherever he was in all this, too. I took one last lick of Cerberus' cock, making him grunt as I ran my tongue from his base to his tip, finding the small hole there and swirling my tongue against it.

Leaning back, I reached out for Lizzie, *my* Lizzie, perfect, with thighs slick with cum, and pulled her onto top of me, crashing my lips against her. I could taste Cerberus on her, feel the fire beneath her skin as her breasts pressed against mine. She rubbed up and down my body as I wrapped my arms around her neck, our tongues dancing around each other's.

It was like a frenzy, an uncontrollable need to feel and touch and come.

"Such pretty little cunts dripping for me, desperate and needy for my cocks." Cerberus used his massive size to tower over both of us, his hands planted in the earth on either side of my head. "My sacred whores, my mates, ready to be bred thoroughly."

My pussy clamped down at his words, every cell in my body agreeing adamantly with him. The heat coursing through me only intensified, running through me in waves. I *needed* him to fuck me, to *breed* me, even if that wasn't technically possible with the implant keeping me happily, and medically-necessarily, child-free.

I held Lizzie's face in my hands, nodding against her forehead between kisses. "Yes. Yes, yes, yes."

"*Please*," she echoed, the desperation in her voice so wickedly sexy. "Claim us."

"As I was fated to do, my mates," Cerberus growled low, and then I felt the blazing touch of his cock against my folds, sliding between them and nudging at my entrance.

The sensation rebounded through that connection as Lizzie felt the same, and it was beyond incredible, beyond intoxicating. It was everything. He sank in a bit more, and we both reeled, arching into each other as our *mate* worked to slowly sheathe himself inside us.

A twinge of pain registered as Cerberus pushed further. The stretch was so intense, but I wanted it all. I wanted him inside me as Lizzie's naked body touched mine, our nipples grinding against each other's, sensitive and throbbing. My clit buzzed as Cerberus slid back and then forward again, pressing, pressing, and the stretch was profound.

And then I was full, so completely full. A thick, hot cock invaded my pussy so wholly, demanding my body melt around it. He thrust in just a bit more, nudging against my cervix.

"Fuck!" The cry escaped me just as one flew out of Lizzie's mouth, and I pulled her down to me, sucking on her tongue as I rolled my hips.

I could taste the lust coursing through her, feel the way this connection was piercing through to the other side. The entire universe, above and below, within and without, could sense this pleasure, feel the way we were claimed by this ancient god of light and dark, son of Queen of the Cauldron and the Beast King.

How...oh, fuck that's amazing...but how...how do I know that?

Cerberus fucked us both, filling us up with his monstrous shafts, and I was blown apart by the sheer bliss zinging through my veins. Something thicker at his base smoothed against my pussy lips, his knot. I was already reeling from the way he stretched me now. Was I even going to be able to take that?

270

You will take me. You will both take my knots, my spend. I will see it dripping down your thighs.

Blinking, I paused for just a moment. Cerberus could speak in my head like Lizzie could. I was hardly surprised, considering he was a fucking elder being from the World of Below, so I just nodded as I kissed her, reaching to her breast and squeezing her nipple between my fingers.

"Temps!" Her words rumbled against my lips. "Yes, harder. Fucking gods, I want to come."

The pace rushed higher, Cerberus pounding into us as we took him more and more, bodies yielding to his. That curved tip of his cock pressed up into my G-spot, and I groaned, whimpering into Lizzie's kiss as my nerves went haywire. I was on fire, certain to burst into fucking flames as our wolf-god rutted us into the dirt, primal and raw.

Echoes sang through the trees, their trunks and branches groaning. The tunneling wind swirled around us, reaching the damn stars. We were in a universe of our own, a realm between life and death where all that mattered was the feeling of claiming each other.

I was so utterly theirs, Lizzie, Caleb, and our ancient mate, Cerberus, destined to find us after lifetimes of waiting.

Pressure built inside me, my clit throbbing, and my sighs and whines were unending as I pinched Lizzie's nipple with all I had. She screamed, this sharp, staccato moan, and gripped my throat, cutting off some of my air. Cerberus' monstrous thrusts rocked us against each other, his cock ramming into me and sinking as deep as possible with each pound.

"Ugh, fuuuuck. I'm...oh, gods, I'm—Ugh!"

Lizzie came hard, her pleasure singing down the connection between us, and I felt her gush, her cum splashing on me as she shook. It was more than enough to tip me over the edge, and as Cerberus' tip collided with that magic spot, I detonated, climaxing so hard that I saw stars.

My depraved, lovely mates...The way you squeeze my cocks... grrrr!

In one commanding jolt forward, Cerberus sank his knot inside me, surely Lizzie as well. My eyes shot open, and I stared into Lizzie's eyes as we both stretched around that thick base of his, locking inside us as he emptied ropes and ropes of cum. The nearly blazing warmth flooded my pussy until it was overflowing, raining down my thighs just as promised.

Cerberus howled into the night sky, the fall moon bright overhead, and the entire cemetery shook from the power of it, reaching into the World of Below. Whatever this meant for the four of us, I knew one thing for sure.

This was exactly how it was meant to be.

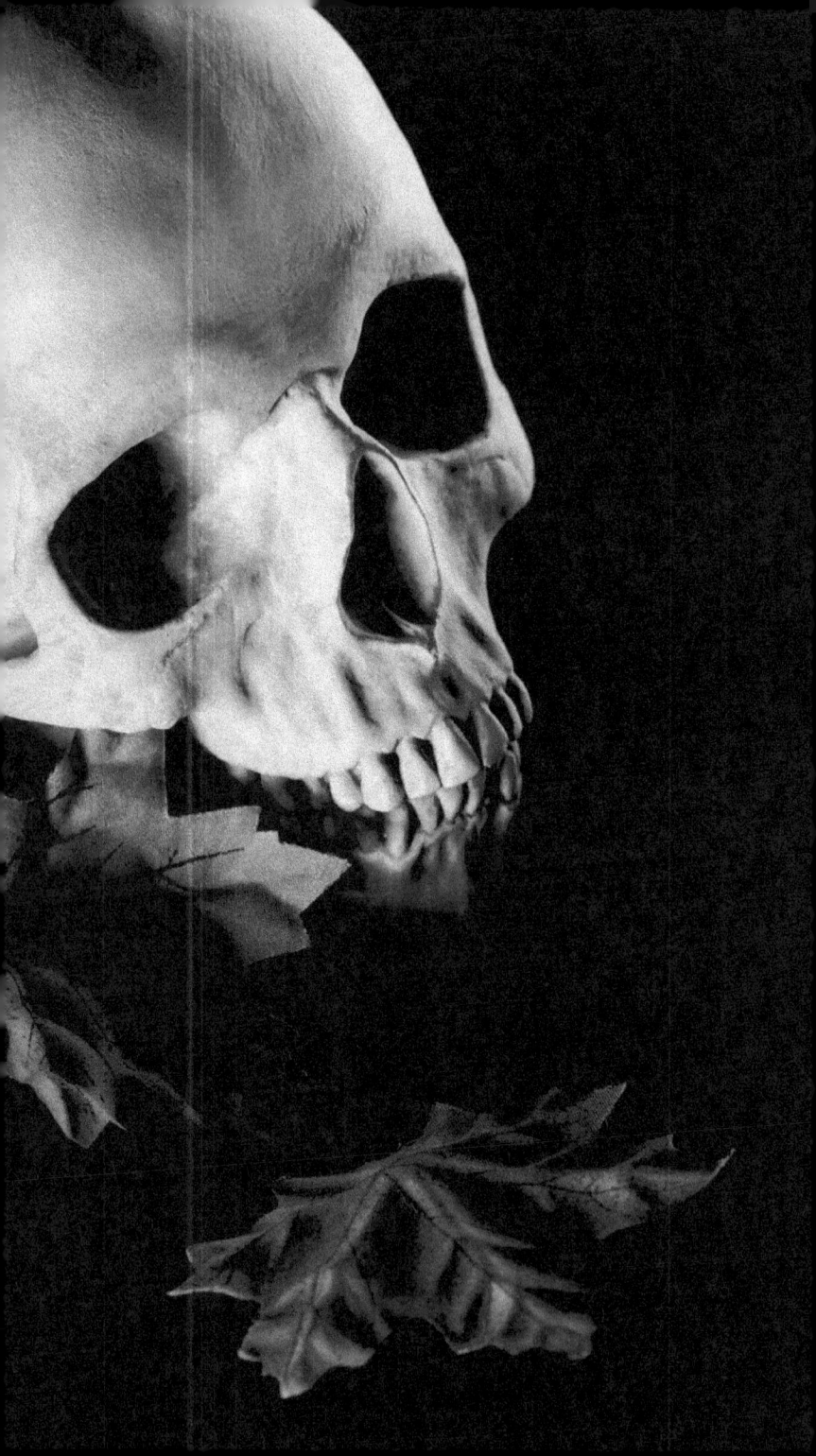

Twenty-One

FROM HIS FOLLOWER'S TONGUE
THE PROPHECY WILL SPILL FREE

CALEB

The ground was cool beneath me, a gentle dew clinging to my skin, and then I was suddenly aware that I had control again. I sat up, wincing as my muscles protested the abrupt movement. The sun was just breaking free of the treeline, the sound of birds chittering back and forth filling the space around us.

Us. Lizzie and Temps. I—

Looking down, I saw them both huddled into each other, sleeping in the flattened patch of fallen leaves and mossy grass. We were beneath a large oak that hung over the cemetery. Wind shuffled through the gravestones, finally extinguishing the ritual candle that had been burning all night. The last remnants of the spell faded; it's working successful.

I touched my bare chest over my heart, rubbing idly. I could feel him. He was still there inside me.

I am, sage. And there is much to be done if we wish to rid the worlds of that heinous malice.

A little thrown, I stared down at nothing. Cerberus was talking in my head, this other part of me now, and yet something so beyond me that I couldn't believe he'd even allowed the soul weaving to happen.

The spell was merely the door. I was always to be with you, to be with you all. Since before my rebirth through the Queen and long after.

Sighing, I shook my head. This was going to take some getting used to.

It's extremely strange to be having a conversation with an elder being in my head, you know that?

I suppose for a mortal it might be odd. I speak to my mother this way in most circumstances. However, that is when I am in wolf form. Even with three mouths, speaking is not available to me then.

Chuckling lightly, I rolled my eyes, sitting up straighter in the grass, which made my back crack. *Did you just make a joke?*

I've been known to—on occasion. But it does not change the fact that we must hurry. The malignance is stirring. It is almost at full strength.

Wait, have you fought this thing before? Lizzie shifted near me, and I traded looks between her and Temps. They looked so peaceful like this. I hated the thought of waking them.

Its last vessel touched ground in the World of Below. My father and mother, though notably more so Mother, were forced to defeat him before it took hold of our entire realm. It was hardly the first time the malignance had affected one of our realms, but Father Paine nearly destroyed us. Destroyed me.

Paine? I know that name. We found it when we were researching the carnival. His son, I think. Jebediah Junior. He's the Ring Leader, the new vessel, it sounds like.

Tension ratcheted up my spine. I didn't like this. If whatever this thing was almost destroyed Cerberus and his mother before, how the hell were we supposed to stop it now? It was surely going to be stronger now that it had a fucking circus cult feeding victims to it on the regular.

I am uncertain what a carnival is or a 'circus cult,' but while you are right to have concern, do not lose faith in our mates. There are four of us now, bound and emboldened. We will stop the false-god. We have no choice.

Sighing, I pinched the bridge of my nose. *Amazing pep talk, Cerberus. Ugh, we'll just...we'll just have to, I guess, huh?*

We need to wake them.

I looked at the girls again, our mates as Cerberus liked to call them, and I hated this all over again. They were in their twenties. They should be nursing hangovers and watching horror movies till four in the morning, not fighting the manifestation of evil.

But life was rarely fair or easy. We didn't get to pick what was demanded of us, and more times than I wanted to think about, people just like them had suffered and died because of this thing.

Relishing one more moment, soaking it in so that I'd remember it forever, I nodded to myself and then squeezed both Temps' and Lizzie's shoulders. They jerked, looking up at me with groggy blinks until twin smiles spread over their faces.

"You're you again." Temps sat up, holding her arm around herself as she reached for my cheek.

I let my face drop into her palm, closing my eyes for a second. "Yeah, I'm me. But Cerberus is still in here."

Hello, little witch.

"He says hi." The girls giggled, and then Lizzie stretched, reaching her arms over her head, which just made her pert tits press up, her nipple hard and delectable.

My cock kicked slightly, and I was getting harder by the second with all this skin on display. Waking up naked with Lizzie and Temps was certainly among my favorite memories, but it was going to be real damn hard to do anything more than fuck them again at this rate.

Your body needs to recover, sage.

Yeah, yeah. Did you have to shred all our clothes? How are we supposed to walk back to the dorms like this?

"Are you okay?" Lizzie put a hand on my shoulder, leaning into my field of view as I pulled my stare away from the ground. "You're like zoning out or suddenly real interested in leaves."

I shook my head with a sigh, dragging a hand through my hair. "No, sorry. I can talk with him in my mind. I was complaining about the clothing situation."

Temps nodded vigorously, her teeth starting to chatter now that she wasn't curled up next to Lizzie. "I second the annoyance about the clothes. I'm freezing. And we can't walk back like this."

See.

Ugh, very well. Have them hold out their hands, and I will direct them to their lodgings. We can travel to yours next.

Unwilling to argue with an elder god, I nodded once and relayed the instructions to Lizzie and Temps.

"I'll make sure to message once I've sorted things out at my apartment. With the very impending rise of this 'malignance,' again, Cerberus' word, not mine, I want to make sure we have everything prepared. I'll craft a few more tonics and such, and we can regroup tonight. Sound like a plan?"

Lizzie stepped up to me, sliding her arms around my waist for a hug before craning back to look up at me.

"It would be a better plan if we could all be together, but yeah. It'll do for now."

I laughed, stroking her cheek and pulling Temps in, too. "I know. Maybe...maybe after all this we can find a way to all stay at my apartment, at least secretly if nothing else."

"I don't want you to get in trouble, Caleb. We can handle a short walk across town if it saves your job." Temps leaned up onto her toe, kissing my cheek, which made Cerberus growl hungrily in my head. "But bamf us or whatever. I'm freezing. My nips are going to pop right off at this rate."

My brow shot up as Lizzie scoffed and said, "My, my, now who's got the potty mouth, Ms. Montgomery?"

Temps knocked her with her elbow, and damn, I just want to go back to my apartment with them, snuggle and kiss and fuck until they couldn't walk, forget all this end of the world shit. But I wasn't *that* horrible of a person. I saved that level of darkness for the bedroom.

I would very much like to see that next time.

That took me off guard, and I coughed slightly as I took the girls' hands, swallowing hard. Was the ancient deity in my head flirting with me?

"Alright, Cerberus, do your thing."

With that, I felt magic rush to the surface of my skin. It was an inferno, just this side of painful as the heat swelled, and then a layer of swirling flame surrounded Temps and Lizzie, blinking into nothing and leaving me holding the air.

They will arrive inside their lodging. I would see no one else look upon their naked form.

Ditto, big guy. Let's go.

And sure enough, using that same pull, Cerberus whisked us through the air, heading back to my far less appealing apartment. Spending a night under the trees as a wolfman truly spoiled me.

Carpet came up under my feet, and I steadied myself, throwing my arms out to catch my balance. The landing was a little rocky, but I couldn't argue with the results. We'd made it back to my apartment in a literal flash, and that certainly beat doing the "Walk of Shame" down Main Street in the buff.

"Well, thanks, buddy."

I cocked my head, still trying to digest everything that'd happened in the past few days, especially last night. Though I'd be lying if I said I wanted things to go back to how they had been before the semester started. Darkness and death to be sure, but having Temps and Lizzie in my life, and now Cerberus, who felt odd at home within me, was something I wouldn't trade.

And would certainly kill for.

Your home feels off, sage. Be wary. I sense something.

Looking around, I couldn't spot anything but the usual pile of books and various folders and printouts I'd left on my coffee table from the other night. The studio was cramped, a single bedroom and bathroom at the back, my open-plan kitchen, living, and dining room seeming untouched.

I don't see anything. Are you sure that—

There!

I turned just in time to see something pull itself out of the shadows, as if it had been a part of them, and leap toward me. Holding out my hands, I gripped the fabric below the neck of this masculine figure, rolling back to absorb the momentum and land with me on top of him, pinning him to the floor.

Cerberus' honed instincts flared through me, bolstering my own, and a menacing growl tore from my throat. Claws extending from my fingers, I held them poised over the man's face, one lined up with his pupil.

"What the fuck are you doing in my apartment?"

Realizing what I was looking at, I sneered as the man, dressed in a shabby, striped clown's outfit, grinned up at me. He laughed, eyes flaring wide, and the sound was empty and wrong, this discordant, warped recording of a laugh, not the real thing.

"Well, I gotta say I figured getting the drop on a guy in nothing but the breeze would be a bit easier." His voice was squeaky, a dull whine that was low on some words and horrendously high-pitched on others. "You got some tricks there the circus could use. Too bad you gotta be dead, *witch*."

He uttered the word with such disgust that I immediately tightened my hold on the grubby, red and white striped shirt, my claws inching closer.

"I promise you, the only dead man talking right now is you. So make your last words useful. What is the carnival doing? Has Paine been sacrificing patrons to this false-god of yours?"

Like flicking a switch, the man snarled at me, bucking against my hold and snapping at my hand with his crooked, rotten teeth. The smeared makeup on his face cracked as he growled, thrashing this way and that. From someone who might have appeared cognizant, this demented clown was all that was left, a thrawl offended for its master.

"*He* is the one! The only path to power and glory! You will be chewed for eternity in his holy maw!"

The fucker dug his nails into my forearm, and without even asking, Cerberus surged inside me, pressing more of himself to the surface. Fur pushed up through my skin, coating me from head to toe, and I watched as the clown's mouth dropped open, his stare wide with terror. Where I gripped his costume, claws lengthened, slicing into the skin of his chest. He hollered out, and I swept a hand through the air, channeling *my* magic to create a soundproofed bubble.

"*Misguided fool,*" Cerberus spoke along with me, a growl that passed through fanged teeth. "*Tell me. Tell me what your 'omniscient' being is up to, and maybe, I'll end you quick.*"

Eyes wild and unfocused, the asshole laughed, a shrieking wail of unhinged dementia. "Do what you will, heathen. I will live in eternity, taken into his welcoming embrace. I will sing in the heavens as his might tears you all limb from limb!"

Rage bubbled over in my blood. This was the same type of bigoted fool as those who had killed my parents. He was giving up his ability to think logically for some promise of power. And what a fucking hypocrite to boot, thinking that he was following some higher being when in reality he was just the pawn of some dark evil. Could he not even see that his own "church," the carnival, was killing innocent people?

What kind of 'holy' fucking god did that?!

Throwing my hand back, I let the full length of Cerberus' claw jut through my fingers, pain flaring but no brighter than the fury roaring in my veins. Towering over the pathetic man, a farce of a missionary for some fucked up cult, I channeled all my inner reserve to give the man one last chance, Cerberus right there with me.

"Tell me. I won't ask again. You spill about your god's plans, or I spill your guts across the fucking floor."

"It is already too late!" The clown didn't even look at me now, his eyes tracking up as he pressed bloody palms together over his bleeding chest. "None of you are long for this world because our god has his final sacrifice. He will walk free this night!"

His eyes found me, bloodshot and peering out from the depths of madness.

"And he'll start with those fucking sluts of yours."

Without thinking, I jabbed my claws forward and into the soft spot beneath the man's ribs, hooking them upward before yanking them free with a loud tearing sound. Blood spurted out of his mouth in seconds, followed by gargling sounds as he choked on his own lifeforce. All I did was watch, watch until the lights of his eyes finally extinguished.

Temps and Lizzie. The carnival will—

It won't have the chance. We will rend them all from their foolish beliefs...our claws finding purchase in their weak bodies.

But despite Cerberus' words, panic infected me. Their god was ready to come out and play; the final sacrifice apparently a done deal. We needed to get the fuck out of here and to that carnival before the big show. I wouldn't lose them. Temps and Lizzie were the best things that had ever happened to me, and if I needed to, I would die making sure they lived to see another day.

Without hesitation, sage.

"Fuck. This is bad. We need to get down there. We need—Fuck!" I drove my fist into the wall near me, aware now that I'd gotten up and started pacing. "The carnival. We need to get down there, but we can't go like this. I need you to back off for just a bit. I'll get dressed, and we'll see if we can sneak inside again. And no snooping this time. We get in, we kill anyone in our fucking way, and we make sure whatever this fucking thing is, there's nothing left to try to raise again."

The transformation eased off, leaving me naked again, and I beat feet to my bedroom, grabbing the first pair of jeans and a shirt that I could find. Dressed, I stuffed a handful of random vials into my pockets. There'd be something valuable in there that I could use when I got to the carnival.

"Alright, you with me, buddy?"

Always, sage. Let's go kill ourselves a cult.

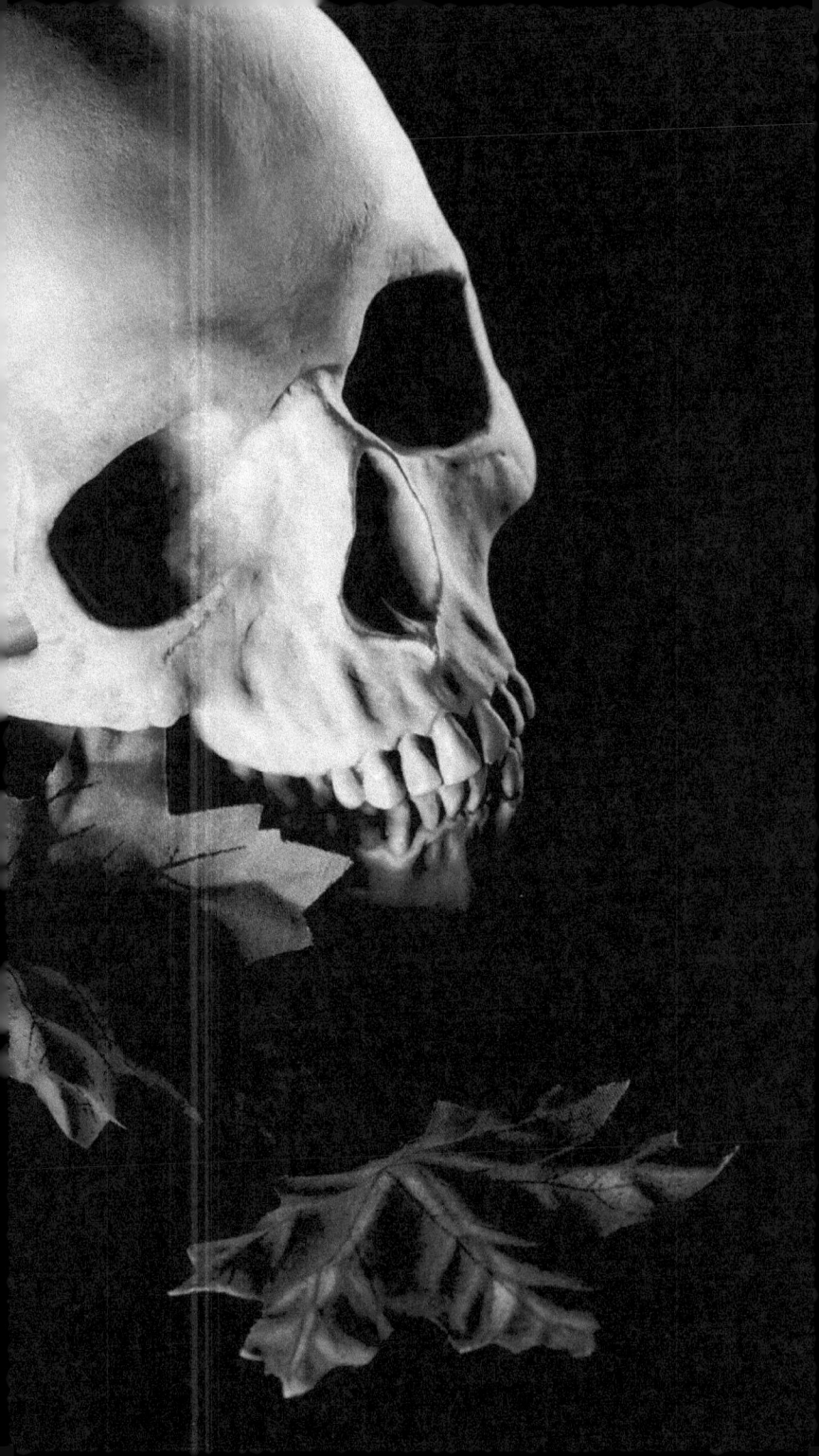

Twenty-Two

LAMBS IN THE LION'S DEN ARE LAMBS SENT TO THE SLAUGHTER

TEMPS

"Would you quit it?" I swatted at Lizzie's mischievous hands, laughing despite my attempt to shoo her away. "I'm trying to get dressed."

"I'm aware." She leaned across me as I stood with my back to the closet, snatching the shirt out of my hand and tossing it behind her with a smirk. "That's why I'm getting rid of that offensive material. Nothing is keeping me from enjoying your perfect fucking tits for a few more minutes."

I rolled my eyes, a smile creeping up the corner of my mouth. Lizzie took a step closer, pressing her bare chest to mine. Two idiots smiling like fools, we wrapped are arms around each other. I stilled for a moment long enough to sneak a pinch of Lizzie's nipple. She gasped lightly, then yanked me to her lips, kissing me like it was the most important thing on the planet.

It wasn't, of course. There was a "carnival cult" to deal with.

Still, I melted into the feeling of her, enjoying every moment because I could never get enough of them. I'd fought this for so long, and now, I couldn't for the life of me understand why. So what if we had entered each other's lives in a "less than traditional" way? Lizzie was mine, and I was hers. Fuck what anyone else said.

"Mmm," she swept her tongue across the seam of my lips as she hummed, and I eagerly let her in, relishing her wicked kissing skills.

Knock, knock, knock.

We paused, both of us eyeing the door as Lizzie said, "Who'd be knocking? Wouldn't Cerberus just bamf him and Caleb in?"

"Umm..."

I was no empath, but something felt weird, a darkness radiating from the other side of the door. Smiling, likely unable to hide my concern from her, I stepped back and around Lizzie, grabbing my shirt and yanking it on over my head as I approached the door.

"Yes?"

"For goodness' sake, Temperance! Would you open the door?"

My stomach dropped and turned to lead instantaneously. I knew that voice. But it was impossible. The school was protected. How in the hell would she even make it through the gate?

"Temperance! Let your mother inside!"

Lizzie was at my side, hauling on a shirt. "How the fuck? Barbara? Am I having a fucking stroke right now?"

"I don't—" My mother continued to pound at the door. "Dammit. She's going to draw too much attention if we don't answer. Just...I don't know. Be on guard or whatever."

"Around the mega bitch, Barbs? Yeah, I think I can manage that."

Rushing up to the door, I turned over the lock and pulled it open, coming face to face with the woman who'd single-handedly made me deny everything about who I was in favor of not getting chewed out by her. Oh, and it was only moments after I'd just been making out with my stepsister.

"Finally. What could possibly have taken you so long to answer the door?" Barbara stood at the threshold, wearing a pale cream suit skirt set, complete with the matching pearls she reserved for church days.

"We were tits out, Barbs. Did you want Temps answering the doors with her nips in your face?"

Shock played over my mother's face, and I had to bite the inside of my cheek to keep from snorting out a laugh. As she scoffed, she pushed herself past me and into the room, standing a few feet away from the door and glowering.

"I see this renowned advanced education has not improved your language, Elizabeth."

Lizzie narrowed her eyes as I shuffled the wet towels from our shower over toward the closet, crossing her arms with her hip cocked out to the side.

"Nope. How'd you even get in here? We have a gate and everything."

"Oh, honestly." Mother rolled her eyes, waving off Lizzie's annoyance like it was nothing. "I demanded that I be allowed to visit my daughters and take them for an important family outing."

Before Barbara could even swing her head back down from her display, Lizzie was right in front of her, fury radiating off her like a dark cloud.

"You are not my mother, and I am not your daughter." Nervous energy peaked inside me as Lizzie challenged my mother. "*My* mother died, and there is not a day that goes by that I wish I could pull the old switcheroo."

They were going to tear each other apart at this rate, and truthfully, I didn't want something happening to Lizzie because my mother pulled a Karen and talked to the school. I shot up between them, stepping in front of Lizzie and reaching my hand back to squeeze hers.

"What's going on, Mom? You said a family outing? We're a bit busy for a middle-of-the-day, no-notice event."

She waved off my complaint just as she had Lizzie. "Nonsense. You'll both be coming. I've been going to far too many of these events by myself, and this time, I'll be presenting my *family*, just like all the other top-tier parishioners."

"You want us coming with you to the church? Are you serious?" Lizzie demanded.

"Yes. Now stop loafing about and get changed into something becoming of two proper young ladies. None of that black crap, Elizabeth." She jabbed a finger forward. "And don't try me either. I have no issue with speaking to the school board about our payments for next semester."

Dammit. She really is that obsessed with all this.

"Alright, alright, Mom. We'll go, just give us a moment to get changed, okay? We'll meet you outside."

"Excellent." She clapped her hands together, smiling like a snake. "Hurry up. Things begin in an hour."

I escorted her to the door, closing it behind her, and then sagged against the wood with a sigh. "Fuuuuck, okay. I'm sorry, but can we just get changed and go to this thing? Maybe it'll keep her off our backs for a while."

When I looked across the room at Lizzie, she narrowed her eyes at me but nodded. "You owe me. Big time."

"I do." Hurrying over to her, I leaned in for a kiss and then landed back on my heels. "So much. You can even tell Caleb and Cerberus that you're owed some loving."

She brightened at that, scampering off to her closet with a grin. "Ooh, good play. You should negotiate more often."

"Well, when this is all over with," I went to my closet, searching through my clothes for that pale pink outfit my mom had gotten me, "I'll definitely think about it. These kinky rules of yours sound fun."

Glancing over my shoulder, I watched Lizzie bite her lip as she pulled free the only white shirt she owned and the weird overdress thing my mom had gotten her last holiday season.

"Done."

"I swear this is the itchiest fucking thing on the godsdamn planet." Lizzie pulled at the neck of the overstretched dress thing, and I fought a laugh.

"Sorry," I frown sympathetically at her, squeezing her hand as we pulled to a stop in my mom's car, "I'll admit that this thing isn't as uncomfortable, but I don't know how I'm supposed to pee in it. I think I'll—"

My words died as I looked out the window and realized where we'd driven. I'd yet to take a car here, so I didn't know how short the trip would be, and every warning bell in my head blared at max volume.

The carnival.

"How the fuck...This can't be right. Is your mom really taking us to a fucking church meeting at the carnival?"

Lizzie kept her voice down as we pulled into a spot, and my mother threw the car into park. I couldn't find the words. We knew that the symbol she was sporting was suspicious, but I'd clearly been in big-time denial. I really hadn't believed that she was actually involved in all this.

I was going to throw up.

"We still made it. I'm so glad I can finally introduce you to Pastor Paine. Ugh, he's a revolutionary. I have never felt as good in my entire life as I have since I've started coming to these. You'll see!"

"I..." I squeezed Lizzie's hand, shaking my head. "I'm not sure I can do this."

She adjusted on the seat as my mother got out and started toward the open flap of the faded red and white striped tent, a line of people already there to get inside.

"We can do this, Temps. We can find out more about what they're doing. A circus holding sermons is seriously less than normal. We can see why no one has said anything."

My heart was so loud in my ears, and I managed a dull nod.

"I'm right here with you, babe. Always." Lizzie pulled my chin toward her, meeting my eyes as she leaned forward and rested her head against mine.

Her presence warmed my clammy skin, and I held onto her. "Okay. Thank you. I'm...I'm alright. Let's go."

Exiting the car, we walked over toward my mother, and I was suddenly so grateful for the clothes we were wearing. They acted like some strange disguise. They were so different from anything we'd be caught dead in that the polyester and starch acted like ingredients to a spell, keeping us nearly invisible to the people around us. And there were so many of them, too. At least forty.

As we all filed in, the seats in the front of the tent, which had been cleared of the red wooden ring and replaced with a pulpit lifted on a dusty, crooked wooden platform. This smaller section of the tent, the stands blocked off by bits of the fabric that could apparently fold in on themselves, was so much smaller than the usual ring. That, of course, meant that while my mother beelined to the very front for the only seat left up there, Lizzie and I were left to stand near the back.

Totally okay with me.

Lizzie? I looked over at her, and she nodded subtly. *Seems safer than talking out loud. Just keep your head down and play it cool, babe.*

I nodded back, ever more grateful for her talents. Then, a single spotlight hit the pulpit, and we watched as the Ring Lead, Jeb Junior, walked up and patted on the microphone to get everyone's attention.

"Welcome, folks. So glad our devoted followers could make it to another sermon. We heed His call."

"And give our will to Him that is higher," the crowd answered.

"Excellent, excellent. And I'm so glad to see that all of you have heeded His call to bring more of the faithful to the tent. Welcome, new faces." I ducked my chin, not making eye contact with him as the people around us clapped softly. "Now, today, we have the most glorious news. He is so emboldened by your faith, your ongoing support of our small traveling parish. My father, rest him, would be so proud."

Ha, I bet. Your dad was a rapist fuckbag who killed kids.

It was too real to be funny, and my stomach coiled into knots as the crowd around us began to sort of move, shifting in unison in a subtle back and forth. They were hanging on this guy's every word as if they were hypnotized by it. Lizzie noticed it too, but the two of us weren't feeling the effects. I was quick enough to start mimicking them, Lizzie right there with me, but why didn't we feel the "faith" like everyone else did?

Cerberus? He knew this asshole was fake. What if being with him protected us somehow?

That's fucking lucky, Lizzie. What if we hadn't performed the soul weaving? Gods, we need to tell Caleb about this. Do we sneak out?

Not yet. I want to see what this is all about.

"Now, He is so close to us, friends. The time is almost here. Come moonrise this very night, our savior with walk among the mortals. The heathens will bow down or be trampled by His might, and it is all thanks to your unyielding faith."

"Praise Him! Praise Him!" everyone chanted, low and strange.

Jeb Junior came around the pulpit and stepped down from the platform, walking in front of the first row. Each person there offered an eager hand up, looking to touch this man like he was some kind of walking avatar for a god. Which, I supposed, wasn't too far off, except for the fact that the Ring Leader was the mouthpiece of an *evil* entity that had been terrorizing people for millennia.

"His field is watered with the essence of His followers. And this night, this holy night where He will pierce through the veil holding Him back, He requires even more from us."

"What can we give?" one person shouted out. "We live to serve Him," yelled another.

"You are all so blessed in His name. Such valuable, devoted

people. The parish's custodians have gathered together ten from this morning's sermon, but alas, one of our brethren has proven false."

"Boo! Cast out the blasphemer!" Chills worked down my spine as the crowd cried out with such hatred, and I grabbed Lizzie's hand, a building dread starting to choke me.

"Yes! Yes, that is right, my faithful! But we require another. Someone of total conviction and faith to stand in for that dreaded waste."

Too many people to count called out, volunteering to be the replacement, begging to be lifted up in "His" name. Lizzie turned to me, and I could see the unease and anxiety peaking in her expression, undoubtedly a reflection of my own.

"I will choose, my blessed congregation. I am His hand, and through me, He will find His missing lamb, to walk it freely in the realm of the Lion."

He was going to take someone, and going by the bodies we'd found earlier, I didn't think it was going to end well for them.

Dammit, Lizzie. What do we do? We can just let this guy scoop someone up and butcher them in front of all these people.

I don't know, Temps. This isn't—Fuck, we almost died last time. We...we need to get Caleb and Cerberus. Look for a moment to sneak out.

Nodding, I made sure that I was standing level with the person next to me, and then slowly, so godsdamn gradually, I began to back up more, putting a hand behind me so that I could feel the tent when I got to it. No one was paying attention to us, and

Lizzie and I got farther and farther away from the main show.

Jeb was still walking that front row, his fingers grazing the people who reached up for him, this massiah among lowly mortals in their eyes. His line got shorter, focusing on just the people in the center of the front row, and I took two more steps back, so close to the exit that I could feel the cool air outside blowing across my ankles.

We're almost there, Temps. We got this. We'll call Caleb right away.

I couldn't bring myself to even think anything back. I was too nervous, too on edge as our escape hung in the balance. The crowd was practically roaring now, overcome by the heightened energy in the tent as they all called out to see who the new "chosen" would be.

One more step, then another, and there. I could feel the rough, fraying edges of the tent. Lizzie slipped out first when I hesitated, something making me look down at that front row one more time.

"You. You are His Chosen. Rise and face the people you save for His glory!"

No.

The world around me dropped away as I watched my mother fling herself up from her seat, a massive smile stretching over her face. She bounced up and down, happily shrieking as she spun around and faced the crowd. The Ring Leader, Pastor Jebediah Paine, Junior, stood at her back.

Something flashed in the spotlight, this white light that forced me to squint as I pulled back. Then Jeb's hand was in front of my mother's neck. Just as realization struck, a line of red appeared across her skin, and then it rained down her white suit, her pearl necklace breaking and scattering across the ground.

The crowd roared in approval.

"Temps," Lizzie was behind me, pulling me backward toward the exit, "we need to—Oh, gods."

The Ring Leader smiled as he held the bloody knife high for everyone to see, my mother's body slumping to the dusty earth as he let her go.

"We need to go. Temps, please." She hauled me backward as I stared straight ahead. "Now."

And then it all disappeared as the flaps of the tent fell in front of me, Lizzie grabbing me by the hand and yanking me forward, sprinting away from the carnival as quickly as we could. My heart pounded, my stomach was on the verge of turning inside out, and I couldn't think.

We just ran. We ran around the side of the tent toward the alleyways that spilled out into the large area the carnival had rented. My legs burned, but we just ran. We ran and ran and ran.

Until, just as we were getting to the edge of the fairgrounds, the metal fence only a few feet away, we collided with something solid and tall, knocking Lizzie and me backward to the dry grass.

"What the hell are you two doing out here?"

Twenty-Three

RAMIFICATIONS HAVE FAR-REACHING WINGS

LIZZIE

Dull pain thudded up my assbones as I craned my head back to see whoever we'd collided with. I was ready to give 'em hell if necessary, but relief shot through me so hard, I actually let out a tiny sob when I saw Caleb standing in front of us.

Temps was quicker than I was, shooting up off the ground and straight into his arms. His brows remained pinned to his hairline as he held her, looking down, confused and slightly out of breath.

"What happened? Temps, you're shaking?" He leaned her back to make eye contact, and I dusted myself off as I stood up, covering Temps with my body from behind. "It isn't safe to be here."

"No shit, Sherlock. Temps..." I sighed, shaking my head as I tried

Not speaking or moving, Temps kept her face buried in Caleb's chest. I watched him put the pieces together, and the shock played over his face before it melted into empathetic sorrow.

"Oh my gods, Temps. I'm so sorry. That's...Fuck, we need to get out of here before they see us, though." He shuffled her up into his arms, carrying her bridal style. "Come on, little flower. I've got you."

I was right on his tail as Caleb carried Temps out of the fairgrounds and toward the alleyway ahead of us. We ducked into a shadowy corner, out of sight and earshot of the carnival, and he set her down, where Temps landed shakily on her feet, her stare fixed to the middle distance and unblinking.

"Baby, I need you to come back to me." I held her face as I moved in front of her. "Don't stay there. Come back to your people. We're all right here."

Caleb stood behind her now, and I watched just his hand shift, turning into this monstrous, clawed appendage covered in fur. A low growl rumbled out of his chest, and in that voice that was actually two voices, he said, "*We will ensure you have your revenge, little witch. They will pay for this.*"

Unable to keep from smiling, I chuckled lightly, which I knew was so inappropriate for the moment. Temps looked up at me at that, though, and I met her eyes as she found her way back to the present.

"Why are you laughing?" She furrowed her brow at me.

"You have a werewolf promising to help you get revenge on a circus." I snorted. "That's wild, babe."

Temps' eyes flared wide, but then she smiled—tiny and still shaken—before a laugh melted out of her. She flung herself into my arms, and I held on tight, letting her just squeeze me.

"I...I think...that I should be sadder. Really, I'm just shocked. He really did that. The woman isn't going to be in my life anymore, but...she'd said such horrible things to us. She...She was a bad person."

I nodded against her shoulder. "I know. It's...It's like we'll never get to see her for the mom she could have been to you. It's no secret I hated the woman. I don't—Fuck, I'm sorry, but I don't mourn her. I mourn that you lost the chance to have a better mother."

"Dammit, that's the most accurate thing you've said in your life, Lizzie." Temps eked out a sob on my shoulder, and then pulled herself back, meeting my stare for a moment longer before she could stand on her own and nodded back at Caleb.

"I'm sorry, Temperance." He stroked her cheek. "And I'm afraid I don't have any better news. When I got to my apartment, someone was waiting. He was clearly sent by the carnival: decrepit clown costume and all. Something is going down *tonight*. We need—"

"The sacrifice," she cut in. "We heard the Ring Leader talking about how 'He' was going to walk tonight. Shit, you're right. I think Big Bad Evil Thing is going to make an appearance."

I thought back to what Jeb Junior had said, the impending doom he was so on about. "He'd asked the followers to bring in more people. Like it was some important thing to have as many people in the tent as possible."

"I can imagine that whatever this thing is, it'll be hungry when it wakes up." Caleb's eyes circled before he landed back on us again, abruptly noticing our clothes. "What the hell are you wearing?"

Both Temps and I laughed, and I immediately peeled off the jacket that went with this horrible overdress-like thing that still itched my skin like a son of a bitch.

"Ugh, I need out of this. I feel like a damn toddler wearing Osbegosh overalls but designed for the Junior Yuppies of America meeting."

"I'm almost grateful for them, though," Temps pulled off her weird suit jacket too, tossing it to the ground, "because no one noticed us in the tent."

"Well, that probably *is* a good thing, considering the cult is looking for more people. Gods, each member was probably recruiting from their own family. Ugh, that's fucked up."

Agreeing with Caleb, I looked back the way we came, the point of the circus tent visible through the gaps in the building. Forty-some people were in that tent, pulling in their children, mothers, and fathers who—

Oh, no.

"Dad! Shit, we have to get back to the house, Temps. There's no telling what your mom did to him before coming to get us. I mean, why wasn't he there? Fuck, what if he's—"

"Hey, it's okay. We'll go now." She turned to Caleb. "Can you do the bamf thing? We need to get back to our house. She's right. The people there were hypnotized. I'm...I'm worried she really could have done something."

"Of course." Caleb glanced to the side, his brows down over his eyes. "You think you can get us there, buddy?"

There was a brief pause, and then Caleb nodded, taking our hands and pulling us in close. "Hang on."

In a flash, we were standing in the front yard of our old house. The white two-story, with its charming trim and blue door, looked quiet, just like it always did, and it still struck me that in the blink of an eye, we'd traveled to the outskirts of Rockport, where it sat.

Jumping into action, I rushed forward up to the front door, pounding on it and trying the knob. But it was locked.

"Dad! Dad, are you okay?!"

"*Step to the side, young morrighan.*" I looked over my shoulder. Caleb's eyes glowed yellow, his hand shifted again, and I nodded as I scooted over, knowing that Cerberus was driving the car right now.

He reached for the knob, squeezing it in his clawed grasp, and then turned hard. The sound of something metal breaking was loud, and then the door swung open. I pushed past him, rushing inside to find my father.

Please, Gods...he's not that big of a dick. Don't let him be dead.

It didn't take long to stop short, my hands flying up to my mouth as I took in the sight of the living room. The place was a mess, cushions and pillows scattered to the floor, the coffee table broken, and shelves and shelves of those dumb knick-knacks emptied onto the floor.

In the center of the room, my father sat tied to a chair, his mouth gagged and his forehead bleeding.

"Dad!"

I was there in seconds, going for the ropes to get him untied. Caleb got behind him quickly, using one of those long claws to slice through the ropes. I didn't even know we had something like that. Was Barbs secretly into knots or some shit? Still, it was probably a lot more likely that she'd brought it with her from the carnival or dug around in the little-used shed outside to find it.

Taking off the gag, which I realized was made of stockings, I held my dad's cheeks. "Dad? Dad, are you okay?"

He blinked several times, my touch seeming to rouse him. When he looked at both me and Temps, he sighed, a cry croaked out as he shook his head frantically.

"Your mother. Barbara. I don't know what got into her. Is she gone?" His arms swung around him as Caleb released him, and he rubbed his wrists, slightly pink and raw from where the rough rope had rubbed against him.

"Yes, she's gone. She's..." Temps couldn't finish, and I didn't blame her.

"Dad, what happened?"

For a second, he tried to stand up, but then he collapsed back down into the chair, and I steadied him to keep him from pitching forward. He was clearly beaten to hell. His forehead injury was obvious, but his shirt was messed up, and going by the state of the room, there had probably been one hell of a scuffle.

"She...she'd come back from an early visit to that church of hers. I didn't want to go with her, as usual. You know I'm just not into that kind of thing. Not like that. When she got back, Barbara asked if I'd go again. When I said I wasn't interested and had things to do for the hospital, she freaked out. She picked up the vase over there and smashed it against my head. I swear to God, I don't know what happened. It was like she was a different person. She threw all her favorite things, screamed about me being a blasphemer. Elizabeth, it was insane. Temperance, I...I don't know what to tell you. I know she's your mother, but I think she needs some serious help."

Temps shook her head, standing to the side with Caleb. "Lizzie, I...can you?"

I swallowed. I knew what came next, and I knew that Temps couldn't do it. I wasn't mad. Hell, it'd been a handful of minutes since we'd seen Barbs die. I wasn't about to put breaking the news to my dad on her.

"Dad, Barbara is...dead. She went to that church thing after this, and...Dad, they're not right. They've been brainwashing people. It's—"

"What the hell are you talking about?" A look of such anger crossed my dad's face that I actually reeled back. I'd never seen him looking like this, and fuck, we needed to call EMTs to look at his head or get him to the hospital.

"I'm sorry. I'm not trying to upset you, honestly. There's some horrible shit going down with that carnival. They're hurting people and—"

"Have you lost your mind, too?" My father pushed out of the chair, wobbling like a baby fucking deer, but he held out a hand, keeping me back when I tried to help him. "No. No, I'm not some idiot. Whatever happened with her clearly got to you, too. There probably is something horrible about that church, and I'm not falling for it. You get my wife on the phone right now."

I didn't know what to do. He didn't believe me. I turned back to Temps, desperate and hurt. Shaking my head, I walked to her. All of this was too much. I'd already been hanging on by a fucking thread, and I was going to snap. I couldn't keep doing this.

"Mr. Montgomery, I swear to you. I wouldn't joke about this. My mother is dead. She was just killed moments ago by Pastor Paine."

"How...You've never been. How do you know his name?" Dad stared at Temps in shock, his skin paling as that wound on his head continued to bleed. "What...She's really..."

Temps just nodded, and when my father looked at me, I held his eye contact. "We saw it, Dad."

"Well, then we need to call the police!" Dad surged forward, and Caleb had to catch him when he started to fall to the floor.

"I think we need to get you checked out first." Caleb draped my dad's arm over his shoulder. "We'll take you to the hospital."

"No! No, I want that asshole arrested. He killed my wife! Brainwashed her! Whoever you are, you call the police. Now!"

"Dad," I rushed forward, putting my hands on his chest, "we can't call them. Okay? We need to get you help. And this is

Caleb. He's a professor at my school."

"What are you doing hanging out with a professor?" Frowning, my father's eyelids drooped, the exhaustion and trauma getting to him. "Shouldn't you be off teaching? It's a weekday. Get the police or get out of my way."

The threat was miniscule considering how my dad had to hang on to Caleb to keep from falling. I directed him backward toward the chair again, looking behind me at Temps and mouthing, "Call 911."

"I am working with Elizabeth and Temperance regarding the carnival. I was there when they came out. I'm trying to make sure they're okay. That *you're* okay."

"I'll be okay when that fucker is arrested."

We all stared, silently conversing about what the hell we were going to do about this. Magic was involved. Deadly cult bullshit powered by some evil wannabe god. We weren't going to be able to call the cops, ever. They couldn't get involved in this. This was witch business, but my dad didn't know shit about that world.

My world.

Sneaking out her phone from her pocket, Temps stepped outside through the front door, which was still open, while I stood in front of my dad, blocking the view. He needed the help. Medical care was something we could at least get him. Caleb stood just behind him, and I looked up, begging him to come up with something because I was at a loss.

I could wipe his memory.

That wasn't Caleb talking in my head. That was Cerberus. I

blinked, trying to school my expression so that Dad wouldn't notice.

What? You want to remove the event? How would that work?

Dad started to fade in the chair, unconsciousness claiming him. It was a good fucking thing that Temps was calling EMTs.

It wouldn't work like that, young morrighan. I would need to remove anything connected to the event. The altercation with this "Barbs," us being here. I could replace it with a new memory, give him something else. But if he is not going to go after this man, if he is going to rest, it needs to be final.

My stomach dropped as I realized what Cerberus was saying. This needed to be big. My father wasn't going to let this go. I could tell that much. He needed something final and solid if he was going to accept it and move on with his life.

He was going to learn about Barbs' death eventually, and I couldn't come back here and pretend like I didn't know the truth. I was good at keeping a secret, but everyone slips up at some point.

This tie we would be cutting needed to be precise and irrevocable.

"Dammit."

Fully passed out, I didn't worry about my dad seeing me, so I paced back and forth. Temps came in through the front door again.

"They're on their way. I didn't give my name. Said I was a neighbor, just in case."

That was damn smart since we were about to wipe my dad's memory of us being here. "Dammit!"

Holding back the tears, unwilling to break, I walked to Caleb, looking past his gorgeous blue eyes to Cerberus beyond them.

"You wipe him. We were never here. He'll learn about Barbs' death soon enough. I...I want you to include us in it—me and Temps. We're dead. He'll never come looking for us, and he'll be safe."

"Are you sure, young morrighan? You would not be able to see him again."

"Yes. Just do it. We'll work with the dean after this is over to have our deaths recorded in town. She'll have the pull. She'll be able to make it like we just died with Barbs. Clean break."

My voice didn't shake. I wasn't trembling or sobbing. I was... okay. I'd been nearly invisible to my dad my entire life. He didn't like my music or style. He didn't like what I was interested in, and he never took the bisexual thing serious. Always saying, I'd find the right guy someday and settle down like it could never be a woman. Like I would change and be the good "trad wife" he'd married someday.

Being dead would put a damper on that.

"Lizzie," Temps was at my side, "we don't have to do this. We can think of another way."

"There is no other way." I looked to Cerberus, whose eyes now looked out from Caleb's form, and nodded. "Do it."

He stepped up to my father, putting his clawed hands on either side of his head. It was like when I'd connected before with my fingers on the temples. My father's eyes fluttered under his lids as if he were dreaming, and then Cerberus stepped back.

"It's done. We need to leave before he wakes."

Cerberus walked to Temps and me, taking our hands. I glanced at both of them, knowing these were my people. These were the ones I wanted with me for the rest of my life, and if I was going to have that, we had a fucking carnival to crash.

"Get us back there, Cerbs. We need to keep that wannabe god from waking up."

Twenty–Four

When The Black Moon Rises, Beware The Lord Of False Promises Bathed In Blood

Caleb

Temps had lost her mother. Lizzie had lost her father, in a manner of speaking. We were three orphans walking into the viper's nest to take out a malignant force we still didn't even know what to call. Death hung around every doorway in this fucking town, and the people I cared most about were paying the heaviest price. While I knew there was no choice moving forward—we'd been roped into this and not only was it personal now, it was extremely pressing—it didn't stop me from wishing there was some way to protect the girls from all this.

Cerberus had smartly teleported us a few blocks down from the carnival, allowing us the opportunity to sneak up to the fairgrounds while keeping an eye on things. It was still surrounded by cars when we first saw it. The parking lot around the shrunken version of the tent was full, and we could all assume that was because the "sermon" was still in session.

"How long do we have to crouch here in an alley? I want to get this over with."

Lizzie was clearly on edge, and I scooted toward her, resting my hand on her knee as she balanced in a squat position, her back pressing to the wall behind her.

"I'm not sure. But we can't go in there with it that full of people. If they could be hypnotized into watching a person be killed and think nothing of it, I would stand to believe they could be hypnotized into doing the killing themselves. We can't handle forty people even with Cerberus' help."

I'm fairly certain I could indeed take on forty mortals.

Restraining my sigh, I mentally spoke back to him. *I know, but we can't kill all those innocent people either. And both of them need time before we run into the fray. They just lost their remaining parents.*

"Are you talking to Cerberus? Does he have any ideas about what to do once we *do* go inside?" Temps eyed me, and I nodded.

"Yes, I'm reminding him that those hypnotized people are innocent in all this, too. But..." Dropping my head, I exhaled, trying to come up with something myself for how exactly we were going to stop this false-god. "...I'm not sure. We don't even really know what this thing is. Sure, it's a malevolent force looking to rule, but where does it come from? What are its weaknesses?"

"Those innocent people could very well have signed up for this shit, too, Caleb." Lizzie wasn't looking at me, or any of us for that matter, but the furious energy radiated off her. "According to Barbs, this church preached some bigoted rhetoric. Bunch of damn prejudicial bullshit about queer people and the BIPOC communities."

"I know you're pissed, Lizzie." She finally looked up at me. "And yeah, some of those people might suck, deserve to be called out on their bullshit, but I can't just let them all die without having any proof."

She started to roll her eyes, but I snagged her by the chin and made her look at me. Holding that eye contact, I didn't blink or hesitate when I told Lizzie the entire truth of the matter.

"There are consequences to a massacre that I won't deal with, Lizzie. But I promise you, if we need to go in there, and any of those fuckers so much as says two words about hurting you or Temps, looses some shit about your worth, I won't hesitate to tear them apart. I said not without proof, not never."

It took a moment, but then the corner of Lizzie's mouth lifted in a smirk. She took my hand when I held her chin and squeezed, staying with me in that moment until she leaned forward and dusted a kiss over my lips.

"I really needed to hear that." She smiled as she leaned back, looking over at Temps, who had scooted closer to her. "Thank you. Both of you. And Cerberus, if he's listening."

I felt that buzz of magic in my eyes that signaled Cerberus pushing forward, likely turning my stare yellow.

"I am, young morrighan. I will say for you all right now that if

someone were to attempt to harm any of my mates, they would be met with the wrath of my claws and fangs."

Lizzie chuckled. "Such a romantic."

Scoffing, I looked around the edge of the building we'd hidden behind, checking the parking lot of the carnival again. It was still packed, but I started to see movement at the exit of the tent.

"They might be leaving soon." I went back to the shadows, crouching in front of Lizzie and Temps. "Cerberus, do you have any other information about what this thing might be?"

Humming magic filled me again, and I felt Cerberus rise forward, taking over so that he could speak through me. I was getting more used to the sensation, but I had to admit that hearing myself with this other voice say things I didn't know was a bit of a mind trip.

"There are several versions of the malignance in the mortal world's religions. They are all shards of truth, none of them whole, but they each mention this entity. The closest to the factual existence it's had since the dawn of creation is that of the demiurge. A chaotic, arrogant being that crafted this false world we have now and keeps people from entering the true higher realm of divinity. That is, of course, a simplification, but mortals rarely understand the complexity of the universe and the several realms within it."

"A demiurge? Like in Gnosticism?" Temps furrowed her brow, coming off her feet and kneeling in front of me. "Those beliefs are from some of the most ancient religions in the world. *They* knew about this thing?"

Cerberus chuckled through me, and I felt that rush of warmth and attraction he had to her well up, magnifying my own.

"A smart young witch. I'm impressed. It is the closest, as I said, not a perfect understanding. The lion-faced serpent was a solid form given by humans. In reality, it holds no shape, but it will manifest in whatever form its followers most desire to see. This is also not a false reality. It's as real as any of the realms. There are multitudes. The entity has been bound to the lines between realms for eons, unable to take physical form. But it has found a way through that by manipulating mortals, specifically this Paine. He and his offspring are oddly resonant with the being. Together, they have sought to overrun the World of Below, as they have other realms such as the Winter Kingdom and Edom. Your mortal world might just be the first to give him form, and form is powerful."

"Fucking hell, Cerbs. The info dump. It's going to take me at least ten minutes to process all that."

Temps stifled a chuckled, and I shook my head, in control again. It was a lot to swallow. And we were still going to have to go up against this thing as a handful of witches and an elder being. What would even affect it?

The sound of car doors shutting and ignitions firing got our attention; the place was finally emptying out.

"What does it feed on? I mean, if this thing is getting power from its followers, will it have issues if that power supply is cut off?" Temps took off the suit jacket that she'd brought from her house, letting it fall to the ground. Lizzie had modified the dress she was wearing with Cerberus' help when we landed, and she added Temps' jacket to the pile of fabric scraps cut from the bottom of her outfit.

She'd made the skirt hit her at just above the knee instead of mid-shin, using the straps that went over her shoulder to create a waistband so that she didn't have to wear it like a pair of overalls.

"I imagine it will cause some issues, yes. The entity, some refer to it as Ninlul, feeds or draws strength from the belief of mortals and other beings. The sacrifices have given it strength, but undoubtedly, it is still heavily tied to Paine. His death would cause issues as well as the destruction of any effigies or magic used to hypnotize or control his followers."

"Okay, I can work with that." Lizzie nodded, and I mirrored it, agreeing with her that something physical to focus our assaults on would be extremely beneficial.

"Alright, so are we ready to head over there?" Temps stood up, pulling her hair into a ponytail with the hairtie she'd worn on her wrist. "Go in the back?"

Nodding, Lizzie pointed at Temps as she found a hairtie on her own wrist and rewound her hair into her signature braid.

"Yeah, I'm thinking a front entrance isn't going to be good. Not that the back door worked well for us last time."

"You did not have me last time."

Temps and Lizzie smiled, patting Cerberus through me, and I couldn't help but grin. "We do have you. But yes, let's go now. While the people are still leaving and the Ring Leader stands a better chance of being distracted."

I held out my hands, the girls taking them as I silently gave Cerberus the go-ahead to whisk us to the back of the tent, wherever it was shadowed and unpopulated. We appeared near the fabric in a line, shadow hanging over us, and a collection of wooden crates in front of us. The little niche would give us a good place to hide, and we all hunkered down again.

"Lizzie, can you find a seam?" I felt around my section of the tent, looking for a way in. "Temps?"

"Yeah, I got one. Hold on, there are ties."

The sounds of cars got quieter and quieter, and the nervous energy radiating through our little group ticked up. We were running out of time. I didn't want to get spotted out here. We'd have so much better chance if we could at least get inside and take on one group of people at a time.

"What are you doing out here?"

I shot my attention up and back, my mouth dropping open as a wave of panic struck. "Dean Owens?"

Oh, we are so fucked.

"Professor Harkert." She stomped closer, coming from the drop-off behind the fairgrounds that led down to the coast. "And students? Ms. Montgomery, Ms. Chamberlain, have you all lost your minds? You absolutely should not be here. This is an active investigation under the purview of the school board. I demand that you return to campus at once."

I couldn't hear cars anymore, and now something stirred inside the tent, the unshakable feeling of people with power just a few feet away.

"Lizzie, hurry." Turning to the dean, I held up my hands, trying to keep my voice down. "Dean Owens, I assure you that we're hear to help the school and this town. The carnival is up to some horrible things, and we—"

"I could have your job for this, Caleb. This is highly unacceptable. You cannot be taking students out into the field for some test when the danger is real."

The blasted woman wouldn't keep her voice down, and she stood there like this proud Head Mistress. She was going to fucking get us caught.

Do you wish for me to shunt her to this campus? I could remove her tongue as well.

Fuck, no. You can't—Ugh, shit.

Leaning up, I yanked Owens down toward me, trying to get her out of sight behind a crate. "It's not some test. We know the carnival is killing people. We know they're involved with a dark entity trying to get into our plane, okay? Would you quiet the fuck down? We can't get caught."

"How on earth have you learned all this?" At least the woman was keeping her voice to a whisper this time. "The school has only just been able to decipher the clues from the body that suggest an entity possessing the Ring Leader, and we've been on this for days now."

She wasn't an idiot, and I appreciated that she was trying to do the right thing. The dean had come here to stop her students from dying. She had no way of knowing the enormity of what was going on. Hell, we'd sort of lucked into it.

Thanks to Cerberus.

"Caleb, we need to move. I got the ties open. Come on." Lizzie gestured with her head, and Temps looked between me and the dean as she poked out from behind the box that provided her with cover.

"Look, it's a demiurge, or that's the closest word mortals have for it. Cerberus has been helping us to figure this shit out. I've got him in my head. He knows this shit better than we do, and—"

"In your head? Cerberus?" Dean Owens' eyes flared wide, the pupil shrinking as she gaped at me. The realization struck her, and I wanted to take it back, to fucking lie to her because we didn't have time for this shit. "Have you performed a soul weaving? Caleb, that is a fireable offense. That magic is forbidden. You have broken a cardinal rule. A violation that I cannot just sit on regardless of the reason why."

"Dammit, Rebeccas, this is bigger than all that. Can't you see? They're going to raise this thing tonight. We need to stop it. You can yell at me later."

She stood up, shaking her head as she backed up toward the crumbling edge of soil. Her heel sank into the soft earth, and she yelped, struggling to get it free as she stood there in her gray, wool suit, the wide-leg trousers and jacket so incredibly out of place for the situation.

"Hey, I heard something around back. Go check it out."

The low voice came from around the side of the tent. We had seconds to get out of sight or we'd be caught and all of this would be for nothing. I turned to Lizzie and Temps, putting a finger to my lips and pointing inside the tent.

"Go," I whispered. "I'll try to get her in."

They nodded reluctantly but slipped inside the tent as quiet as a mouse. When I turned back to Rebecca, frantic energy rising up the back of my throat to choke me, I thrust out my hand, doing what I could from hiding to loosen the dirt and set her free.

"Please, Rebeccas. Just get inside with us. We can talk about this when he world isn't fucking about to end."

"You performed a soul weaving," her voice carried too much on the wind. "No. No, I will not—"

Footsteps, loud enough to hear beating the earth, and they were right around the corner. *Dammit.*

With little other choice, I backed up into the tent, peering out at her from the shadows and gesturing for her to follow. She just shook her head, defiant, and then her eyes went to the side.

"Well, well, what have we here?"

I let the fabric close, frozen there at the gap as I listened to the exchange.

"You will not have another soul!" The sound of magic cracking through the air was a soft rumble, but a smug chuckle followed it.

"Parlor tricks ain't going to work with me, sweetheart. I'm one of His chosen."

Another crack, this one booming and final before a thug followed, and I swallowed hard, silently cursing. He'd fucking killed her. The stubborn woman wouldn't get into the godsdamn ten, and now she was dead.

Fuck!

"Aw, He'll be so please. Bit of food for our god to snack on once the old show begins, and He wakes up. I'm getting in real good with the Ring Leader now."

Footsteps thudded in the other direction, the shuffle of something being dragged following them. I waited until it was silent again, and then it was just me, left in the darkness, and the quiet as the cult claimed another victim.

Twenty-Five

ILLUSION STANDS IN THE MIND, A TWISTED THREAD YOU MUST UNWIND

TEMPS

I had heard the voice outside the tent while Caleb was dealing with the dean. Lizzie and I had looked at each other, eyes wide in the dark as the panic choked me, for what felt like eons, before a faint light at the seam got our attention. I took off for it, wanting to get to Caleb, and felt Lizzie hot on my heels. I remembered how this place had acted before, and I held my hand out behind me, seizing her hand so that I didn't lose her.

But we couldn't find Caleb.

As soon as we got to the flap where he'd come in, he was gone. Nothing but blackness lingered around us. The tent, this fucking cult, had set up traps so that they'd be ready for us again, or anyone else, for that matter.

"Dammit, I'm sorry. I couldn't get to him." I shook my head, my voice a whisper, and I turned to face Lizzie as tiny circles of light began to blink on behind her.

"It's alright. I know you tried. It's this fucking place." Music started to play behind us, sweet and tinkling noises that felt plucked by the tiny metal fittings inside a music box. "Ugh, what now?"

She turned around as a shape took form, this constellation of lights making sense as a hazy red glow filtered out from behind it. It moved, circling over and over, a familiar sight from memories of my childhood. But I dreaded what I might see now inside this cursed carnival tent.

A carousel.

"We need to keep moving forward. You remember what Caleb said. He'll do the same. He'll keep moving, and we'll find him where the paths converge."

Lizzie raised a brow at me, her mouth in a straight line. "You sure about that?"

Sucking in a deep breath, I grabbed her hand and nodded once. "Yes. I have to be. I choose to be. We're magic, too, Lizzie. We can fight back against this."

With a smile, she pulled me over for a quick kiss. "Damn skippy, babe. Let's go."

The dim red glow behind the carousel brightened with each step we took closer, the music that played from it an odd juxtaposition compared to the sinister vibes it gave off. The top of the carousel was lit with those little lights, revealing the shapes carved into the worn wood at the top. They were depictions of little scenes, like you might see on the typical ride, but these weren't cute.

Bodies being torn apart, fingers deep inside skulls, the silhouettes were all violent and wrong. In some, I thought I saw the pieces of people being eaten, and my stomach flip-flopped. Things lingered in the shadows around us, unwilling to come into the light, and it flickered, revealing dozens of pairs of eyes.

"Keep it lit." I held up a hand, conjuring a bit of light in my palm—one of the first tricks I learned when I was studying this stuff on my own. "They won't come toward the light."

Lizzie held up a hand, closing her eyes briefly as she forced herself to conjure up the glow. She didn't do this type of magic as much as me, and I focused with her, calling up more of my own inner power to help her get a ball of illumination floating above her palm.

The creeping sounds in the dark corners stayed put, and we both silently agreed to hurry up and get onto the carousel to come out the other side.

"What the fuck?"

As we got closer, Lizzie was the first to notice the horses. These weren't the pretty ponies and occasional "circus" animals that we'd expect. The black stallions' eyes all glowed an eerie yellow, their bodies purposefully missing chunks, rib cages, and bones exposed.

"Fucking zombie horses? Are you serious?" Lizzie squished me against her as we stepped up onto the revolving platform, keeping me close to her.

"I'm going to assume we should steer clear of the mouths."

"Smart."

It hadn't looked that big when we were walking up to it. Hell, the carousel looked like it had a whopping three horses on it when we stepped on. But now, the spinning ride picked up speed, and with each revolution, more horses and odd creatures appeared on new poles, which seemed to genuinely stab through their bodies.

The machine whizzed faster, and Lizzie and I had to walk against the rotation to attempt reaching the other side of the thing. That's where the back of the room was, where the exit would be on a non-haunted ride. However, with it moving this fast and new animals popping up, all missing skin and eyes, it was getting almost impossible to navigate without bumping into one of them.

"Fucking—Ugh. Try to step inward over here." Lizzie pointed to her right, closer to the central mechanism of the ride.

Angling that way, I held tight to her hand as we slipped between two horses. They didn't move, but it was like their stares tracked us, and the one to our left, the one whose mouth was way too close for comfort, seemed to stretch just a hair, like it was inching its teeth forward.

"Lizzie, I don't—Ah!"

I yelped as just in front of us, an elephant appeared on the carousel, popping up from the floor with a shiny gold pole sticking out of it. The thing looked worse than the horses, its trunk hanging half cut off, and its ears ragged and torn. One chunk in particular looked like it might have been a bite mark, and the ribs showed too, intestines still coiled inside it and held in place by the bewitched wood and lacquer construction.

My foot slipped, and I pitched backward as Lizzie got around it. Her shoulder yanked as I stumbled, and for a moment, I didn't know if I should let go or not. She gripped me tighter, though, keeping me from twisting to the left, my face inches from the horse's open mouth.

Its teeth snapped down, chomping at me. "Fuck! Lizzie, go!"

All around us, mouths clacked down, wooden teeth crunching together as the inanimate animals surged to life, a freakish showing of impaled creatures, decaying and baying loudly, trying ceaselessly to devour us.

Lizzie took off, keeping her fingers laced through mine, and I ran with her, doing everything I could to fling us toward the back half of this carousel. We were so close, and my thighs burned as we started to gain ground on the speeding ride.

Whineying rang out near me, and I stopped short as one of the horses closed its teeth down on my skirt. I pulled against it, the fabric loudly tearing, and then another animal, a peacock, burst through the floor. It sent me flying forward as I did my best to tumble out of the way, the wooden platform unforgiving as I rolled, smashing my knees and elbows into it.

"Temps!"

I turned over my shoulder to see Lizzie with her braid in the grip of a zombified monkey, my stomach dropping through the earth.

Oh fuck.

Standing, I took off for her, looking for anything that I could use to whack the damn thing and get it to let her go. That elephant was close, trumpeting its broken horn in this horrible sound.

The trunk. Oh, dammit, gross.

I got to it, careful to keep my fingers and appendages out of mouth range, and I grabbed hold of the trunk, wrenching it hard in one direction. The wood snapped, making the animal go silent, and I ran to Lizzie, swinging as hard as I could into the monkey's head. It smashed clean off, splinters flying, and I dropped the trunk to grab her hand.

We ran for the back of the ride, not looking behind us but only forward as we rushed for the way off. Reality seemed to stretch and thin, and the sounds of laughter from the sides of the ride crescendoed. The shadows were closing in, the lights on the top of the carousel blinking out one after the other.

"The light! We need to conjure it again!"

Holding out my hand with Lizzie's fingers knotted in mine, I forced the magic there, calling on hers too. We screamed as we both pushed the ball of light to appear and grow, swallowing up the area around it. That pull on reality lessened, and we used everything we had to leap off the carousel and into the dimly lit doorway, the red glow behind it faint and pulsing.

Unsure how much time had passed, I came back to myself, lifting my head off the floor, Lizzie on the checkered tiles next to me. Everything ached, and as I looked around, trying to get my bearings, all I could do was groan.

"A funhouse. Amazing."

Lizzie stood up, pulling herself off the floor with a low moan of pain, and held a hand out to me, helping me up. Her braid had come free in several places, and she was sporting a bleeding lip. It probably happened from hitting the ground when we jumped, and I looked down to see that my knees were bleeding too.

"We get through it. Just like the last time."

I nodded back at her. "Right. Okay, don't let go. I...I hate these things."

"I know, babe. I got you."

We looked down the narrow hall ahead of us. It was dark in her, only enough light to just make out the walls and floor. Things on the walls glowed, little figurines and dolls, their empty eyes watching us as we slowly crept down the first passageway.

"Hehehehe!" A clown figure jumped out from the corner, snarling through his laugh as he held a massive, round saw blade up, the thing secured to a baseball bat. "Come and play, girlies!"

"Run."

Lizzie switched hands with me, getting me in front of her as we dashed past the clown. His faded outfits were torn and stained— brown and red splatter covering him from head to toe—and his makeup was streaky and splotched from being worn for who knew how long.

We took off down the only option forward, rushing down

another hall as the sound of a chainsaw screamed from just the other side of the wall. There was only the single path onward, and Lizzie and I didn't take any chances with slowing down, sprinting through the twists and turns and running into the sides more times than I could count.

Light appeared as we rounded a corner, and my heart surged in my chest. "Lizzie! Look!"

"Don't stop for anything, Temps! Go for it!"

Powering toward the exit, my lungs screamed, more animatronics popping out from corners as we zig-zagged through a section of oddly angled pony walls. A Jack-In-The-Box opened, screaming as it leaped out and drove a knife downward. I stumbled back, but the point of the blade caught my shirt, tearing down from my collarbone to my already injured knee.

"Temps!"

I kicked wildly as Lizzie tried to run up to me, looking back for her just in time to see another clown appear from below a section of the short wall. He stood up, wielding a massive meat cleaver with jagged edges. Blood coated the blade, which was spray-painted with red stripes; the handle featured a swirling red and black pattern, reminiscent of a lollipop.

"No!"

I rolled as the Jack-In-The-Box swung forward again, grabbing hold of the knife in its hand and using all my strength to break it free. The thing was so much bigger in my much smaller hands, a white painted blade with a smiling clowface drawn on in Sharpie. The eyes were Xs, and the red smile was finger-painted on with what had to be blood.

My skin burned where the long cut traced down my skin. Each step to Lizzie was so fucking painful that I nearly fell to the ground. But that godsdamn clown held her shoved against the wall, his cleaver at her throat, the points of the broken metal pressing into her skin.

As I dragged myself closer, I forced down the pain and realized that the clown asshole wasn't right. His exceedingly pale skin was stretched too tight, and even from the side, I could tell that his hair was made of ropes, rough jute that frayed this way and that.

It also covered his eyes and mouth, sewn into the skin in Xs.

"Holy fuck." I reeled.

This thing was dead. This wasn't a human in costume, either. It was too real. The Xs on his mouth when all the way back to his ears, but he was somehow still talking.

"Come on, pretty little thing. Don't you know you're prettier when you smile?" He lifted the cleaver to Lizzie's mouth, angling one of the points at her cheek. "I'm just going to make it easier for ya. And you're gonna scream all pretty for me."

"Fuck off!" Lizzie kicked at the clown's crotch, making contact.

He lurched, pulling himself in, but as she tried to run for me, he snagged her by the braid. She halted, the clown yanking her to his chest. I needed to move quicker, but my vision was going hazy as I leaked red all over the damn floor.

"Now, now, little slut. You know you want it. Why else would you dress this way?"

I shook my head, trying to focus while this undead creep reached around to Lizzie's front and groped her breast. His bony, blood-stained fingers wormed down her stomach, balling up her skirt and stuffing between her legs even as she squeezed her thighs together.

"Oh, fuck no. You get your hands off her."

I used everything I had to run forward, and the asshole didn't even seem to notice me until I was pulling Lizzie out of his grip and throwing her behind me. I didn't hesitate, jamming the blade in my hand up into his stomach. He dropped to the floor, the knife in his guts, and I turned to run back to my girl.

"Go!" I pointed behind her. "The exit!"

A low growl reverberated through the air from the shadows. This fucking place wouldn't quit, and I just focused on sprinting straight ahead, zeroed in on the way out. Lizzie stood at the threshold, waving her arm frantically like it was actually going to get me moving faster. Then, her eyes flared.

"Behind you!"

Squish.

I heard it before I felt the pain. The sound of my skin tearing and the wet slice as my blood bubbled up around the wound. The knife I'd used stuck out of the spot below my collarbone, my nerves screaming as the injury registered. I gasped, unable to keep moving forward.

"No!" Lizzie took off from the doorway, running toward me in slow motion.

Or was that just me slowing down? Everything felt so far away.

And then that feral growl was everywhere around me, so loud

and menacing and omnipresent. I could feel it in my bones, and then a hard yank, making my skin burn again. A massive black shape, furred and snarling, stood over me where I slumped to the floor.

But it faced the clown, two clawed hands moving like lightning, they tore into its body until it was in little pieces on the floor. It was disgusting, but I couldn't find it in me to be nauseated.

"Don't fucking touch what's mine."

Two voices speaking as one. I knew that sound. Then a bunch of scuffling sounds as the world went dark, my eyelids too heavy to keep open.

Twenty-Six

COME ONE, COME ALL, TO THE BIG TOP SHOW & SEE EVERY TRICK UNDER THE SUN

LIZZIE

"'emps! Temps!" I shot Cerberus a glare, tears streaming down my face. "Fucking do something!"

He sank onto the floor next to us, the floor under Temps turning more and more red. With his claws, he reached into Temps' shirt, ripping the hole made by the knife larger. The stab wound was grizzly, this slice through her warm tan skin, which was steadily losing color as she bled out. I didn't know what I expected him to do, but licking across it wasn't it.

The swipe revealed more of the injury, and he grabbed my hand, getting me to push down on the area right above it.

"There is no poison. That is good." Cerberus sucked in a breath at

the wound, sniffing Temps's blood. "*And no malignance. I will beseech my mothers.*"

"Your mother? What the fuck would she—No, it's not important. Go."

I watched as she shut his wolfen eyes, holding a clawed hand over Temps's shoulder. Energy hummed around him, and that dark connection I'd noticed before—the way he seemed to be this creature of nature and death—swirled in the air.

Frantically looking around us, I made sure that no more surprises lurked in the shadows, doing what I could to keep the ball of light glowing in my palm. I wasn't the alchemist. I wasn't the proper spellcaster. I did things on instinct and intuition. But I knew those assholes didn't like the light. So, I went with what Temps had shown me.

Come on, baby. You can't leave me.

The call in my blood toward her zinged, perking up as Cerberus began to growl our words that I couldn't understand. Threads of gold appeared beneath his hands, and I watched them tighten, threatening to snap.

"*There is resistance.*"

"Well, I don't give a shit! Get her stable!" I looked down at Temps. "Don't you dare fucking leave me! Don't you dare! I need you!"

The golden threads wavered in the air, vibrating like a tuning fork. Cerberus grabbed my hand, thrusting it between them. I could feel the ghostly heat rumbling over my skin, and I snapped my eyes up to his.

"Will you give to have her? Will you bind so that your fates are entwined permanently?"

A sharp chuckle bit out of me. "Aren't they already? Temps is my life. I won't lose her. I won't have *you* lose her."

Cerberus nodded, one of his eyes going blue as Caleb appeared at the surface, their voices speaking as one.

"Agreed."

The chords of gold went taut around my skin, looping around our joined hands and squeezing down. They cut into our flesh as they sank deep, and a few drops of blood trickled down from both me and Cerberus. Even Caleb's brighter red blood was there. It landed on Temps' wound, seeping in.

Light emanated from our little group, and just beyond it, standing at the threshold with their hands joined, stood two women. One had light hair cascading down to the floor in a white dress, the other nude with long black braids trailing into eternity and horns perched on her.

"What in the holy fuck?"

More warmth blazed at my back, and I turned over my shoulder. Two more women stood there. One had blazing red hair and antlers, this time, a black eye and a gold eye. The other looked like it could have been Temps except for being so much paler. Dark hair hung down, mingling with the fabric of her deep blue dress.

Four booming voices called out into the room. *"It is done."*

At once, the entire room flashed white before going dark again, and I sat on the floor with Temps lying there, Cerberus receding some, so that it was this hybrid between him and Caleb.

"Temps," I held her cheek, rubbing my thumb back and forth over her skin. "Temps, baby."

"Temperance!" Caleb's voice rang out. "You heard Lizzie. Get back here!"

He reached forward, his hand covering mine as he held her. *Zap!* Electricity launched through us, this arch I could feel ring through my head to my toes and then back to Caleb and Temps. My concentration on the light faded, and in the darkness, almost too dark to see, a faint glow emanated from Temps' chest.

"Fuck!" She shot upright and into our waiting arms. "What the...Did I almost die?"

Nodding against her shoulder, I let my tears fall. "Yes. Yes, you fucking did. Don't do that to me ever again."

She chuckled, Caleb chuckled, and he squeezed both of us. "Promise."

Creeeaaaakkkk...

We all looked to the shadows, bubbling laughter getting louder and louder. They were coming. This was far from over, and we still had to make it to the center. I had no doubt that the ring would be in the middle of all this. That's where the "big show" was going to go down.

"We need to move." Caleb stood up, offering his hands to both Temps and me, and only wearing his pants. "The door."

"I see you got casual," I smirked at him, forcing that ball of light into my palm again. "Looks good on ya."

He snorted, rolling his eyes. "I'm just glad Cerberus left me with my pants this time."

A loud pop sounded from the distance, followed by that sourceless laughter. It kept repeating from the shadows until I could see the edges of figures forming there, each one holding a fistful of balloons. They each popped one, the noise so fucking loud and bright.

"Time for the show, folks! Step on down! Try your luck!"

They stood just out of the direct light, swinging their various blades out in front of them. Temps screamed as one slashed by her face, this long machete with polkadots painted on it. Blood splattered over the blade and handle, I peered into the darkness to see a massive man, six feet at least, and so round that it almost looked fake.

"We need to go! The exit's that way!" I pointed at the door, which seemed so fucking far now, and we all took off, the figures dogging us in the shadows beyond where my light reached.

"Come on! Try your hand! Come see The World's Largest Man!" The machete streaked through the light, slicing Caleb's arm as we ran past.

He growled, raking his claws through the air and catching on the fabric of that oversized man's clown suit. We ran, heading toward the threshold that glowed red from the seams. But an enormous sledgehammer smashed down into the tiles in front of us, busting them into tiny shards.

I shifted my glow that way, Temps now able to conjure up her own light at our backs. My stomach dropped as I saw what stood in front of us.

Mangled limbs at wrong angles, all four of them, worked to hold the sledgehammer, two heads craning in our direction in a sharp jutting motion. Only two legs held up the figure, all clad in those same dilapidated clown costumes, and the one backward hand gripped the sledgehammer toward me. It hoisted it up into the air again, smiling at us, too wide and too many teeth.

"Come play! Test your feat of strength, puppies! We'll even let'cha get the first swing before ol' KitKat!"

"A conjoined twin?" Temps stumbled near me. "What the fuck? What's—"

"I think the 'freak show' has come to us girls." Caleb reached into the pockets of his pants, pulling out three vials and shoving two and Temps and me. "Throw 'em. I'm not sure what they do."

"Now, now." KitKat swung wide, and I had to duck under the huge, weighted head of the hammer. "No outside treats!"

"Ah!" I rolled, the sledgehammer colliding with the floor behind me in a deafening crash. Temps and Caleb darted to the other side, and I forced myself into a crouch so I could get moving again. "Meet at the door!"

We all got the message, and I ducked back as the conjoined twin sang again, barely dodging the long reach of the weapon. I sprinted toward the door, a fucking pipe organ starting up in the background as the "freaks" giggled relentlessly. Big Boy went after Temps and Caleb, slicing through the air with that machete.

"Hold still, folks! You're ruining the trick! You know, the part when..." I watched Temps flash her light up in his face, and bright illumination revealed the horrific, torn flesh and stitches holding him together, each patch a different skin tone. "...I slice myself a new addition!"

"Oh, little witch," a sing-song voice called behind me, and I risked a glance over my shoulder to see the twin barreling toward me, weapon poised over its shoulder, "hold still! Imma make some heathen paste! Eat it up and send it to Him, too! He loves to chomp on some abominations, too! Crunch those witches—"

I threw the ball of light on my hand to its face, and it screeched, reeling back as the sledgehammer came down again, demolishing the floor.

"—between His teeth!" The words came out on a horrible roar, a boom that shook the room at a pitch so low I almost couldn't understand it.

As the light made the twin clear enough to see, I hucked the bottle Caleb gave me right at its face. In a whoosh, the liquid erupted into flames, burning down the front of the twin. It screamed, dropping the sledgehammer and clawing at its flesh as it charred and melted off. The smell was fucking awful, making me gag.

The hammer.

I leaped forward, snatching the weapon off the floor just as the twin reached for me, rolling out of the way and back toward the door. I took off for it, leveling the head of the hammer with the doorknob and swinging away. The locked panel flew open, wood chunks hitting the floor.

"It's open! Come on!"

Caleb hooked a clawed hand under Temps' arm and hauled her toward the door as he ran. He was a lot faster, even in hybrid form. Temps cranked back her other arm and lobbed the vial she held at Big Boy. It smashed against his face as he ran into her light, making him stop.

"No! Argh!" He bellowed so loud, and I watched in horror as he struggled to catch pieces of his sewn flesh as the sloughed off his face. The green mist that wafted over him from the vial leaked down his body, and more and more of his patches came loose, tumbling to the ground as he literally fell apart.

Holy fucking shit.

Temps and Caleb made it to me as a little pile of skin and fat and muscle piled up on the floor, still screaming about putting him back together. The suit of people this thing had made for himself was all in shambles, like discarded fabric on the floor. I gagged again, tasting bile at the back of my throat.

"I will never not see that in my head." I shook, still reeling as Caleb grabbed me, still holding Temps, and threw us all through the door.

We hit the floor on the other side of the doorway, and it disappeared behind us. Fluffy, musty dust puffed up around us as we pulled ourselves to standing. We were in the main tent. Thankfully, we were off to the side, not in the center, and to our left, a row of cages sat next to a gap in the wooden stands.

"Caleb?"

He turned to a cage near the end of the short row, hurrying toward it as I pulled Temps into my arms. "Are you okay?"

"Yeah, I'm...well, I'm right where you are. The shoulder is okay, sore but okay."

As we looked back over at Caleb, he stood at one of the cages, gripping the bars in both hands. I took Temps' hand and hurried that way, shocked to see that Dean Owens was inside. Her suit was a mess, torn and stained with blood from a wound that'd dried on her head and some I couldn't see on her legs.

"You're alive. Fucking hell, let's get you out of there." Caleb threw back his hand, his claws extending all the more, and he slashed down through the bars like they were butter.

The dean took a step forward, collapsing into his arms when she couldn't walk. Temps and I helped to keep her upright as we all walked her over to the side of the tent, leaning her against the subtly moving fabric.

"Get our guests lined up in the center of the ring."

A familiar voice called out from across the ring, and we pulled the dean into the shadows with us as we hid behind the stands, peering through the slim gaps between the slats of wood. The Ring Leader came out with that same pair of performers from the trapeze. The two of them held a line of chained people, all dressed up like black-and-white clowns with much newer-looking costumes.

They led the sacrifices—because that's totally what they were—to the center of the ring, parading them in a line until they reached just in front of this massive rune that had been painted on the ground. The trapeze performers shoved them down to their knees, and I counted the people.

There were nine of them—the previously mentioned faithful

who'd been chosen that morning.

"Excellent." The Ring Leader walked to the center of the ring, standing in the middle of the rune. "We will begin."

"Shit, Caleb, it's starting. What the fuck do we do?"

I looked to him, Temps on his other side, and he shook his head, his expression grim. "I don't know. I—Fuck, I'm not sure what's supposed to stop him. We need to take out the Ring Leader, probably. Those trapeze people."

"And how do we do that? He's about to open up the portal!" I whisper-shouted, gesturing at the circle where the Ring Leader, one Jebediah Paine Junior, stood with his arms outstretched toward the sky.

"Which means he'll be vulnerable." The dean spoke in a pained whisper, pointing at the rune. "He's going to channel the demiurge. Those sigils. He's going to soul weave it."

Like Caleb did.

I focused on the circle where Pastor Pricktips was chanting low. He needed to focus on the spell, concentrate, and when Caleb had done it, there was a brief window when he'd been completely gone to the spell, wrapped up in the magic.

"It could work." Temps looked down as she thought, her eyes searching as she waved a hand in tiny, frantic gestures. "But we'll need something to keep the sacrifices safe. If even one of them dies, it'll trigger the spell to begin."

"I can create a barrier." Dean Owens grunted as she pulled herself to the edge of the stands, leaning on the wooden slat at her chest, his lids looking real damn heavy. "I'll keep them protected for now. You three, or four, I guess, take out that piece of shit."

"We have no choice." Caleb looked between Temps and me, his body shifting again as Cerberus came to the surface completely, taking over. *"Target your attacks. Focus on Paine. Call up the power in your blood, your ancestry."*

I took their hands, reaching into their heads because I couldn't let the dean hear me.

I love you, weirdos. We do this, or we go down fighting.

They held my eyes, sending those messages back at me as the dean worked her fingers through the air, a shimmer of magic appearing around the chained group.

Here we fucking go.

Twenty—Seven

AND BENEATH THE WANING MOON, THE BEING OF DARKNESS SHALL RISE

TEMPS

As quietly as we could, the three of us slipped out from under the stands, walking closer to the open section that led down to the front row. Pastor Paine stood in the ring, his arms up high as he waxed on, the threads of his strange working shuttering through the air. He wasn't a witch. This wasn't innate talent or a deity that was giving him the power to conjure up change.

It was the demiurge, and everything about the working reeked like rotten meat and burnt hair.

"Blessed are His children, who shape the earth in His Will!" Paine kept his arms aloft as he looked down at the sacrifices, their muted cries muffled around gags I couldn't see. "Do not heed His will and be made a meal for the God That Devours! All you fucking heathens, foolish sheep being herded to the slaughter, you will see in Him the face of your destruction!"

The rune on the floor began to glow, the red lighting flaring at the bottom of Paine's face, making him look like the demonic terror he was. A bass thrum rumbled through the ground, and from the lines drawn into the floor, the earth began to crack.

He's close. Wait for the moment he lets go.

Lizzie split off from her place next to me, moving toward the opposite stand and crouching slightly as she slipped forward. I did the same, trying to make myself small as Cerberus stalked forward. The wavering light around the people the circus stole flickered, that red infecting the bottom. I turned back to look at Dean Owens. She was clearly struggling, her hand outstretched over the wooden beam, fingers shaking.

"I welcome You into me, God of All! Take hold of your child and raise me up so that I might carry out Your will!"

Paine's eyes rolled back, and he began to hover off the ground ever so slightly.

Now!

Cerberus rushed forward, speeding across the tent until he could make the leap for Paine. Lizzie popped out from behind the wooden cover, her hands shooting forward as she screamed a primal call. The trapeze performers noticed Cerberus and then, growling as they sank down into the haunches. One took off for Cerberus as the other rushed for Lizzie. I could feel the pull of her powers; this compulsion was sent to the trapeze performer's head. She gripped her skull, screaming. Lizzie forced the weight of shame to the surface, making the woman double over, her eyes going bloodshot and feral.

I had to take care of the other one going for Cerberus.

A spell is desire made manifest.

Sucking in a deep breath, I found that reservoir of power within me, this gentle hum to it that I remember feeling when I'd first woken up after being stabbed. I'd sensed them there—Cerberus' family, the ancient elders of Winter and Spring, Summer, and Autumn. I could feel the woman whose line was a part of my own, and I called for them, demanded my desire be made real.

"Stop him." The snarling man, his costume coming undone as his body contorted into a grotesque version of muscular, too bulbous and veiny, leaped for Cerberus and then dropped as my power seized him. "Keep him down. Don't let him up. Let Cerberus get to Paine."

He thrashed on the ground, this way and that, and I had to fight against his strength, breaking out in a sweat as I forced him to stay planted on the earth.

But it worked.

Cerberus sprinted past, not stopped by the man, and he smashed into Paine, sending him flying as Cerberus tumbled purposefully and came to a skidding stop just in front of him, growling. Paine shot up from the floor, his body broken and bent at odd angles. He snapped himself back into position, wrenching his head back to the front.

What the hell? Is he dead?

"Fucking mutt! You will not stop His ascension! My God

will rise! My line of Paine and suffering will be whole and everlasting!"

Paine reached through he air, taking hold of Cerberus the way I had his minion. Cerberus dug his claws into the ground, refusing to be moved. He fought through the hold, crawling across the dusty ground toward Paine.

"Arrgh!"

Shit. The man I held surged forward, getting his arms beneath him. I tried to press down again, but my arms shook. He reached back for something, and I twisted my hold, flipping him onto his back as I sucked in a breath. Whatever he was doing, I had to stop it.

But the power inside him wasn't backing down. I could feel the change in the air, the way it smelled off. The demiurge was coming, and the cracks beneath Cerberus and Paine stretched wider.

"Lizzie!" I shouted over, chancing a glance at her and how she was maintaining the other one. "He's too strong. I need you to get her down!"

"I'm fucking trying!" She stepped forward, her hands twisting in the air as she increased the volume. The woman screamed louder, but she still wasn't out, not enough that Lizzie could help me.

Dammit! Think, Temps!

A blade soared through the air, and I just dodged it, snapping my attention back to the man I held down. With a quick jerk, I focused every ounce of my magic on his neck, yanking to the side. A snap echoed around the ring, and he went still.

"Oh, thank gods."

"Temps!" Lizzie gestured behind me as I looked over, and I followed the line of sight to Dean Owens.

The knife was lodged in her stomach beneath the wooden beam, her arm still outstretched. She blinked at me, and then her wrist dropped. I screamed out, eyeing the tracking to the shield around the people still chained in the center of the ring. That bubble of iridescence faded, and even Pastor Paine noticed it, his red eyes gleaming.

I bolted forward, rushing toward the ring so that I could get to those people and at least break their fucking chains. The remaining trapeze artist swung out at me as I moved to dash past, her fingers in claws as she foamed at the mouth, her eyes bleeding.

"Die, witch!"

"Lizzie!" I rolled under her attack, landing on my hip in the ring. The ground was hard beneath the dust and hay, and pain zinged through my bones. "Shit! Help!"

I could hear her steps before I saw her, rushing up toward the stark-raving woman, sent into this broken reality by Lizzie's gifts. She slashed at her, producing a knife from somewhere just like her buddy had. Lizzie kicked at her hand, grabbing a hold of her head as I ran past to the sacrifices, Paine steadily closing in on them.

Swiping my hand through the air, I sent a gust of force toward the Ring Leader, shoving him back a few steps. Cerberus growled as he tried to turn himself around, still slowed by Paine's attack. I needed to disrupt his concentration.

A head shot.

"Aaaaiiieeee!!" I shot my eyes to Lizzie, her fingers stuck into the woman's temples.

The performer's skin turned more and more red, stretching around her eyes like an expanding balloon, and with an ear-piercing, wet pop, her skull detonated, crimson chunks flying out everywhere.

"Oh my gods, oh my gods..." Lizzie turned to me, her stare horrified and wide. "I...Fuck! Temps!"

She pointed with a blood-stained finger toward the center of the ring, where Father Paine raised his hand over one of the people chained at his feet. They shrieked in muffled pleas, begging for a mercy they weren't going to get from someone like Paine.

He couldn't kill them. He couldn't start this. We'd never make it out of here if the fucking demiurge were summoned entirely.

"Wren, help!" I threw out my arm, and from the ground around the sacrifices, a wall of ice shot up out of the ground, closing around them like a cave.

Looking down at my fingers in shock, the tips were coated in a thin layer of ice, melting on my skin as I stood there.

Well, holy shit. That's not—

"Blasphemous whores!" Paine smashed his fists down onto the frozen barrier. "I'll fucking peel your skin off your bones! Fill your corpses with my seed and make you the hosts for His

Beasts!"

In a flash, Lizzie was at my side, grabbing my hand. I swallowed down the fear as I looked at her, nodding toward Cerberus.

"We need him up. Help me."

She furrowed her brow, the unsure flicker in her eyes as noticeable as her shaking. "I...Temps, I'm not you. I don't have some crazy line to call on."

"You're a morrighan. You see and touch death like no one else can. Make him feel it. We just need a second, one moment for Cerberus to break free. He'll tear through him. You can do this."

She looked from me to Paine, who hammered down on the ice in front of him, chips of it flying off as he clawed at it relentlessly.

"Shit." Reaching out her other hand, Lizzie focused on Paine, and I watched as her eyes turned black, smoke appearing around her fingers.

I squeezed, anchoring myself to her presence, and shifted my focus from bolstering the ice to Paine. He was still mostly mortal. He could break. I focused on the cells, the little bits of emptiness between them, and the bonds that held him together. I remembered how an alchemical solution could break those bonds to create something new, and I pictured his blood filled with that solution.

He faltered, snarling at us as his eyes began to bleed. "He will eat you whole! Nothing will stop His arrival! Nothing!"

"Mom," Lizzie whispered, her body thrumming next to me, "Wren. Queen of Cauldron. Queen of the Shadowed Summer Sun. Those gone, walking the paths of the next world. I have a wayward soul for you to claim. I mark him in your names!"

A brand flared to life across Paine's chest, the earth cracking beneath his feet, and he screamed. "Nooo!"

I felt something snap in the ether around us, the shadows lengthening around Paine. And then I saw him, towering behind the Ring Leader, an Angel of Death.

"Say hello to your father."

Claws jutted through Paine's abdomen, the finger and arm following as Cerberus speared his hand through the fucker's middle. Gore dripped from the werewolf-like forearm, and the glowing red of Paine's eyes faded into nothing. The rune rumbled, a roar from somewhere I couldn't fathom ricocheting through the ring, but then it stopped, the cracks sealing up.

Yanking his hand free, Cerberus let Paine's body flop to the ground, and I dropped to my knees, exhausted as Lizzie gasped.

"It's...done?" Cerberus met my stare as my question hung, nodding. "Oh my gods."

Lizzie's arms were around me, and then I released my hold on the ice. The world moved around me as Cerberus rushed to the sacrifices, tearing through their chains before touching each of their foreheads. They passed out unharmed, and I had a feeling he'd wiped them. That was...a lot to see.

"We need to go," he said, sprinting up to us, shifting back into Caleb. "He could hear sirens."

The cops were not going to understand this, so I nodded, letting Lizzie pull me up. My attention went to the stands where I knew the dean was still lying.

"I don't want to leave her here." Caleb shot a glance that way, and in a blink, Dean Owens was lying on the ground in front of me.

"She tried, you know. She tried in the end." I knelt down, taking her hand. "Get us out—Oh my gods!"

Dean Owens squeezed my hand as the sound of sirens got loud enough for all of us to hear. She was alive somehow.

"Rebecca?" Caleb grabbed her other hand. "Fucking hell, hold on. We'll get you out of here and to—"

"The school board," she croaked out, blood coating the inside of her mouth. "They'll..help."

"Right." Nodding, Caleb took all of our hands as best he could, his eyes closing. "Buddy, get us out of here."

The world was shifting again, and I felt that tug on my body just as red and blue lights began to light up the outside of the tent.

Twenty-Eight

STAGNATION CANNOT FOSTER GROWTH, ONLY CHANGE CAN DO THAT

CALEB

It'd been twenty-four hours since we left that tent, and... so much had happened. Thankfully, we were able to get Rebecca to the school board for healing, but I was forced to leave almost immediately after dropping her off, trusting Temps and Lizzie to report back to me. That many powerful mages in one spot would have picked up on the soul weaving I'd done, and I would've lost my job in a heartbeat.

I'd been grateful to hear that she would be making a slow but steady recovery when my partners returned to my apartment, and none of us was ashamed to say that we almost immediately passed out.

Now, awake and snuggled into my bed with them, I stretched

over to my nightstand where my cell was charging, and picked it up to see if we'd missed anything during the night.

"Well, anything?" Temps rolled onto her side, looking up at me from her position next to me in the bed.

"It looks like the authorities blame 'odd cult behavior' for the bodies and horrendous crimes committed by the carnival. The headline says, 'Son of Infamous Killer, Pastor Jebediah Paine, Found Dead in His Carnival of Horrors.'"

"Ha, well, shit. That's pretty damn accurate, actually." Lizzie lay on my other side, her arms folded behind her head as she looked up at the ceiling. "Wonder how they're going to explain those 'freaks' we fought."

"It looks like a lot of it disappeared after we killed him. The circus tent's rooms and shit were mostly gone. There's no mention of the house of mirrors or funhouse."

"More like a not-so-funhouse, thank you very much. We almost died in there. Ugh," Temps shuddered, "fuck that place."

Pulling her under my arm, I kissed the top of her head, scrolling away from the news and to the emails the school had sent.

"Classes are paused until the board sorts this out. And they've expressed interest in me continuing to teach, so I think we're clear on the soul-weaving front."

"Thank gods," Temps said, nuzzling into me. "I feel weird saying it, but I'm glad that the dean was able to see how necessary it was because she was right there in the tent with us."

"Umm," Lizzie leaned up onto her elbow, glancing at me with that uncertainty she disliked so much behind her eyes, "any word about the townspeople who were killed?"

I knew she was getting at Temps' mother, and undoubtedly she was curious about her father as well. I went back to the article, scrolling through the paragraphs that speculated why Paine had done all this. We knew well enough that this was a family corruption. Jeb had been just like his old man, falling into the depths of malignant power and trying to use it for his own gain.

As we rested last night, Cerberus had filled the three of us in more about what had happened in the World of Below with his parents and Jeb Senior. He'd corrupted an entire portion of the Underworld and very nearly spread his plague through the entirety of it. It'd taken his mother everything she had, as well as the Beast King in several forms, to defeat the man.

It made sense that shortly after, the demiurge would cook up another plan involving Paine's son.

Refocusing, I found a section of the article about the people found inside the tent's backroom, and the surviving victims who'd nearly been killed by the cult extremist before an unknown person or thing had killed him.

"It says that there are twelve confirmed victims and nine survivors. The survivors were blindfolded so they didn't see what happened to Paine, but report hearing an animal attack. The names of the lost aren't listed 'for the privacy of their surviving families.'"

"I wonder if the police have talked to my dad yet."

Temps and I glanced at each other before eyeing Lizzie, concerned for her obviously, but also feeling guilty. At least I was. I'd been the one to wipe him thanks to Cerberus making a home in my soul, and I could feel what it was like to take those memories away.

"Are you okay, Lizzie? I know it was hard to lose your dad." Temps reached over me, taking her hand.

"I'll be fine. It's just...weird." Lizzie smiled at both of us, cocking her head to the side. "But I have you guys. I feel less alone than I ever have, I promise you."

"Speaking of," Temps shuffled about in the bed, sitting up tall as she looked both of us in the eye in turn, "what are we going to do about this? Like, are Lizzie and I going to keep living in the dorm? Or are we living here? Do we tell people? Do we not?"

I couldn't help but laugh. Temps was certainly the planner of the two of them, and part of me really appreciated that she wanted to get this all straight. I wasn't a wishy-washy type of guy myself. I liked knowing my place, our place, and it felt good to know that she'd been thinking about all this. Hell, it felt damn great to hear her mention living here. I wanted both of them with me all the time.

"Fuck, babe." Lizzie rolled her eyes with a smirk. "Just lay it all out, why don't you? Haha, I mean, you gave our poor professor like four seconds to think about it."

"Actually," I shrugged, pulling Temps to my lips for a forehead kiss and then yanking Lizzie up under my arm, "I've been thinking about it since we first had sex. I'm a planner, too."

"Really?" Temps stare softened as she leaned in, and I was holding these two amazing women in my arms after all the fucking hell we'd just been through.

"Yes, little flower." I squeezed them tight. "And...I'd love it if you both lived here. I just...I didn't want to be pushy. I have a tendency to throw myself into something completely, and I knew that would be the case with you both, even more so. You're...mine."

And mine, sage. I chuckled, rolling my eyes. "Cerberus agrees."

"I want to stay here. I want us all to be together. Lizzie?" Temps glanced at her with her brows up.

"Umm, duh. Of course, I want to stay. Not that your apartment is much bigger than our dorm. But the company is much better."

"Fair." I grinned, squishing Lizzie some. "But I do still think it's smart to keep this under wraps. At least until neither of you is officially my student anymore. You'll have your dorm for show, but next semester, you can move the rest of the stuff in here."

"Sounds like a plan," Temps declared, nodding with a smile. "But does that mean we need to lie to the dean?"

"Of all the people who get to be privy to this, I think Rebecca will actually understand. She also owes us big time for saving her life, so we have some leverage there."

"Maybe during the rest of the year, we can work on finding a bigger place?" Lizzie sighed, looking up at the ceiling like she was imagining it. "I'd like something with a garden. And I'm sure you'll both need a room for all your alchemy shit."

We all laughed, settling in with absolutely no plans to do anything else for the rest of the day except enjoy each other's company.

"And a room for all the toys. A proper sex dungeon so we don't have to go visit that club unless we want to."

Temps stared at Lizzie in shock, but all I could do was grin, from ear to fucking ear. That sounded like a fantastic idea. Even so, I could make due without one for the day. Cerberus growled inside my head, happily agreeing.

"The kitchen will suffice for today."

Both of them stared at me, that humming sensation warming my skin and eyes as Cerberus crawled to the surface.

Yup, I can definitely get used to this.

A WEEK LATER...

"Thank you for coming. I've been looking forward to finally getting the school year started again, and I wanted to discuss a few things with you all."

The dean sat behind her oversized wooden desk, the dark room of mahogany and gothic architecture smelling like old books and incense. She smiled across at the three of us as we sat in the brown suede chairs before her desk, her fingers gently crossed as her hands rested on the desktop. I was glad that she was looking better.

"Of course, Dean Owens. How can we be of service?" I knew Rebecca would appreciate the decorum, and right on cue, she smiled over at us.

"I would like you to return to teaching spell casting for the remainder of the semester while I look for a new hire, but in the spring, I'm elevating you to the post of alchemy professor."

Nodding, I offered a gracious smile, putting my hand on my chest. "Thank you, Dean. I look forward to being back in the laboratory."

"As for you two," she flicked her eyes to Temps, "Ms. Montgomery, I have passed you for spell casting. I think the show you put on at the carnival was quite enough of a final exam. You'll be moving up to alchemy with Professor Harkert... as his assistant. Formally this time."

Smirking, I restrained a laugh, but leave it to Lizzie to snort for all of us.

"And Ms. Chamberlain, you too have passed spell casting. Though I know your interests do not lie with alchemy. Instead, I would like you to consider joining the Evening Tides. They are a group of psychics and empaths with renowned abilities who are responsible for the school's protection. They have not had new blood in some time, I'm afraid, and with you joining, as well as a new faculty advisor, as I have dismissed the previous for his lack of oversight into the situation, I'm sure that—"

"You fired the head of the school board committee? I thought that windbag would never leave."

I couldn't stop the remark, and Rebecca did her best to hold back her grin. "Yes, well, he was less than helpful during this trying time. He couldn't see the talents you both possess, even you, Caleb, and we do not need that type of rigidity here."

Temps and Lizzie were practically glowing in their chairs, Lizzie's excited aura filtering out of her and smoothing against mine, and no doubt Temps' as well. She'd gotten quite good at manipulating emotional energies and projecting them on others or pulling them away.

It was spectacular when we were fucking. Which, of course, gave me so many ideas for when we got home.

"I accept." Lizzie grinned, nodding as she stood up from the chair and walked to Rebecca to shake her hand. "Meet your new student-faculty advisor. Nothing like a morrighan to set the 'wipper snappers' right."

"I—That was not what—" But Rebecca stopped, Lizzie giving her a look I couldn't see. "Very well. You've both earned the reputations floating around campus now."

"Ooh, we have reps, Temps." Lizzie spun back around, holding out her arms so that we could loop ours through them. "We best not let the power go to our heads."

Without another word, she marched us to the door, slick, warmth energy rushing off her in waves. I could taste the lust she sent us, spicy and demanding on my tongue. And then she whispered into our heads.

I think we're ready to try that thing with Cerberus, don't you?

We'd been planning something special, doing the research, and I turned inward, listening for his response.

Yes, young morrighan. We most definitely are.

Epilogue

BOOKS CLOSE, BUT THE STORY IS NEVER REALLY OVER

CALEB

Lizzie's lips pressed to mine as the three of us stumbled into my apartment. I kicked the door closed behind me, hearing it lock as Temps most likely used her magic to flip the thing over. She was just behind me, her hands reaching around for the buckle of my belt.

A dark chuckle left me as I leaned Lizzie back, nipping at her neck. "Did you already make it? Or are we going to have to pause so you can cook?"

"You know Temps is the chef around her, and yes," Lizzie smacked my hand away, getting up in my face again as she jumped, forcing me to catch her, "she did make it. It's on the counter."

Temps rounded us, still undoing my belt now with Lizzie's ass just above her hands. "And you need to be naked to make it work."

Even with my eyes closed, I rolled them, kissing Lizzie while I waited for my pants to drop to the floor. Soon enough, they did, and I stepped out of the pile and carried Lizzie to the small island in the middle of my kitchen that acted as counter, table, and, right now, bed.

Temps hurried over, swiping her arm through the papers I had spread on the top and grabbing the small bottle of enchanted oil we'd concocted. The stuff, improvised from an alchemical text about separating the mind from the body for astral projection, was hopefully going to allow both Cerberus and me to be active at the same time.

Over the past week, we'd all discussed our connection, as well as the proclivities and acts we wanted to try. A proper kink conversation, complete with lines and veils, and we'd all agreed on wanting our ancient being to come out and play.

I distinctly recalled saying, "What on earth gave you the idea I was straight?"

Lizzie slid her tongue between my lips, Temps grabbing hold of my boxer briefs and yanking them down. I groaned into Lizzie's mouth before setting her down on the island. She smirked at me, Temps climbing up onto the marble surface as well, all grins and devious intent.

"Take off each other's clothes." I narrowed my eyes, watching hungrily as the girls stripped each other.

They'd worn their uniforms to the meeting with Dean Owens, and their fingers moved with deft precision as they both slid off the other's jacket, moving to the buttons of the shirts and freeing them one at a time. I worked on my own, taking off my tweed jacket and flinging it somewhere before unbuttoning my shirt enough to yank it over my head.

New scars littered my body from the cuts and claw marks obtained from the carnival, and I felt Cerberus shift inside me, equally as ravenous.

If this works, sage. We're going to need vats of that oil for how much I'll be playing with all three of you.

I grinned, tilting my head as Lizzie shoved Temps' sleeves down, the shirt dropping to the floor. Temps' skin glowed in the soft yellow light from my Edison bulb lamps, scattered throughout he room to make it all the more warm and subtly seductive.

I'll be happy to make it as quickly as I can, Cerberus. What will you look like in this spirit-like form?

His laugh echoed in my head as Temps kissed Lizzie's bare shoulder, her finger sliding down the fabric of her shirt and the strap of her bra. Neither of them wore much in the way of bras, and I was always ever so grateful for that.

The wireless garments were lacey and stretched over their thin bodies, their hardening nipples standing out in the fabric. Lizzie's was black where Temps' was a deep wine color, and soon enough, they were gone, revealing their scrumptious little breasts, pert buds at the tips aching to be touched, sucked.

I imagine I will look more like my true form, a humanoid wolfen figure with three heads.

That's a lot of mouths, Cerberus.

He just laughed again, and as I stood there naked, I stroked my thickening erection, watching our girls unzip each other's skirts and fling them to the floor. Lizzie made Temps lie back, hooking her fingers under the waistband of her panties and dragging them down her legs. Temps' thighs gleamed, her skin slick from the wetness dripping from her pussy.

Lizzie crawled back up Temps' body, starting to lower her mouth toward that delicious sight.

"Ah, ah. I didn't tell you to get started yet." I cocked a brow, gesturing down at her panites with my head. "Lose them."

Temps sat up, helping Lizzie out of the underwear, and before either of them could do more, I used my magic to call the oil to me.

"You two have a job to do. If I remember correctly, this is supposed to coat my entire body." I shook the bottle playfully. "Who wants upstairs and who wants downstairs?"

Lizzie hopped off the island, grabbed the bottle, and dropped to her knees. "I'll get this part."

A sadistic smirk lifted the corner of my mouth, and I watched as she uncorked the bottle and poured a healthy amount of oil into her palm. Temps maneuvered the bottle up to her hand, taking some before she lifted on her knees and pulled me closer to the island.

"Fine with me." She rubbed her hands together, planting them on my chest and massaging the oil into my skin. "I get kisses here."

She dusted her lips over mine, gentle and almost shy. I wasn't having any of that, and neither was Cerberus, for that matter, so I grabbed Temps by the back of the neck and crashed her lips down onto mine.

"And who says I don't?" Lizzie mused, and I moaned as her hands ran up my thighs only to close around the base of my shaft. She squeezed, rocking her fists in tiny motions. Then her lips brushed against the head of my cock before parting around it as she sucked me into her mouth.

For once, I couldn't find the words. The energy swirled higher, my skin buzzing where the oil touched me, and before I knew it, Temps had the bottle floating over my back, the cork out, and it rained the magnificent stuff all over me. Sure, it wasn't a precise application, but it didn't need to be, and the sexual magic was already blazing as Lizzie opened her throat for me, letting me fuck that bratty little mouth.

Temps tongue danced with mine before she leaned back with a grin, holding my stare as she began to chant the words.

"Spiritus terrae, spiritus inferorum, vos obsecramus ut spiritum vestrum lupinum volare sinatis."

Cerberus recited the words in my head. *Spirits of the earth, spirits of the World of Below, we beseech you to allow your wolfen spirit to soar.*

"Da formam filio tuo et permitte ei gustare carnem omnium sociorum suorum."

Give form to your child and allow him to taste of the flesh of all his mates.

The energy mounted, surging higher as Lizzie worked my cock

in and out of her mouth, dragging her tongue up the underside where my piercings were. I kicked in her grip, precum oozing from my tip, and my skin felt like it was on fire. This desperate urge for something filled my blood, but I couldn't name it. It was nearly unbearable, feeling empty and needy and almost drunk on the compulsion swelling in my veins.

"Holy shit."

Temps voice made me flick open my eyes, Lizzie stopping and letting out a tiny gasp as she stumbled up to her feet, her back hitting the island as she peered over my shoulder.

"What?"

At first, I just looked down, and that was enough to have my mind reeling. Smoke-like tendrils streamed from my skin, gently crawling through the air in this endless circulation. They never left me, anchored there as I turned this way and that.

But then I remembered.

Following the rivulets of shadow up and behind me, I turned, and against the odds, there stood a massive werewolf-like man, his body covered in short, silky black fur and two other heads perched near his shoulders. His muscular body much much more human than wolf, and his face was a terrifying yet gorgeous hybrid of both.

"Holy shit." Temps smacked my shoulder as I peered up into these impossible yellow eyes, intelligent and hungry.

"That's what I said."

Cerberus smirked, eyeing Temps over my shoulder with just the flick of his glowing stare. "*Hello, little witch.*"

The air thrummed, and from my side, Lizzie reached out, dragging her fingers down his impossibly thick arms, the muscles profound and stark. His entire body was like a work of art, almost chiseled from stone, and I couldn't stop myself from scanning down his abdominals to his waist.

He was naked, a massive bulge, still sporting that black fur, and hiding what I knew he was working with. But as he roamed his stare over us, that agonizing need nearly sending me to my knees, Cerberus dropped his hand to his crotch, stroking over the bulge until a rosy pink tip emerged from within.

Whoomph.

My blood shuddered. "What the hell is that?"

Chuckling, which only made it worse, Cerberus extended a clawed hand, wrapping it around my throat as he squeezed just enough.

"You are in heat, sage. Because I demand it so. I want to watch as you break apart for me. As you cry for my spend, begging me to breed you."

"Gods, yessss..." I groaned, my cock twitching as Cerberus pressed himself against me, his shaft rubbing against mine as he freed it and held it to me.

He felt like molten against me, so damn hot and unyielding, and before I could think, he angled me back over the island. Lizzie and Temps were to either side of my head, and I could tell by their lidded gazes, they were feeling the effects of the heat, too.

"Sit on his face, young morrighan." Cerberus scooped under Lizzie, making her squeak as he hoisted her up. *"Our sage looks*

so very hungry."

Breathless, Lizzie straddled my head, leaning over me so that her lips pressed to Cerberus' middle mouth as her pussy hovered over my mouth. I reached up for her hips, pulling Lizzie down. My tongue speared through her soaked folds, and I began to furiously circle around her clit. She gasped, arching over me, but I didn't let her retreat for even a moment, holding her to me as I traded circles for driving my tongue inside her.

"Fuck!"

"Sweet witch, that mouth of yours looks rather empty. Take our cocks."

I couldn't see, but I could hear Temps get down from the island, coming over to where Cerberus had our shafts in his grip, squeezing them together as I balanced backward on the island. It was a good fucking thing he was so strong, and I wasn't that bad myself.

As it was, the edge of the island dug into my shoulders, but I hardly gave a single fuck, needing all my *mates* so fucking badly.

Then Temps' mouth was on my cock, her lips sealing around us where Cerberus held me pressed to him. He stroked us both as Temps sucked on us, bobbing up and down. All the while, I feasted on Lizzie's perfect cunt, swirling and flicking, stuffing my tongue inside her and then replacing it with my fingers as I pulled her clit between my lips and combined that suction with more flicks of my tongue.

"Oh, fuck...oh, fuck. Oh, fuck. Oh, fuck!"

Lizzie's fingers speared through my hair as she cried out, warmth gushing around my fingers. I pulled back just a hair, hooking my fingers into her G-spot and fingering her hard and fast. She came apart, squirting over my face and tongue. I eagerly lapped her up, marveling at her taste as she climaxed for me.

And I wasn't stopping, not until her legs were quivering and she could hardly move.

"*Yes, sage. Make our morrighan flood.*" Cerberus storked us together harder, Temps' mouth clamped onto our heads as she sucked furiously. "*Such a good witch. Go to our morrighan and take her hand again. I would see you riding her fist every damn day.*"

The warmth of Temps' mouth disappeared, and in a few moments, she was up on the island, lying across the surface as she pulled Lizzie from straddling my head to kneeling over her. I craned my head back to see them kissing, Lizzie's fingers going straight for Temps' gleaming cunt. She slid them past her folds, dipping one inside as her thumb rubbed Temps' clit.

"*I've not even begun with you, sage.*"

Again, faster than I could think, Cerberus spun me around, bending me over the island. The cool marble was heaven against my overheated skin, and I reached across it to Temp's nipple, pinching as Lizzie stuffed her fingers inside her.

Cerberus stood behind me, and that bottle of oil vanished over my shoulder before something cool dripped down my ass.

Oh fuck.

I hadn't done this for anyone. I was usually always the top, but that need inside me was too strong to deny, too incredible. I wanted Cerberus to fuck me until I collapsed. I wanted that knot shoved inside me, stretching me.

"That I can oblige, sage."

His shaft rubbed along my crack as he kicked my feet wider. The smooth head of his cock pressed to my hole, and I clenched before he pushed my lower back down, growling. I needed to relax as much as I could. Cerberus swirled his head against the tight right of muscle, and my entire body fucking melted for him. It felt wild and new and so damn good.

"Fuuuck."

Claws digging into my hips, I opened my eyes, not remembering when I closed them, and stared at those smoky tendrils again. They connected me to him and glowed gold as I felt a rush of euphoria from Temps and Lizzie. Our psychic was reverberating the pleasure again.

Gods, I love when she does that.

Just as I glanced up at them, my cock throbbing as I watched Lizzie's hand disappear inside Temps' wet cunt, Cerberus sank into me. I gasped, arching, and he pressed in another inch. I was achingly full of him, stretching around that monster dick. He started up a rhythm, back and forth, going deeper and deeper with each trust.

"That's it, sage. Take my cock. Feel me breed your tight, little hole like a good boy."

The wolf was calling me a good boy, and I was over the damn moon for it, so many puns intended.

At once, he was fully seated inside me, his knot hot against my skin. He pumped in and out, rutting me as I feasted on the sight of Temps' moaning while she took Lizzie's fist. Cerberus was so big, giving me everything he had, and that heat he'd brought out inside me flared with so much relief and pleasure that the precum dripped from me.

"Cerbs...ugh, I need to come. *Please*." I spoke through gritted teeth, shifting so that I could stroke my dick. "I *need* to."

He smacked my hand away. "*I will make you come, sage. You're going to take my knot and then cover my fist with your spend before I breed you.*"

Grabbing hold of my shaft, Cerberus pumped his fist up and down my length as he fucked me. His hand glided over my piercings, his thumb rubbing right down the middle of them. I jerked in his hold, Cerberus sinking all the way inside me until his knot began to press in.

"Shit!"

It was nearly too much of a stretch, the pain mingling with so much pleasure. But I only wanted him to continue. I wanted him to finish, to fill me up, to *breed* me. I wanted to be his good boy, his whore. I wanted him to scream my name as he came inside me so much I could practically taste it.

Faster and harder, he stroked me, and I felt that burning need to come in the tip of my cock. His knot completely filled me, and then I felt him swell, his shaft thickening.

Oh, fuck yes.

"Lizzie!" I looked up at our girls, watching Temps come around Lizzie's hand, her tongue lapping at Temps' clit. "Yes, yes, yes.

Right there. Don't stop. Ugh!"

Cum trickled out of Temps' pussy while Lizzie hungrily slurped at her. Cerberus growled behind me, pushing as far in as he could, and just as Lizzie glided her hand free, licking up the juices on her fingers, he squeezed the base of my cock, patting it against the palm of his other hand.

I saw stars, orgasming hard enough to steal my breath as I emptied myself into Cerberus' hand. It went on, ropes launching from me as my shaft kicked, the intense sensations downright marvelous. Just as I finished, he took his hand around my side, and I reflexively turned over my shoulder to watch him.

Cerberus licked his tongue through my cum, scooping it into his mouth as he snarled greedily. My jaw dropped on its own, and then he was covering my mouth with that same hand, making me taste myself as he fucked me with abandon.

"*Urgh!*" His roar echoed through the kitchen as he came inside me. "*Breeding my good boy, my tasty sinner.*"

Warmth filled me so entirely, Cerberus spurting his cum deep into my ass. Another short, sharp orgasm rocked me as I tasted myself on his palm, his thick cock spearing me as his knot stretched me. So much damn heat as he pumped every drop of spend into my asshole.

"I don't think I can stand." Temps whispered from somewhere above me, and I heard Lizzie chuckle, agreeing with her.

"And you, sage? What are your thoughts?"

I smiled as Cerberus stood behind him, waiting for the moment to slow down enough that he could dismount.

"We're definitely doing that again."

Acknowledgements

Thank you, monster fuckers! This book has a piece of my soul in it, and for as dark and twisted and sensual as it is, I also know that it is heavy and honest, and forces us to look at life in all of its wonderous flaws and contradictions. I love Cerridwen and her Beast King. I love the way she grows and changes so much while still claiming that spring child that she'll always be. So thank you for taking a chance on this story, and I hope you enjoyed the journey as much as I did.

As always, this book also wouldn't have come to fruition without the support of some truly amazing people. My author friends for sharing their resources with me, my first-look readers, and, of course, my ARC readers. A special shout-out to my Patrons— Samantha, Brittany, Erika, Becks, Mandy, and Denis.

To my PAs, Halla and Jasmine, thank you so much for helping me to manage all the other things while I was throwing myself into the book. To my ride-or-dies, Ally and Rachel.

To family and friends who have helped me form a support system I know I can count on. To my author bestie and incredible friend, Tori, you always support my unhinged, especially niche ideas, and I adore you for it.

And to the one and only Ryan. You have been there for me through thick and thin, and you've never told me to give up, even when I really felt like it.

Thank you for listening to me rant, offering ideas and suggestions, and putting up with my ramblings about monster genitalia and how I always need to step it up a notch with each book. I love you with all my heart forever and ever.

Books by RE Johnson

THE NEWBORN CITY SERIES

Affinity for Pain- The Newborn City Series Book 1
Burn the Bone- The Newborn City Series Book 2
Calling Evil Forth- The Newborn City Series Book 3 (TBA)
Series Relaunching in 2026

NEWBORN CITY UNIVERSE

Cherry Cobbler- A Valentine's Day Newborn City Shifter
Novella

SAN DOMINGO NOVELS & NOVELLAS

Till Death Do Us Part- A Monster Horror Romance
A Final Girl Halloween Kinktober Series (October 2025)

THE SHADEPORT HERMETICA

The Evil Within Us- The Shadeport Hermetica Vol I (July 2024)
The Evil Around Us- The Shadeport Hermetica Vol II (Summer
2025)The Evil Beneath Us- The Shadeport Hermetica Vol III
(2026)

MONSTROUS SHORTS & MORE

The Night Garden- A Monstrous Short

A Solstice Sin- The Solstice Seasons Novellas I

Shadowed Summer Sun- The Solstice Seasons Novellas II
The Solstice Seasons Duet Omnibus

These Unhallowed Halls

Necromancy- The Keepers Mate Duet I

Resurrection- The Keepers Mate Duet II (2026)

Up from the Earth- The Equinox Seasons Duet I

These Unhallowed Halls- The Equinox Seasons Duet II

PATREON EXCLUSIVES

His Black Alchemy- A Dark High Fantasy Monster Romance Serial (Ongoing)

WEBSITE EXCLUSIVES & ANTHOLOGIES

The Macabre Dance of the Sanguine Six (Website Exclusive)

His Bloody Survivor (Website Exclusive)

In The Company of Monsters (Website Exclusive)

Tales of the Scorned- The Red Queen

We Shall Rise- Blood Is Thinner Than Water

Fallen- In Darkness We Shall Rise

Loving Proudly- Don't Look Back (February 2026)

The Bloody Demise Duet Anthology (2026)

To get your hands on all the goodies, check out linktr.ee/ rejohnsonauthor

Stalk Me

Want more?

Join the Demon Club on Patreon

Like RE Johnson on Facebook

Join RE Johnson's Demon Club Reader's Group

Follow RE Johnson on Instagram

Join the RE Johnson Street Team

Sign up for their newsletter at rejohnsonbooks.com

All links available at linktr.ee/rejohnsonauthor